LOST SOUL

ALSO BY T. G. AYER

Young Adult Paranormal

THE VALKYRIE SERIES

Dead Radiance

Dead Radiance Audio

Dead Embers

Dead Embers Audio

Dead Chaos

Dead Chaos Audio

Dead Wrath

Dead Silence

Joshua - Dead Radiance

Joshua II - Dead Embers

Joshua III - Dead Chaos

Joshua IV - Dead Wrath

Joshua V - Dead Silence

THE HAND OF KALI SERIES

Fire & Shadow

Blood & Gold

Time & Fate

Fury & Virtue

Spirit & Soul

THE DARKWORLD ORIGINS

Pyros (Logan)
Ailuros (Kailin)

~

THE DARK SIGHT SERIES

Dark Sight
Cursed Sight
Vissarion
Shadow Sight
Dark Prophecy
Cursed Prophecy
Shadow Prophecy

~

THE APSARA CHRONICLES

Immortal Bound
Gods Ascendent
Dominion Falling
Vengeance Born
Last Legion

~

A SEASON OF ASH AND BONE

Heartfyre

~

Lost Soul

A SkinWalker Novel #2

Cover art by Eduardo Priego

Editor: J.C. Hart

ISBN-10: 0995112533

ISBN-13: 978-0995112537

LOST SOUL

USA TODAY BESTSELLING AUTHOR

T.G. AYER

For Patti Larsen.
I couldn't ask for a truer, more steadfast friend – with a foot, shoulder or ear always at the ready when the time requires it, you have been my rock on more than one occasion.
Thank you.

CHAPTER 1

MY BODY BURNED, MY OWN brand of fire searing its way through my limbs.

I flung the covers off, trying to convince myself they were the reason I was too hot. But even as I lay there in a thin cotton singlet and briefs, I couldn't seem to cool down. I wiped damp tendrils off my sweaty forehead, fingers tangling with my unkempt mane.

My forearm burned, throbbing accusingly at me.

My gaze avoided the area of my forearm where the burning heat and the constant throbbing emanated. I didn't want to see the blue-green color of my skin. Nor did I want to see how far the poison had spread, threading its deadly toxins through my veins, through my flesh. I didn't want to be reminded of the reason I was relegated to my bed, too weak to move, too weak to work. Too weak to save anyone, least of all myself.

I hated weakness in any form. It pissed me off.

And time wasn't standing still waiting for me to get my act together.

I sighed and swallowed, my throat convulsing, my mouth a

furnace of its own. My eyelids were so hot and heavy I could barely keep them open. They drifted shut of their own accord.

I hated being so helpless. Greer was still in the In-Between and Anjelo and Mom were still in Wrythiin. The longer I languished in my bed, the longer they would suffer at the hands of Widd'en's men. They would remain at the mercy of the Wraith Army while I was chained to my mattress by pain and poison. I gritted my teeth, my fingers twisting the edge of the sodden sheet.

Despite my frustrations, I was still sprawled in bed, waiting for Logan to figure out how best to rid me of this debilitating poison. Hopefully I wouldn't die before he finally honed his Fire enough to help me. Not that I was ungrateful or impatient with him. He needed to learn how to control his power better so he could properly treat the poison.

I balanced my weight on my good hand and raised myself off the bed, shifting until I rested on my elbows. A wave of nausea gripped me so badly I slumped flat on my back and shuddered. So much for trying to sit up like a normal person. Nausea tightened my throat and I began to breathe in and out very, very fast, trying to exhale away the urge to hurl. I hated throwing up. I'd been doing too much of that lately. Slowly the desire began to recede and my throat relaxed.

But now I needed the toilet. Badly.

Sighing, I gritted my teeth against pain and nausea and pushed myself into a sitting position. No matter what additional privileges the bedridden were allowed, the last thing I needed was for someone to find I'd wet the bed. I teetered on the edge of the bed, gripping the mattress as the world tilted. I swallowed hard, blinking at the wave of dizziness that washed over me. I extracted myself from the dampened sheets still clinging to my body. Muscles clenched, I launched myself onto my feet and remained hunched over for a moment, holding onto the mattress for support until I felt a little more steady on my weakened knees.

After a few shaky moments, I managed to hobble to the bathroom on wobbly legs, making it there and back to the bed without dying. That was a good sign. Seated on the bed again, I was so tempted to lie down and rest. With every move I'd made, my body screamed that I'd be better off lying down. My body was probably smarter than I was.

But I was partially up. And I was damned thirsty.

I glanced at my nightstand, giving the pile of empty water bottles a disgusted glare. No way could I fill any of those long, thin things in my mini bathroom sink. The way I saw it, I had one of two choices. Head back into the bathroom, huddle over the sink, and drink from cupped palms, or make a trip to the kitchen for an actual glass of the stuff.

But the kitchen was very, very far away. I sighed—sometimes being an invalid was all so overwhelmingly hard.

Sometimes it would be so easy to just give up. But I didn't have the luxury of giving up.

I moved and the dark blue shadow of my arm swam into my vision. Green and blue veins stood raised and fat as if the poison had thickened and now formed a slow-moving sludge in my bloodstream. The Wraith poison had worked its way through my body, covering my skin with tiny threads of navy and purple, casting a gray-green tinge to my complexion. I looked like I was morphing into some kind of water sprite or kelpie. I shuddered.

Moving slowly, I got back on my feet. Knees trembling, I held my heart in my hands as I navigated the endless expanse of floor between my bed and my door. I had nothing to hold so I could so easily face-plant at any time.

Nope, chin up, think positive, one foot in front of the other.

I stiffened my legs and moved forward, looking straight ahead and hoping that would help my balance. Step by step I breathed slowly until only two feet remained and I realized I'd made it.

Almost fainting with relief, I grabbed onto the open door and held on by my fingernails, my knees quivering as they threatened to buckle under my weight. Thankfully, the kitchen counter sat only about ten feet away from my room door. If I could make it from my bed to the door, I could make it to the kitchen. Half-way there anyway.

I let go of the door, flexing too-stiff fingers, and moved ahead slowly. I made it to the sink without kissing the floor.

The counter took my weight and I rested my elbows on the cool marble; then leaning forward, I listened to the frantic thudding of my heart. When my head stopped spinning, I reached for a glass from the wire rack, held it with shaking fingers and filled it, drinking until my thirst was quenched. I shuddered, my body feeling the effects of my journey.

Looks like it's back to bed for you, Odel.

Alpha or not, a girl had to know when to admit defeat. I needed rest and the kitchen was as far as I dared go. I filled the glass again and turned when the kitchen, floor, counter and all, began to spin. My stomach churned and the muscles in my abdomen clenched.

Too light-headed to do anything, I sank to the floor, my knees at last losing the fight to hold me up. The heavy-bottomed drinking glass slipped from my grasp, falling straight to the wood floor, smashing into a million pieces. As the glass hit the ground, water burst from it like a geyser, spraying droplets all over the kitchen. And all over me.

Good job. Now who's going to clean up this mess?

Lying where I fell, my face rested close to my poison-wreathed arm. I stared at it as it throbbed and pulsed, as if the poison had taken on a life of its own and was just waiting for the next moment to advance further into my flesh.

Who knew a tiny piece of Wraith-sword could be this deadly? It seemed fate had conspired against us all: against me who had found and killed the soul-suckers, against Grandma Ivy who'd given me the armband for protection, and against my mother who'd sacrificed her life to ensure my sister and I would be safe from harm.

CHAPTER 2

THE LAB WAS COLD AND silent as Logan breathed deep, drawing the fire through his body and centering the molten energy within his mind. The mouse shivered in his hand, its sickly green eyes staring up at him, its expression sad and pleading. The little, large-eyed white-furred creature had been shaved to reveal its bare skin, enabling Logan and the lab-techs to assess how well the fire was progressing in killing the poison.

He felt a twinge of regret at using the innocent creature. He'd needed a suitable test subject to ensure he could find and perfect the safest method of neutralizing the poison. Now the naked mouse wriggled in his hand, its body streaked with the purple and green stains of the insidious venom.

The colors guided his thoughts to Kailin, and his gut twisted at the pain and agony she continued to endure from the poison.

Logan wanted to move faster. To hurry. The longer he took the more Kailin suffered, and if there was anything he wanted more, it was to free her from the bindings of the Wraith poison. But he had to keep reminding himself that he needed to be accurate much more than he needed to be fast. What good was rushing if he didn't get it right?

The mouse squeaked as if he knew his time had come. Logan concentrated, harnessing and building the power in his mind, drawing it into a mental bowstring, pulling it taut but letting it go in a steady, controlled stream.

He stared at the animal, watching for the slightest change.

Logan could feel the heat surging throughout his body. He hoped his magic wouldn't be as destructive as the last time he'd tried this. He needed to know there was some hope for Kailin. Two weeks had passed since she'd returned from Wrythiin, two weeks since they'd discovered the poison infecting her system, and two endless weeks of suffering. His visits to Kailin always ended with him returning to the lab and working himself half to death. He hated seeing her suffer.

The mouse squeaked again and Logan blinked. Now, he stared at his palm and the forgotten rodent struggling within it. He grasped the mouse, thumbed the skin below its eye, and pulled it down to examine the whites. Clear. He turned the mouse over in his hand, examining the skin closely. Only the faintest threads of grays and blues and purples remained, and they were fast disappearing. Seconds later the mouse, re-energized, twisted within his hand, trying to gain his freedom.

Logan gave a half smile. "Sorry, dude. You're alive, but probably only long enough to die another day." Logan scanned the lab and wondered what other experiments they had in store for the little naked mouse. He preferred not to know.

After securing the mouse in its cage and making the necessary notes on the file, Logan shucked off the white lab coat and slipped on his black leather jacket. He couldn't wait a moment longer to get to Kailin.

The fire worked.

Now he just had to make sure it worked on Kailin.

~

Kailin

Despite the warmth of the wood floors, cold seeped into my flesh and bones. I shivered but I couldn't move; I just lay there and stared at puddles of water and glass shards, listening to the thud of my heartbeat in my ear.

Useless. That's what I was. Totally useless until I found a way to rid myself of this poison. Until then, I wouldn't be able to do anything about saving Greer or my mother or even Anjelo.

A growl ripped through my throat, my anger and frustration finally spilling over. Long pent-up emotions battered my defenses, shoving through, releasing in the sharp snarl of my panther. She'd had enough. She'd taken the beating of the poison too, hated feeling useless as much as I did.

I'd longed for release and maybe my panther form would be the best way to achieve that. A little question hovered at the back of my mind. What would happen to my body and the body of my panther should I change while the poison was so prevalent in my system? Would I harm my panther?

But she didn't seem to care about the danger. My ears lifted, pointed, flared out. My eyes burned, the particular sensation of my panther eyes coming forth. Another growl and my jaw lengthened, hardened, my nose now picking up every odor surrounding me, including the sickly scent of the poison flowing thick and strong beneath my skin.

My hands transitioned smoothly into paws, my fingernails curving into deadly-sharp claws. I stretched out, lengthened my back, and let the panther take charge.

My feline was about to take full control when my ears flicked, angling toward the door to my apartment. A sound filtered through from a lower floor in the building. Someone was coming up the stairs. My nose twitched, scented the air. I began to sink back into my human form as he knocked hard on the door.

LOGAN.

Logan frowned as he climbed the last few stairs to Kailin's floor, laden with bags of Chinese takeout. He'd been so sure he'd heard a very feline growl come from the apartment just a second ago, and though he strained to hear more, the sound didn't come again. Still frowning, he reached Kailin's door and paused.

Taking a deep breath, Logan knocked.

CHAPTER 3

LOGAN RAPPED ON THE DOOR again and waited. He knew Kailin would take a bit of time to answer. He hated seeing her so weak. Her strength was one of the things he'd always admired about her.

He frowned, then dug into his pocket for her key and shoved it into the lock, thankful she'd relented and given him a spare. He'd visited her a few times, bringing her food or just coming over to keep her company.

At least today he was able to give her some good news.

He entered, kicking the door shut with his heel, his hands full. He'd brought Chinese since they'd both be famished after the treatment. Kailin wasn't in any condition to have cooked today, and he wondered if she'd eaten at all.

The door to her room stood ajar, the view to her empty bed unhindered. He scowled and hurried to deposit the food on the kitchen counter. As he turned to search her room, a low moan caught his ear.

He rounded the counter to find Kailin sprawled on the floor surrounded by broken glass and splattered with water. More water puddled on the floor around her.

"What the hell happened?" Logan's stomach tightened as he rushed to her. He knelt at her side, lifting her up to support her head.

She gave him a sheepish smile, her face pale and drawn. "I needed a drink. Room service didn't answer."

He snorted, noting the feline peak to her ears and the enhanced almond shape of her catlike green eyes. "What were you trying to do? You know a transformation could sap whatever little energy you have." He knew he nagged, but seriously, the girl had to be forced to take good care of herself.

The last two weeks had been an endless battle that had everyone, including her family, hovering between frustrated and helpless with her pig-headedness.

"Come, let me get you back in bed." She was silent as he scooped her up and strode to the room.

Safely tucked in, she gave him an inquiring, hopeful look. "Any progress with the fire?"

Logan nodded and hid a smile. Kailin never wasted a second getting to the point. "That's why I came. It's working so I thought I'd come over and administer a treatment. At least you can feel a little better until the process is perfected."

"Well, what are you waiting for?" She raised an eyebrow.

He shook his head and spun on his heel. Heading for the kitchen he said, "First, I'll get you that drink before you die of thirst."

"I wasn't dying of thirst." He could hear the pout in her voice.

"Yeah, I wonder why you forced your way to the kitchen when you're so weak." He shook his head as he returned from the kitchen with two full glasses of water. Handing one to her, he set the other on her nightstand. By the time he turned back to her, she'd drained the glass.

She gave him an ironic glance and handed him the glass back. "Funny that. I must have been thirsty."

"Okay, now that you're ready, we can begin." He rounded the

bed to sit on the empty side, closer to her left hand. He got comfortable, shucking off his shoes and curling into a lotus position before reaching for her hand. His chest tightened at the sight of the purple and blue skin, the veins so dark they appeared black, crawling ominously along her arm, up to her neck, even tracing its way across her temple.

Her racer tee hid nothing. Blackish veins tracked their way across her throat and neck, disappearing into her cleavage. He bent to her feet and turned her instep to get a better look. The poison had left not a single part of her body untouched. She let him inspect her body without a fuss. Strange for Kailin. He studied her face, took in her sunken eyes, the dark circles around them.

Logan gritted his teeth, more determined now than ever to help relieve some of her agony. Simple pain-relieving drugs were pointless given her Walker species, and tranquilizers weren't an option unless he wanted her permanently unconscious. Once he'd suggested using a Synthe strain to relieve some of her agony. The look she'd given him had been enough to chill his blood. Fury had turned her eyes feline in a heartbeat and he knew never to mention such a thing again.

"Right. Get comfortable." He held her hand within his palms as she shimmied down among the pillows to lie flat. She looked at him and waited, her eyes expectant. "Ready?"

At her nod, Logan breathed deep and hissed it out. He shut his eyes and let the calm filter through him, centering his thoughts, his energy, his power. Her skin was feverish against his fingers but he kept his eyes closed and soothed the hitch in his breath.

He moved his hands up to cup her arm from the elbow to the wrist. Placing one hand on either side of her forearm, he breathed in and out, bringing his ever-present, simmering fire to the surface in a controlled stream. Heat pulsed through his body and pooled within the palm of his hand as he directed the energy to Kai's arm.

His skin touched hers and electricity sparked between them. The bed shifted and Kailin moved beside him. He didn't open his eyes. He sent the energy into her arm, channeling the power in small, concentrated bursts into her flesh.

Slowly, he opened his eyes, sure of the flow of energy around his body and through his palms into Kailin's arm. His hand covered the worst of the infection and he steeled himself against the urge to peek.

The heat simmered and pulsed between their skin and he met Kailin's eyes. Her expression was languid and sleepy. "How do you feel?" he asked.

"Tired. And calm." She swallowed and shifted. "It's hot."

"Uncomfortable hot? Or manageable hot?"

"I can handle it." She smiled and sighed.

"Tell me if it becomes uncomfortable." She nodded but he wasn't sure he believed her. He trusted Kailin to bite down on the pain no matter how bad it was. That was Kai.

He bit back a smile and concentrated on her hand, sending stronger pulses of heat into her arm, alternating them with short bursts of faint fire. Slowly, he began to increase the strength of every pulse. He snuck a quick glance at Kai. Perspiration dotted her forehead, a few droplets running down her neck.

"You okay?"

"Yeah." She nodded but her cheeks were pink and her pupils dilated. Her body was reacting to the stress of the treatment and he had to keep a close eye on her. But he didn't stop. Not yet.

He examined the skin of her forearm. The network of black veins had faded to a dark blue and what purple blotches that still covered her bare skin had paled.

It was working.

He watched Kailin but kept up a strong, steady stream of energy, unrelenting. Steady, strong pulsing of the fire made for a more lasting effect of the treatment. Not that it would cure her. That would hopefully come later after he'd fully perfected it.

He glanced up and met her tired eyes and she smiled. "Thank you."

"Don't thank me. The process isn't perfected yet. This is just maintenance." He kept his voice measured and controlled, but when she frowned, he knew she had sensed his frustration.

She shook her head. "Don't rush it, Logan. You can only do what you can do. No more." Concern gleamed in her eyes. "Besides, I don't want you to get hurt. Or to hurt me for that matter." She tempered her admonition with a smile.

Logan tensed his jaw, his hand still firmly attached to hers, fire still pulsing through her arm and through her bloodstream. "Yeah. The thing is I do need to rush it. You can't be lying about here for weeks on end. You have important things to do."

"So you feel that by taking your time with the fire, you're delaying me?" Kai shook her head again. "Don't be silly. If I have to wait, I'll wait. I'm still not sure where I'll go first—back to Wrythiin for my mother and Anjelo, or to wherever it is Greer got to. So don't be hasty and rush. You want to get the process right so I'm strong enough to bring them back, to fight if I have to."

It was the most that Kai had spoken in days and it exhausted her, her face growing paler, the corners of her eyes tightening.

"Okay, don't get all worked up." He raised both his eyebrows.

She threw him a glare and he merely smiled back then turned his attention to her arm. At last he felt it was time to take a peek. He raised his palm and peered at the bruised skin, at the wound left by the broken shards of the Wraith's sword. He sighed, relieved and removed his hands, revealing her forearm. "It worked quite well."

She examined her arm, tilting it this way and that. The purple and blue splotches had faded to a light dusting of color, the dark veins now looking more normal and green as they should. "Well done, Mage. I can't thank you enough."

"How do you feel?"

"Exhausted. And starving." She laughed as her stomach chose that moment to emit a growl.

"I've got it covered, Ms. Odel." Logan rose from the bed and headed out to the kitchen leaving a perplexed Kailin staring after him.

I watched Logan leave the room and suppressed a small burst of laughter. He never ceased to amaze me. Propping the pillows up behind me, I leaned back and relaxed, exhaustion pulling at my eyelids.

"Hey. No time to sleep yet, lazybones. Eat first, then rest." Logan returned with a tray filled with takeout boxes, chopsticks, and two glasses filled with juice.

He threw a napkin at me and resumed his position on the bed, this time settling the tray between us. I ate until I was sated, noting Logan's hunger and the lines of exhaustion on his face. The treatment had taxed him as well.

We didn't speak until we'd finished eating and Logan placed the empty tray in the kitchen. He returned and sat beside me on the bed, propped against the headboard, his bare feet crossed at the ankles.

"How are you feeling?" I asked, turning to look at him.

"Tired. The healing is taxing." The dark circles under his eyes confirmed his words.

"More taxing than throwing fireballs I take it?"

The corner of his lip turned up. "Way more." He ran his hands over his face as if he wanted to wipe away the tiredness, then scraped his hands through his hair making it stick up in fifty different directions.

"You should rest," I said.

"I am resting." He grinned when I glared at him. "Now tell me what you're thinking."

"About what?"

"About what your next step is. I thought you'd intended on finding out where Greer went and saving her first."

I looked away from him, not wanting to meet his eyes as I spoke. "Maybe Greer can wait. I think I need to get my mother and Anjelo out first. Who knows what could be happening to them?"

"And who knows where Greer ended up and what's happening to her."

I still refused to meet his eyes. The silence rang hollow for a moment, but when I spoke, I couldn't keep my voice from sounding defensive. "Look, if our roles were reversed, I'd be the last person Greer would save first." It had been bugging me for a while now, especially since I'd had plenty of time alone to mull it over.

I knew Greer very well. Logan didn't. I sighed. "Greer isn't the happiest person around. She's always had a dislike toward me—perhaps because I was more Alpha than her. And then maybe because she ended up Pariah. And I remember her reaction to Mom when she saw her in Wrythiin. Greer despises Mom more than she dislikes me." I shook my head. "I honestly don't understand her, Logan. What could possibly have been going through my sister's mind for her to stand by while Niko did all those horrible things? For her to support Brand? I honestly can't say that I even know who Greer is anymore. And the scariest thing is, what if we never really knew her at all? Just like with Niko." I shuddered. Tara's visions had made so much more sense when we found out Greer had hooked up with Brand.

"I understand how you feel. And maybe she wouldn't be the first one to come running to save you should you need saving, but she could be in way more danger than your mom and Anjelo. Both are being held captive as far as we know. And your mom is definitely an asset to the Wraiths. Let's hope they consider Anjelo an asset too. And I'm pretty sure your mom will bargain Anjelo into safety."

I smiled. Logan was right about Mom. She was one tough chick and she wouldn't back down. And something told me she knew the Wraiths and Wrythiin better than anyone else. Anjelo would be safe with Mom.

That left me with Greer.

I took a deep, reluctant breath. "I guess you're right. Maybe I knew it all along." I sighed, rubbing the bridge of my nose. "First we have to find out where she went when she jumped through the portal."

"Finding Greer should come first. If she ended up in the Bahamas and is currently sipping margaritas and working on her tan, she's definitely low priority."

I snorted. "You're a funny guy." I grinned at him, then asked, "So we'll need someone to scry for her?"

"How much do you know about scrying?"

"A tad more than nothing," I answered with a shrug.

"Okay. I can put a request in for a Tracker. We'll get one to you as soon as possible."

"A tracker?"

"Yeah. A Mage with the ability to scry. Some of our Trackers are extremely powerful. They will need personal belongings of the missing person to help get a lock on their location."

"But I don't have anything of Greer's." My heart sank. Just when we had the opportunity to find her, we hit a dead end.

"You don't have anything? Letters? Clothing?" Logan frowned.

I wanted to laugh. It wasn't as if Greer and I had spent much quality time. Our most recent close encounter had more to do with throwing punches and hair-pulling than with sisterly heart-to-hearts.

That was it.

I sat up stiffly. "I think I might have something. Could you check the coat stand beside the front door? I need my leather jacket—I wore it when Greer and I fought in Niko's lab."

Logan nodded and headed for the coat rack, returning quickly with my jacket. Greer hadn't held back when she'd fought me. At the time, I'd been certain she would've killed me given the chance. I inspected the entire coat then whooped softly as I picked at two long strands of white-blonde hair.

In the struggle, I may or may not have grabbed her hair. I grimaced, pushing away ironic thoughts of cat fights as I held the strands out to Logan.

He dug into his pocket and retrieved a rolled-up plastic envelope. He held it open and I dropped the strands into it and watched him seal the packet.

"Good. So we have her hair. Will that be enough for the Tracker?"

"I'm pretty sure there isn't anything better for a tracker than biological objects like skin, hair and blood." Logan rose and placed the plastic bag on my nightstand. "I'll get the Tracker organized and ring you to confirm the time. I'm hoping it won't take too long."

I nodded. "Thanks. Let's get this show on the road."

"That's the right attitude. Now you and I both need to get some sleep." He moved to the door. "Will you be okay?"

"I'll be fine if you have to leave." I smiled up at him. "Although you are welcome to stay. You'll be even more exhausted by the time you get to your hotel."

Logan hesitated as he looked at me, then grinned that cheeky, sexy way that sent shivers up my spine. "Okay. I'll make the call for the Tracker then hit the sack."

I smiled as he left the room to make his calls. I threw off the covers and headed into the bathroom to brush the garlic from my breath before I crashed. My reflection in the harsh fluorescent light was far from comforting.

In two weeks, I'd wasted away. My face was gaunt, cheekbones sticking out like one of those runway models who lived on a daily diet of a small block of cheese and painkilling drugs. My eyes did seem brighter though. Most likely Logan's treatment.

When I returned to the room, he was standing beside the bed, a pillow in hand, looking a bit lost.

"What's wrong?"

"I need a rug or a blanket."

"Why?" I frowned. "Aren't you sleeping in here?"

"Hell I am." He snorted and went to the closet I pointed to. "If I sleep in the same bed as you, I'll certainly not be getting any rest." I suppressed a laugh. He held the blanket to his impressive chest and strode to the doorway.

"Enjoy the couch then," I called as he pulled the door almost shut behind him.

Then he stuck his head into the room again. "Oh, and we need to be at the Tracker's place after breakfast tomorrow morning—about nine thirty. Jess said she'll meet us here."

I stretched a salute as he winked at me and disappeared into the living room.

CHAPTER 5

I WOKE TO THE PUNGENT aroma of fresh coffee and dashed from the bed thinking I had overslept. A glance at the clock assured me I hadn't. I had half an hour before Jess arrived and we had to head out to meet the Tracker and nerves were already twisting my stomach into a bundle of knots.

Unable to resist the coffee, I headed to the kitchen to pour a mugful of caffeinated goodness. Not that it woke me up or gave me a buzz or anything. Same as with alcohol, caffeine did nothing for a Walker's constitution. I just loved the taste of the drink.

Logan sat on the sofa, threw me a wink as he caught my glance, then turned his attention back to his phone. The guy worked too hard.

Coffee mug drained, I headed for the shower, scrubbing away the sleep and the exhaustion, and enjoying the heat at full blast. Enjoying the feeling of energy and life coursing through my veins. I breathed deeply, so grateful for being able to stand on my own two feet without being weak-kneed and light-headed, that I was, for one silly moment, light-headed.

When the knock sounded on the door, I strolled out of the

room feeling fresher and more pumped than I'd felt for weeks. Logan gave me an appreciative once-over as he hurried to the door.

Jess walked in. "Hello, Kailin. It is good to see you looking well." The Titan, an Immortal I was glad I had on my side, gave me a serene smile. "Ready?"

"As I'll ever be."

"We'd better get a move on then." Logan rose and we headed out to his car. We weren't much for conversation as Logan drove toward the suburbs that hugged the fringes of the city. Leafy tree-lined, doubled-storied homes and innocent-looking streets seemingly untouched by such abnormal things like demons and paranormals.

Logan drew up in front of a white Victorian double-story, complete with a cute little attic that looked out over the street. I followed him and Jess up the stairs to the stained glass-windowed doorway, rubbing nervous hands on the back of my jeans. I hoped I wasn't going to regret this.

When the door swung open and a dark-haired, jeans-clad girl opened it I hid a grin and hoped she was the Tracker. If so, I had a feeling things would be okay.

Logan held out a hand and the girl smiled and took it, shaking it warmly. "Hey, Logan."

"Hey, Mel."

Jess kissed and hugged the girl and glided serenely into the house and Logan turned to introduce me. "Kai, I'd like you to meet Melisande Morgan. Mel, this is Kailin Odel."

I shook the Tracker's hand, scanning her pale face, black hair and silvery eyes. She screamed gypsy even with the jeans and goth boots. Must be the deep purple peasant blouse peeking out from under her black leather jacket. I decided I liked her.

Other than her clothing, there was nothing about her that spoke of her powers. No jewelry proclaiming her magical skills, no pins or signs of witchcrafts around the house.

She smiled and said, "I'm glad to meet you. Although these types of meetings aren't always under the best of circumstances." She gave a wry smile and I shrugged, understanding what she meant. "Let's hope I can help you find who you're looking for." She looked over at Logan then back to Jess. "Shall we begin?"

I hadn't expected her to be this efficient and professional, but I wasn't complaining. The quicker we found Greer the better. She led us through to the dining room and we gathered around the large wooden table. I withdrew the little plastic packet from the pocket of my jeans, placing it in the center of the table.

"Ah. This is perfect. It should be a simple enough matter to track the owner of these strands. But first, may I know a little about her?" She tilted her head to one side and waited.

"We're looking for my sister, Greer. She's twenty-one and a Panther Walker." I'd been about to tell Melisande that Greer was Pariah, but she didn't need that piece of information. It was always hurtful to think about. For me and definitely more so for Greer, that as a Panther Walker she would never be able to fully transform. That somewhere in her genes, something had gone wrong and she was broken and could never be fixed, would never fit into normal Walker society. Would always be an outcast.

I blinked away the thoughts and concentrated on the tracker.

"Alright then. Ready?" Melisande smiled kindly and I knew she thought I was suffering from grief for my missing sister, but she couldn't be more wrong. I did want to find Greer, but out of duty, not love. I still hadn't forgiven her for trying to kill me.

I nodded and leaned forward. I wasn't sure what I'd expected. Maybe a map and a crystal on a piece of string. I'd seen that in an old movie once. That was the most I knew about scrying. But Melisande did nothing of the sort.

She sat back in her chair and breathed deeply in and out, in and out. Was she putting herself into a trance? She startled me when her eyes popped open and she reached for the packet.

Emptying the hair into her palm, she placed her other hand over it, holding both palms together in a praying clasp.

She sat back again, allowing her hands to remain on the table. She did her controlled breathing thing again and fell into a silent rhythm that began to lull me into a calm too.

When Melisande finally spoke, I almost jumped. "I can see her."

Jess leaned forward. "Where is she?"

"She is angry, very bitter. Almost mindlessly angry." Melisande hadn't answered Jess's question. She'd seemed not to hear her.

"Where is she, Melisande? You can see her. Can you see where she is?" Jess asked, her voice holding not a hint of impatience.

Melisande hesitated a moment then answered. "The Graylands. She's in the Graylands." She opened her eyes, looked straight at me, and frowned. "I thought you said she was alive. Wait . . . She is alive. I feel her living soul. But what is she doing in the Graylands?"

I leaned forward until my chest nudged the table edge. "I have no idea. She's been missing and we just needed to find out where she was."

"I've found her for you. But the Graylands . . . It's not easy to get into. There're rules against entering the plane of the dead."

Jess placed a hand on Melisande's arm. "You did well, Melisande. Thank you. Now that we know where she is, we can concentrate on finding a way to get her home."

Melisande nodded, her eyes still clouded with confusion, concern, and a touch of fear. "You will get her out?" Her gaze went from Jess to Logan. "I would help but I have no power to get there and back."

Logan nodded. "We understand. Don't worry. We'll get her out. Kai's dead set on it, there's no stopping her." Logan smiled.

She gave a small nod. "She must be retrieved or she will go out of her mind," Melisande said softly. "It won't take much to send her over the edge, for her to go completely insane. Don't waste any time."

My heart clenched and I paid little attention to Logan as he assured the Tracker we had no intention of wasting time. I squeezed my temples as if that would help the crazy swirling in my brain.

No matter how indifferent I'd been to Greer's predicament, Melisande's words certainly changed things.

I had to save Greer. And soon.

CHAPTER 6

We said our goodbyes and left a solemn-looking Melisande on her doorstep sufficiently placated with the promise we would get Greer out of the Graylands as soon as possible.

Once Logan drove around the corner I asked, "Why was she so upset?"

"Probably because she feels helpless." He shrugged. "Mel is the kind of Tracker that gets in, gets the person out. She gets the job done. And in this case, she couldn't because Greer was in the Graylands and the Graylands is off limits. I'd bet it's never happened to Mel before—having to find a soul in the Graylands still alive."

"Yeah. I can totally understand her frustration." I snorted. "What now? How do we get into the Graylands? How do we get her out?"

"We will need a DeathTalker," Jess answered from the back seat.

"What's a DeathTalker?" I frowned.

"They're Light Ethereals with the ability to travel between life and death, between the veils. They communicate with the dead, so they have a good understanding of the Graylands and will be able to show us how to get there."

"Okay, hold on. What exactly is the Graylands? I didn't ask when Melisande mentioned it because I didn't want to disturb her, but I'm not exactly familiar with this place."

"It's an In-Between plane," Jess replied. "The place the dead pass through on their way to eternal rest. It is also a place in which the dead remain if they are unable to find their way to their destination."

"You mean it's like Purgatory?"

"Something like that. The demon realms have easy access to the Graylands. Demons live there, make it their job to entice the dead to join them, to do their bidding."

"So what happens to the dead if they do the demon's bidding?" I asked.

"They return to this realm in a ghostly form, most often one with deeper malevolence."

"Like poltergeists?"

Jess nodded. "The ghosts are angry and demented, forced by the demons to do their bidding. Possessions, disturbances, destructive hauntings, unexplained murders. The list goes on."

I sat back for a moment, absorbing her words. "So this stuff is real." Cold fingers slithered down my spine. "What would a demon do with a living person in the Graylands?"

"I am assuming a possession in a similar fashion to the dead. They could bring the human back to the living realm and use them as a familiar to do their bidding here. There is no doubt that Greer is in mortal danger. If she resists a demon, if she angers one enough, they could kill her. And a mortal who dies in the In-Between will stay there for all eternity." Despite the seriousness of the topic, Jess's face remained serene and unaffected.

An icy chill set between my shoulder blades. Greer's potential fate was worse than I'd expected. I shuddered to think of what my family would say when they heard.

I tried to refocus. "So a DeathTalker can help us how?"

"They can show us the way in. Tell us what to do and what not to do. What weapons work and what do not."

"A survival guide to the Graylands." My words came out a croaky whisper.

"I couldn't have put it better myself," Logan spoke for the first time in a while. "Jess, have you ever heard of a Walker being stuck in the Graylands?"

Jess shook her head then pulled out her phone. Odd looking at an Immortal with a mobile phone. "I shall ask Nerina to meet us here." She lifted her head to look at me. "Oh and Nerina will need the strands of hair too."

I nodded but Jess had already returned her attention to the message she was typing out. Did the DeathTalker have a PDA as well? But I was being stupid. They were all people just like me. It would be like assuming a feline Walker wouldn't use a mobile because he turns into a cat every now and again.

Jess clicked her phone shut and pinned her gaze on the back of Logan's head. He cleared his throat as I swiveled to him. "There's something we need to discuss with you."

"Okay." I smiled, a little nervous at the change in tone of the conversation.

"Omega wishes to make you an offer." Now I knew why he hadn't yet broached the subject with me. Why he'd needed his superior to push him into it.

"What kind of offer?" My voice was cool, matching my expression.

"Omega would like to offer you a position."

"A position? So am I to assume Omega's help to locate and rescue Greer is dependent on my decision to join?" My voice dropped a few degrees. He'd better not say yes. And the longer he took to answer me, the more furious I got. "Was that what all this was? A way to show me the lengths Omega can go to help me just so that I'd be encouraged to join?" I wasn't against the art of manipulation. I just didn't like being on the receiving end of it.

"No, Kai. That's not what this is at all. You know I wouldn't do that to you. And neither would Jess." With a nod of his head, Logan urged Jess to agree. When I turned my head to the Immortal, I knew Logan was right even though I could see he was afraid he may be wrong. Jess had told me her duty was to protect and guide Logan, and one part of that was to be of assistance to me because I happened to be the Ni'amh or whatever it was she'd called me.

"Logan is being honest with you, Kailin. Neither of us has manipulated you in any way, nor do we have any intention of ever doing so. We are merely messengers of Omega in this instance. They see you as an asset. Someone who will be an advantage to the organization. Maybe even someone who can do a lot of good. But I am not here to sell the position to you. That decision you must make on your own."

"And whatever decision you make will have no impact on the help we give you," added Logan, his face strained. "You can trust me on that. And you can trust Jess."

"Okay, I believe you." For a moment, I remained silent as I considered Omega's offer. I had no idea what their agenda was. "But I can't make a decision like that right now. I've got too many things going on. Can it wait?"

"I'm sure it can wait," Logan assured me.

But Jess leaned forward. "Do not take too long. It is best to make the decision and accept or decline rather than drawing it out."

"I agree. I won't take too long. But in the meantime, I need to make plans to retrieve Greer."

Both of them nodded.

Jess's phone beeped and she flicked it open. "Nerina will meet us here tonight."

I frowned as Logan drew up in front of my building. It wasn't even midday yet. I wasn't keen on waiting for so long. "Why so late?"

"The DeathTalkers work best at night. They use the shadows to travel between the veils."

"I see. Okay, so maybe in the meantime, I'll pay my father a visit. Keep him up to speed on what's going on." I jumped out of the car, enjoying the strength in my limbs as I stretched, then bent over and looked at Logan. "So how long will this treatment last? When do you think it will start fading?"

Logan's lips turned up as he gave a small shrug. "Probably anywhere from two days to a week. You'll be the first to notice the wane in your strength levels. Try not to overtax yourself though. If you put yourself through anything very rigorous or stressful, it may negate everything I just did."

I grimaced. "I guess that also means no transforming?"

"Sorry." He didn't look sorry. "No transforming."

"Fine." I glanced at Jess. "You guys want lunch?"

"What? Are you cooking?" Logan raised an eyebrow.

I withdrew my mobile from my pocket and flicked it open. "Nope. But I am ordering."

Logan grinned and so did Jess, but both shook their heads. "Sorry, but we have to get to HQ. Paperwork. And I'd like to get more work done on the fire technique."

I grinned as they escaped my hospitality, leaving me to my thoughts of Greer and her impending insanity.

CHAPTER 7

S ILENCE HUNG HEAVY IN THE apartment as I pottered about feeling a little useless. Sunlight streamed into the living room, and a cool breeze played with the curtains. I made sure my weapons, crossbow, knives, and scimitar would fit in my rucksack.

I'd learned a costly lesson not so long ago. Never underestimate an opponent and never go anywhere unarmed. I'd gotten complacent thinking the hunt for a psycho Walker killer couldn't be as dangerous as killing Wraiths. That my strength and abilities meant I would be near-invincible.

Could I have been any more wrong?

I opted to leave the bow behind and safely strapped my knives to my ankles, well hidden by my boots. Tucking the scimitar into a leather satchel, I turned to leave my room when my gaze caught the obsidian Wraith sword, hanging on the dining room wall like a souvenir from my travels. An unlikely weapon to hide well. My arm throbbed, as if the wound answered the call of the inflicting weapon.

I shook my head and headed to the door. I was shrugging my

leather jacket on when a key jiggled the lock and someone shoved the door open.

"Grams?" I called out, simultaneously thrilled and annoyed.

"Hello, darling. I'm home." Grams sighed, dropped her keys onto the dining table, and left her duffel on the floor to come to me. She wrapped me in one of her loving, jasmine-scented hugs and I gave her a returning squeeze. Then she held me away and inspected me head to toe. "How's your hand?" Her voice got motherly and demanding, although I didn't miss the tightening at the corners of her eyes.

I recalled how she hadn't wanted to leave me when work had called her out on a job a week ago. But I'd managed to convince her that between Lily, Iain, Tara and Logan, I had plenty of people looking in on me and I'd be fine. In the end she'd left, but she hadn't looked happy and she still had that unsatisfied, almost guilty look on her face now.

"It's fine." I didn't give in to the urge to touch my forearm.

"Let me see." She moved forward.

"It's fine." I repeated and tried to step away, but she got that look in her eye and said, "Kailin Odel, please take that jacket off this minute and let me look."

I sighed, defeated. Shrugging off the jacket, I dragged up the sleeve of my pullover and stuck my forearm close to Grams' face. She bent her head to inspect the wound, pressed her finger into the sensitive skin around it, and nodded. "Good. It's healing."

"Not by itself it's not." My tone was dry and I enjoyed the almost startled look she gave me.

"What do you mean?"

"This bloody wound has had me flat on my back since you left. Logan's been treating it with his fire. Seems the fire is the only thing that can take the poison away—at least for a while."

Grams' face purpled. "Are you insane? What if he sets you alight with his fire? Playing with a Mage's power is too dangerous, Kailin."

"Don't worry, Grams. Logan's been practicing his technique and his control. We know how dangerous it can be. He's been very careful."

"As long as he's being careful." I tugged at my arm but she didn't let go.

"I'm sure he will be. I doubt Omega would want to take responsibility for my exploded hand."

Grams shuddered delicately. "Don't even use the word exploded." Then she linked arms with me and walked me over to the sofa. "Sit. I have something for you."

"Okay," I answered slowly, warily.

She hurried back to her duffel, digging around inside it for a while then withdrew something wrapped in black fabric. The moment she turned to me, I knew what it was. The magic in it seemed to resonate with my blood, my bones. Even my breath hitched as she sat next to me.

I said nothing as she opened the fabric and placed the bronze armband in my hands. "So that's where it went," I whispered.

I'd searched the apartment for the armband, wanting to examine the damage Widd'en's sword had inflicted on a piece of armor meant to protect me from anything but I hadn't found it. Eventually the pain had taken its toll on me instead and I'd forgotten my search. Now, I stared at the armor piece and for a moment considered giving it right back to Grams. What was the point in keeping the damned thing if it didn't actually do its job?

Instead, I turned it over to inspect the damage.

There was none.

The metal had been repaired perfectly. So well I couldn't tell it had ever been damaged.

I frowned at Grams. "I took it to be repaired."

"Who in the world is capable of fixing something like this so well?" Grams didn't answer. I turned to face my grandmother, taking in her unusually young features with a narrow eye.

"Grams, I think you owe me some answers. And I don't think I want to wait anymore."

She looked at me, but didn't really see me. Her mind was probably fighting a battle between reasons to tell me or not to tell me whatever it was she'd been keeping from me all this time. Then she sighed. "I guess it's time to come clean."

"Please." The dryness in my voice didn't go unnoticed, but to her credit, she said nothing except offer me a tiny raised eyebrow. "Tea?" I asked.

"Yes, please." She nodded. I stood and headed for the kitchen, pottering about with the kettle, cups and tea bags, giving her time to arrange her thoughts. She cleared her throat and smoothed a hand over her cargo-clad thigh. "So I'll start from the beginning. When your father first met Celeste, we never thought the relationship would go anywhere. My son had always been a stickler for the rules. But Celeste, she affected him in a way no one ever had. Bad enough she was Human, but a Mage? Corin had tried to keep her magic under wraps, but the Walker High Council eventually found out the truth."

I raised an eyebrow. Everyone seemed to have been aware of my mother's species and talents besides me. I poured water and waited as the tea steeped and Grams spoke.

"Corin hadn't always secluded himself in Tukats, hadn't always submerged himself in Alpha duties. He'd been part of the organization I work for since he'd reached his Change. Headstrong boy. He'd wanted to prove himself, make a difference. Help paranormals like us who are in danger."

My eyes widened. My father had always seemed like such a stick in the mud. It was near impossible to imagine him as part of any organization that sounded like Omega.

"Wait a minute," I blurted out. "You work for Omega?"

Grams shook her head. "Not Omega. But something like it. I'll get to that soon."

I shook my head and swallowed my annoyance, then brought

the tea to the coffee table in front of the sofa. I sat, but didn't feel very relaxed at all.

Grams continued. "It was at Sentinel that Corin met Celeste. They fought their feelings at first, but the more they were thrown together on missions, the harder it became. Eventually, everyone just gave up and let them be. How could we rail against a relationship with a Mage when all paranormals worked so closely together, Walkers, Mages, Ethereals, Immortals? It didn't make sense in the end. So they married, and Celeste chose to be less active in Sentinel work when Iain and Greer were little. She returned briefly. And then you came along."

There was a reminiscent smile pasted on Grams' face as she blew on her tea and took a sip.

"You were such an adorable baby. Everything seemed perfect until you showed signs of recognizing the Wraith markings." My head shot up and I stared wide-eyed at her. She nodded. "You were almost two. We'd gone out for lunch and passed an interior décor shop Celeste wanted to scope out. She did tend to think about work more than was necessary, so it was nice to see her relax. It didn't last long, mind you. You reached for the shop door and began to trace the coral-colored marks the Wraiths leave behind. Celeste was horrified. She grabbed you and we got the hell out of there as fast as we could. Back home, Celeste had no idea what to do. She sought the advice of the Elders without telling them she suspected your power. They confirmed it was highly likely her power could be handed down to any of her offspring. I think Corin and Celeste had thought a Walker/Human child would not inherit her magic. But you did. Greer and Iain were older and neither one of them showed the signs, but there was always the possibility they would develop later."

I pushed a plate of cookies toward Grams but she ignored them, taking elegant sips of her tea, her eyes staring off into a different time and place, memories and long-ago hurt. "And then came the prophecy."

"The prophecy?" I asked. Her words held echoes of Jess's tale of the Ni'amh. "Does that have something to do with me being this Ni'amh person?"

Grams' eyes widened and her entire body stiffened. She looked like she was about to crush her teacup in her palms. "How do you know about that?"

"Jess told me, but she didn't explain anything about it."

"Okay. Let's get back to that." Grams waved the question off although I could see how hard it was for her to concentrate on telling the story now that she knew I knew. "When Celeste heard about the prophecy, she knew she had to protect you, and your siblings too. That's when she left. Your father was devastated, but he also knew she left to protect your family, to ensure no harm came to you. She made him promise to keep you in Tukats until you were grown, if not forever. He promised. He did everything she asked, but I think he never forgave himself for letting her go. And when you rebelled and wanted to leave, it crushed him because he felt he had failed her. It's why he only agreed to let you go if you came to me so I could watch you."

"But you're barely around, Grams. How much watching can you do when you're traipsing around the world every other week doing whatever it is you do?" There was a cold edge to my words but she ignored me, and I turned back to study my tea, now too cool to enjoy. I couldn't decide if it was the brown cream floating on the surface of the tea or the story Grams was telling me that turned my stomach.

"Although Corin and Celeste had agreed not to keep in touch, I certainly hadn't. I saw Celeste often. Made sure she was okay. She stayed mostly off the radar. Continued her demon hunting and missed Corin and her family terribly. I was her only link, passing her photographs of all your milestones. She especially hated not being there for your change until I reminded her that clan law would have prohibited her from being anywhere near you during your time of Change."

My head shot up again. Mom had told me the same thing when we had spoken in Wrythiin.

Grams paused and my stomach twisted. A shadow crossed her face as she paused just a little too long. "There is something else I'd meant to tell you, but I didn't feel you were ready at the time. Now is as good a time as any, I guess." Grams met my curious gaze. "The armband belonged to your mother."

CHAPTER 8

"WHAT?" I STARED AT HER, shaking my head in disbelief. It was all so much to absorb. "Is that why you gave it to me?"

"Yes. I knew you were hunting. We'd seen the signs of it around the city. I checked with Celeste to see if it was her and when she said no, I knew it had to be you. And you needed protecting. The portal key was also your mother's. She'd had a few created to allow her easy travel back and forth between this world and the Wraith world."

I nodded. "That's why she was so pissed when I told her about the key. She said she was going to kill you."

Grams laughed. "That's Celeste. Ever the protector. I had tried to convince her to come home now that I knew you'd started hunting. I didn't tell her, of course. She had enough to worry about. But she refused to listen. She'd only stop when she was certain you were safe. She also knew there was another hunter in Chicago and she had set her mind to finding out who it was. Of course, I thwarted her every move and it was getting a tad tiresome."

"So putting me onto Storm who guided me to Tara, and

giving me the armband and the key was your way of looking out for me?" I wanted to be angry at what seemed to be my whole life being controlled by my grandmother, but could I really be pissed when all she was doing was making sure I had everything I needed? She had never interfered in my hunting. She had never even tried to stop me, directly or indirectly.

She nodded, her face filled with lines of worry that hinted at her true age for just a moment or two. "I could only do what I was able. Prophecies are dangerous things. Not to be messed with. We are not allowed to try to change or influence fate."

I was curious. Jess hadn't given me the whole story, just bits and pieces and hints at how important I was, but nothing concrete so I could understand how I could be better at being this Ni'amh. "So what does this prophecy say?"

Grams looked pained. As if even contemplating telling me physically hurt her. "I'm not even sure I should be discussing it with you. There are dangers to knowing one's fate." When she paused, I glared at her. "I can only tell you the gist of it. It says,

'And she who wields the obsidian blade, whose eyes part the Veil of the worlds, she shall be the champion of all the Olde Ones.

She is the Hunter and the savior and destroyer of the world.'

You can see why this prophecy isn't exactly likely to generate mass celebration."

I snorted. "Typical. Hone in on the one negative word in the entire thing." I sat back feeling a sense of awe and shock at having heard the words of the prophecy for the first time.

"Quite right. But that is what the council fears. There's more to the prophecy though. An entire book filled with predictions, all so convoluted and mysterious that the council's had people trying to translate it for decades."

"Interesting." I pushed the now-abandoned cup of tea away from me and sat back, pursing my lips. "So, can we get a hold of a copy of what's been decoded so far?"

"I'm not sure. Might have to bend a few rules."

"So bend them. I need to know what they say." It came out harsher than I'd expected, but Grams didn't seem to mind.

"I'll see what I can do."

"And Sentinel? What are they?"

Grams sighed, resigning herself to finally telling me who she worked for. "Sentinel is similar to Omega in that we perform the same functions, investigation into paranormal disturbance and related crime, protection in case a species is in danger or has been revealed, exorcisms, tracking, things like that. We also help out the Human police with tracking missing persons, but we try and do so discreetly. People still look at so-called psychic trackers as if they're witches in disguise."

"So what's the big difference between Sentinel and Omega?"

She grimaced. "Sentinel has existed for centuries. The organization has been around for as long as our history has been recorded. It changed its name every so often, but the structure and purpose of the organization have never changed."

"So they have something to do with the Supreme High Council?"

Grams sighed and pressed her temples. "I guess you could say for all intents and purposes they are the Supreme High Council. Sentinel acts as the formal investigative arm of the Supreme High Council."

"Oh." I tried to process everything she'd just said, the part that Grams worked for a pretty powerful organization. "So why didn't you help me when Lily and Byron went missing?"

"Because you already had Omega on the case. Sentinel and Omega have an agreement not to step on each other's toes unless absolutely necessary. Both organizations have the manpower and the technology to do the job properly. A few years ago, the High Council decided it was best to not go head-to-head with Omega. They are too big, too powerful, too tenacious to get rid of. So the High Council decided to let them operate but to continue to keep an eye on them."

"Keep an eye on them? How?" Grams raised her eyebrows and I gasped. "You mean you have a mole in Omega?" I snickered, liking the way the High Council thought.

"More like *moles*." She emphasized the plural. "So we keep an eye on them, and in the end, the paranormal world is policed and taken care of. I do think that's what matters most in the end."

"But the High Council does suspect Omega has an agenda that's not in keeping with theirs?" I asked, wondering if that job offer had anything to do with their agenda.

Grams nodded, and suddenly, I was glad I hadn't decided to join Omega on the spot. "Omega's organization is derived from an offshoot branch of the High Council called the Council of Enoch. Enoch and his followers disagreed with many of the Council's methods of attending to paranormal policing and laws. They wanted to be more stringent. They wanted to learn more about the different species' physiology. They were radical in many ways. Much too radical for the High Council to sit by and accept. They were stood down and it seemed it had been what they were waiting for. Almost immediately, they set up their own council and got the word out that people had a choice as to who they called for help. The High Council tried to remain discreet, believing that centuries of loyalty would stand for something. They were wrong to a certain extent. Those who saw the High Council as old and too set in their ways saw Omega as a new beginning, especially with the world on the cusp of a technological transformation. But both organizations are equally powerful, equally effective. The only difference is that the High Council still functions as the umbrella overseer."

"So their Council of Enoch still answers to the High Council."

"They want to play by the 'rules.' They want people to see a semblance of hierarchy so their own regulatory actions will be accepted. They don't want to let go of their access to the power of the High Council."

"Of course. The High Council legitimizes their entire organization." I nodded. The more I learned about Sentinel, the High Council, and Omega, the more fascinating things became.

"That's right." Grams looked drained. The truth often takes its toll. I stared at her and marveled how she'd been there, watching out for me all along, without me even realizing it. It had seemed a bit convenient that she'd arrived with the armband just before things hit the fan with Niko. Even more so when she'd appeared out of nowhere to tend to my Wraith sword wound after the Wraith Lord had injured me and disappeared with Anjelo, Niko, and Greer.

"How did you know?" When she looked up at me with questions in her eyes I continued. "About my injury...that the Wraith had injured me? Did you know?"

She nodded. "Coming home to the apartment all torn up, I knew something bad had happened. My nose gave me a pretty good idea of what had happened here, but I called Sentinel to access the mole. It didn't take long for them to report back your position. And as it turned out, a call to Iain confirmed he'd already been taken to you. So it all worked out well in the end."

I took a deep breath and felt a surge of love for my Grams. I leaned over and wound my arms around her for a cuddle. "So does this mean you're going to stop flitting in and out of here so mysteriously?"

"Yes, I think it does." She squeezed back.

"And no more secrets about Sentinel?"

"No more secrets," she whispered into my ear.

"Okay, since we're not keeping secrets, I have two things to tell you."

"Go on."

"Logan brought a Tracker in. I wanted to know exactly where Greer was before I decided who I was going to find first. But now that you're here, I have a question." When she tilted her head expectantly I continued. "Can't we split the job? You go for Mom and I'll go for Greer?"

"Unfortunately, that's not as easy as you think. The Supreme High Council forbids any kind of travel to the demon planes. And they've gone as far as to use powerful magic on the Veil between the worlds to prevent us from entering. Only a demon may enter the demon world."

"Then how did Mom get into the Wraith world?"

"Because she's a Demon Hunter, like you. She is the Hunter and she is the only person able to travel between the planes at will. And now, of course, there is you—a Hunter even more powerful than Celeste."

I folded my arms, resigned to the task. "So there isn't anyone who can help me."

"I'm sorry, honey. I would have come earlier. I know this is difficult for you, but with Celeste imprisoned, you're the only one who can get her out of there."

"That's okay. It was just a thought." I couldn't deny I was terribly disappointed.

I wanted to pout, but Grams brought me back to my senses. "So, about the Tracker. I assume she told you where Greer is?"

"Yeah. She's in the Graylands." Even saying the name gave me a chill.

Grams went deathly pale and sat up stiff and frowning. "The Graylands?" She whispered the word as if saying it out loud would make it far too real. "How is she going to get out of there?"

"I'm going to get her out," I said firmly, more to convince myself than anything else. A part of me still resisted the decision to find Greer first.

"But, how? I know you can get in because it's a dark plane. But how will she pass through the Veil if it's locked and warded against her? The protection spells won't allow her to pass."

Grams was right. This was more complicated than I thought. "I'm seeing the DeathTalker tonight. I'm sure she'll be able to tell me how to do that."

"Who are you seeing?"

"Her name is Nerina." Gram's eyes lit with recognition and she smiled. "You know her?"

"Yes. Both Omega and Sentinel often use the same outside contractors. There are operatives who have remained unaffiliated with either organization, like Nerina and a few Trackers I know. There are lots of them I do believe."

That gave me an idea but I filed it away to think about another time. Maybe I could turn down Omega's offer, but make a counter. The idea of an unaffiliated operative was far more appealing to me, especially when I much preferred being my own boss.

"Do you want to be here tonight? For the meeting with Nerina?" I offered. She was Greer's grandmother after all.

But Grams shook her head. "You don't need me. And it would probably make things a little uncomfortable—Omega and Sentinel in one room for a tracking. Just keep me updated on what she says." Grams patted my knee and shifted on the sofa. "I have some errands to run."

"Errands, Grams?" I raised an eyebrow and smiled at her.

She gave me a sheepish grin and laughed, the sound echoing around the room. The light was weaker outside—we'd spent a lot of time talking. "Okay, I have some Sentinel stuff to do. I'll be home later." She leaned toward me and hugged me tightly. "Take care of yourself, Kai."

I hugged her back, then extricated myself from her arms. "It's only going to be a few hours, Grams. I'm sure I'll manage," I answered dryly.

She shook her head at me as if she believed there really was no hope for me, then grabbed her bags and headed into her room. A few minutes later, she left with a wave and another warning to take care. My mind was going a mile a minute and I barely noticed her departure.

CHAPTER 9

AS SOON AS GRAMS LEFT, I headed out, walking the few blocks to Tara's shop at a steady pace. It was nice to be outside in the late afternoon sun. I hadn't seen sunshine much in the last few weeks.

And now, although the fire treatment had rejuvenated me, I was still strangely tired. I was careful to not tax myself in case I totally undid all Logan's hard work.

I pressed my hand to my injured forearm. The flesh around the wound was still sore to the touch. More painful than this morning. The day had definitely taken the oomph out of me.

Tara's shop came into view as I turned the corner. I shoved the door open, listening to the tinkling sound of the bell above the door. Tara sat at the counter, perched on a high chair, bent low over a contraption that looked like a microscope on steroids. She had a syringe in her hand, the barrel filled with deep purple liquid. Probably working on bullets like the ones she'd made for my crossbow.

"Hey you," I called out as the door shut with a whoosh. The place smelled warm and dusty. Sunlight streamed through the front window, reflecting off the various shelves filled with an endless number of weapons.

Tara beamed as she watched me approach the counter, but she didn't put the syringe down. "I've just got to finish this bullet, then you'll have my full attention."

I waved her away but she already had her head down and didn't see. "Don't worry about me. I can wait."

She smiled, her attention on the microscope. I strolled around the shop, examining the weapons covering every spare inch of space on the surrounding shelves. Weapons from every culture, every time period, every metal known to man. I could just imagine Tara and her mother collecting these daggers and swords and pistols and bows, storing them over the centuries. The shopfront was more a museum than a weapons store. I couldn't understand how Tara could bear to part with any of them. The amount of history each piece held alone would surely be on an art collector level.

A rustling at the entrance to the inner apartment drew my attention and Gracie, Tara's mother, walked into the store. She made a beeline for me. "Kailin, my dear, what a horrible time you have had."

She held her palms out to me and I placed my hands on them. Her face remained serene, calm with an edge of steel to it. Tara's mother was no ordinary woman. Even now she exuded a regal air, but without the airs and graces of human royalty. Referring to her as Gracie seemed somehow disrespectful, demeaning to her standing, to whom she really was, a queen of the Ethereal Fae, a queen whose line held the unique power to mold metal, a substance known to cause great weakness to all Fae, and yet Gracie and Tara honed the element like it was any other natural substance.

"Now tell me, how are you feeling, my dear?" She drew me to the counter and waved me at the pair of stools opposite Tara.

"I'm feeling much better today in fact. Logan used his fire

magic to heal me, so today's been better than most days." I perched on the stool and smiled under her scrutiny.

"Ah yes, the young fire Mage, Logan. Tara has filled me in. Now, my dear, any news on your mother or your sister?" I was startled to see how very concerned she was about my family.

"No news on Mom, but we now know where Greer is. We just have to figure out a way to get her out." I sighed. Whether the sigh was fatigue or frustration, I didn't care to know right now.

"And where exactly is she?" Gracie's eyes never left my face, and across the counter, Tara tensed as if she too were eager to hear my revelation.

I hesitated only for a moment. This was the reason I was here anyway. "Greer is still alive but she's in the Graylands."

The silence that followed was palpable. "Kailin." Gracie breathed my name, shock filtering through each syllable. "The Graylands. That is bad news indeed."

"I'll find a way to get her out," I said, my voice brooking no argument. Somehow, I felt the need to reassure her that I'd complete my mission.

"But nobody is allowed to enter the Graylands. Only those who traverse the worlds: demons, the dead, and those who have the power to project their minds into the dead realm. I do know some Olde Fae who can enter the Graylands and the Demon worlds, but to have a living human trapped in the land of the dead and damned... Nothing like that has ever happened before."

The Fae Queen was visibly upset at the news. Across from me, Tara's movements had stilled. I met her gaze and she too had a look of hopelessness and sorrow in her eyes. I hesitated only for the briefest moment. "Don't worry. I'm going to the Graylands to bring her back."

"But the portals are spelled. Nobody can pass through." Tara shook her head.

"I can."

Tara reached for my hand. "This is insane, Kai. Nobody can go there, nobody alive can enter."

"Nobody besides the Ni'amh." Beside me Gracie uttered the words in a hushed whisper.

"Mother," Tara admonished her, "you know that's just a silly old prophecy. Besides everyone knows the Hunter goes back and forth between the planes all the time."

"You know of the Hunter?" I asked, staring from mother to daughter.

"Of course. The Fae court has worked with the Hunter on numerous occasions. We owe her many debts. As she owes us a few too."

"Mother, be honest. The Fae owe the Hunter more than she will ever owe us."

Gracie laughed although her eyes didn't reflect her amusement. They seemed to be staring off into space. "You are right as always, Tara," she said absently. Then she slowly turned her gaze to me and gave me a thorough once over. Her eyes narrowed as they studied my face. "The coloring is right, skin, even the shade of hair and the physique."

"Mother, what are you babbling about?" Tara asked the question though her eyes remained on her microscope.

"I'm not babbling, dear. I think I just figured out who we have standing here in our shop today."

My chest tightened as the Fae queen held my gaze. Tara snorted. "Mother, I think you may be fevered. You know exactly who Kailin is."

"Not really, Tara. Not until now."

Tara clicked her tongue and pushed away from the microscope to reach behind her for a small box. "Mother, please try and make a little sense. Kailin's going to think you are soft in the head."

"Kailin knows exactly why I'm not soft in the head, don't you,

Kailin?" Gracie turned to stare at my face again. "How did I not realize it before? It was right here to see all this time."

"I'm sorry, Gracie. I didn't know myself until very recently," I answered, feeling truly apologetic for some reason. I felt uncomfortable knowing that Gracie may think I'd hoodwinked her all this time, but that made no sense because this whole Ni'amh story was nobody else's business but mine.

"Know what?" Tara faced me with her hands on her hips and her cheeks getting redder with each moment that passed.

"That I am the Ni'amh."

I could cut the silence with a knife.

"What?" The word came out a strangled shriek. "What are you talking about?"

"My grandmother told me who I really am. My mother is the Hunter. Celeste."

"You have got to be kidding me." Tara sat on her stool with a small thump, looking slightly lost. She had totally forgotten about boxing up her newly made cartridges.

"No. Not kidding. Believe me, I'm as shocked as you are." There wasn't any need to tell her that I'd known I was the Ni'amh for weeks, just that I hadn't had any idea how it was connected to both my mother and me until recently.

Tara sat, slack-jawed and eyes wide for a little too long. Then she blinked a few times.

"Kailin, this means that you are able to traverse the Veil and enter the Graylands. It also means if you are venturing into demon territory, you will be needing demon-grade weaponry," said Gracie. She turned to the still silent Tara. "Darling, close your mouth and box your syringes. We have a lot of work ahead of us."

"I quite like the sound of demon-grade weaponry," I said, smiling at Gracie and Tara.

"Um. Yeah, demons don't die easily. They need special ammunition, a lot like the Wraiths. In fact—Oh." Tara paused and stared at me with an odd expression. "Is that why you've been able to track the Wraiths? You're not a Wraith Hunter. You're a Demon Hunter."

I grinned at Tara. "Yeah. I'm a Demon Hunter."

"And not just any Demon Hunter, one of the greatest Demon Hunters to ever walk the earth," Gracie said.

"And the Demon Hunter who also spells the destruction of the earth," Tara responded, her eyes darkening with sadness.

"Tara, be silent. As with most prophecies, it is often the interpretation that causes hysteria. We cannot define exactly what the prophecy says. Just because it mentions the word 'destruction' does not mean Kailin will end the world." Gracie patted my hand. "That's just narrow-minded thinking. There is far more to the prophecy than just the ramifications of a single word."

Tara slowly turned her still wide-eyed gaze to Gracie. All she said was, "Yes, Mother."

CHAPTER 10

GRACIE'S WORDS REMAINED ON MY mind for a long while after I left the shop. I watched the sky darken outside as I ate my takeout dinner, barely tasting the usually delicious burger. Grams hadn't returned, as expected.

At seven I heard Logan's knock on the door and opened to find him with Jess. And nobody else.

"Where's Nerina?" I asked, looking around him at the empty corridor.

"She'll be along soon. She prefers not to walk the streets like the rest of us have to." Logan smiled as I shut the door and the three of us gathered inside.

"We are ready?" Jess asked, looking from Logan to me.

We both nodded and she closed her eyes for a moment. The action struck me as odd but not surprising. Something else I'd just learned about Immortals. They were on a telepathic network with DeathTalkers.

Interesting.

Before I could do much else but breathe in and out, the air shifted in the corner of my vision. I turned to watch empty nothing darken and twist, gray shadows of every shade from darkest metal to palest gray. A fluttering like feathers or fabric sounded as the gray mass of shadow coalesced into a more solid collection of swirling, dancing fabric.

The whirlwind settled to reveal a girl. She could have been anywhere between eighteen and twenty, but her silvery eyes gave away nothing.

"Greetings, Jess. Greetings, Logan." Then she turned to me. "And greetings to you, Ni'amh. I am honored to meet you."

My heart stuttered. I didn't want to be referred to as the Ni'amh. Talking about it was one thing, but people using it as my name? I didn't like it. Not one bit.

"Please, call me Kailin. I'd much prefer it." I couldn't help the slight edge to my voice, but if the girl noticed, she didn't react.

"Very well, Kailin. As you wish." She nodded, the silver in her eyes turning and twisting although her face remained neutral. "We can begin as soon as you are ready."

"Where would you feel most comfortable?" I asked, waving a hand at the apartment.

"The table is fine."

"Now, you have a personal item I can use to find her?" asked Nerina.

I withdrew the plastic pouch and placed it in her upturned palm. She opened the packet and dropped the strands onto her hand, her face remaining expressionless. That fight with Greer was certainly coming in handy.

Nerina closed her fist and sat against the backrest of the chair.

Silence blanketed the table.

An invisible breeze ruffled the DeathTalker's hair, playing with the soft gray silk of her flowing dress. Everything about her was gray. Even the strands of her thick, lustrous hair were washed of all color.

She lifted her chin, her neck straightening until she looked at me. But she didn't see me at all. Her metallic eyes shifted color so smoothly, becoming a pearly gray, the change sending shivers up my spine.

Her fist tightened over Greer's hair and she opened her hand, splaying her fingers wide.

Nobody spoke.

I blinked as a gray-white mist rose from the strands of hair in her palm, swirling and twisting like an incandescent snake. It rose, curling toward Nerina's face as if she called it to her.

She probably had.

The smoke reached her and she breathed it in. It flowed smoothly toward her face, then twisted and broke apart into tiny little smoky dregs of gray, like torn bits of fabric. Then the sinuous shreds of gray disappeared into Nerina's nostrils as she continued to breathe in.

Nerina shuddered, her sightless eyes still staring in my direction. She let out a soft breath, more like a gasp. "I see her. A Panther Walker. She lives and yet she walks the Graylands." She spoke as if she was not surprised. Logan or Jess must have filled her in on Melisande's tracking results.

Jess leaned to her. "Is she in danger, Nerina?"

Nerina's gaze didn't waver. She just stared straight ahead, transfixed on whatever it was she was seeing, on wherever it was that Greer's hair had taken her. She puffed a soft breath again and whispered, "She is prey. She is hunted."

We'd known that was possible. A human in a dead land must be big-time demon fodder. But just having Nerina say it out loud made Greer's retrieval all the more urgent.

"So she is not safe," said Jess as she spoke to Nerina. "Is she hurt?"

"She was injured, yes." The DeathTalker spoke slow and soft, as if she spoke in secret and didn't want to be overheard. "Old wounds. A few of them. They were inflicted when she entered the Graylands. But I can feel the wounds have healed."

"Are you able to communicate with her?" Jess asked.

Nerina shook her head. "She is blocked to me. Perhaps it is because she is still alive. When I perform the Calling, the soul I am normally trying to contact is no longer alive. There is an empty space within the soul I can fill, which allows me to communicate with them, through them. In this case, the girl is closed off from a joining, so I cannot speak to her directly."

A shaft of disappointment ran through my gut. I'd expected more information from Nerina but we were nowhere further than we'd been after talking to Melisande. But Nerina continued to speak.

"I can sense her, though. Sense her emotions. And I think she can tell I am there with her." After a small pause. "She thinks I am a ghost."

"Apart from the injury you mentioned, is she okay?" I asked without thinking. I gave Jess an apologetic glance but she just inclined her head as if to say it was okay.

Nerina gave her head an almost violent shake, sending her silvery gray hair shuddering around her face. "No. Her mind is unstable. Her thoughts are frantic, distorted. She has a deep anger in her. And a profound bitterness." Nerina paused. "Has she always been this way?" And even though she spoke to me her eyes remained out of focus.

"A little," I answered, not so sure how much to say, not so sure how much I wanted people to know about Greer's emotional issues. "But what you are describing seems much worse than she has ever been."

"I suspect the Graylands have begun to affect her mind," Nerina said, and she gasped softly.

"What happened? What's wrong?" I leaned forward wanting to shake the DeathTalker until she said something.

"There are demons around her." Nerina frowned, her porcelain forehead wrinkling. "But she does not seem afraid of them. She seems impervious to them."

"She is a strong Walker. From an Alpha pack. Perhaps she managed to overcome one or two of them?" Jess suggested.

"Perhaps." Nerina wasn't convinced. She frowned. "I can tell you no more about the girl than this." The milky cloudiness in Nerina's eyes faded and she was back with us. "My connection to her is gone. But I can give you information of her location."

"Thank you, Nerina. That would be very helpful." Logan provided the DeathTalker with a pad and paper and on it she wrote an address.

"The Graylands, the land of In-Between is referred to as such because it is an intangible place. But it has structure and form to those who occupy it. Unlike the other planes, the Graylands do not have their own makeup. It is a mirror image of our plane that is devoid of color and light."

"It looks like this world?" I asked.

"Yes. From the buildings to the street names to lakes, mountains, and trees. The only difference is there is no power, no color. Only shadows and an endless twilight." She pushed the pad toward me and I turned it around, frowning at the scrawl.

It took me a few moments and then I grinned. "I see. You said the world was ours in a mirrored form. Ninety-five Gilligan's Way. I know where that is." I tapped the table with my forefinger. "So what will I need to take with me?"

"I would suggest food as nothing grows in the dead lands. There is no commerce, no markets, nowhere to purchase items that do not exist. So you will need sustenance. And weapons. If something exists here in this world it will exist there. If it is created here it will 'become' there. So you do have a choice with weapons. You may leave them here and pick them up there or you may take them with you."

Yeah, demon-grade ammunition and weapons. Tara and Gracie had that covered. "Food and weapons. Got it. So how do I get in?"

"That is something you will have to discuss with the High Priestess."

Jess shifted in her seat. "I thought you would be able to tell us how to get in?" Jess didn't seem to like the idea of consulting this High Priestess. The set of her jaw made that clear.

"You will need a portal key. And unless you have a working key that opens the Veil to the Graylands, you will need to have an audience with the High Priestess to make that request."

Jess gave the tiniest shake of her head. She didn't like it. I thought of Grams and the High Council. Maybe she could speak to them for me. Nerina shifted her chair back a bit before standing with the tips of her fingers touching the surface of the table. "Please contact me as soon as you are ready. I will accompany you to visit the High Priestess."

Then there was a fluttering of gray and a gusting of shadows and Nerina disappeared.

CHAPTER 11

LOGAN SIGHED AND SAT BACK in his chair. "Well that does make things complicated."

"Isn't there somewhere else we can get a portal key?" I asked, hoping he'd say yes, although from the look on his face, I wasn't prepared to bet on it.

"There are other places but the DeathTalkers would probably be the most compliant." Then he snorted. "Not that *they* are the easiest of the races to deal with."

"What's wrong with talking to their High Priestess?" I turned to Jess.

"She is not the easiest person to bargain with. Her sense of fairness is a little warped at the best of times."

"Then why is she the leader if she's not such a nice person?" After the question left my lips I realized how naive I sounded.

"She was next in line," Jess answered with a shrug, although the darkness in her eyes didn't imply a nonchalance.

"That would explain it," I said, my tone dry. I swallowed the desire to laugh. "Yet you say she is the easiest option?"

"She is," replied Logan. "There are necromancers we could contact who would happily help." I perked up. Necromancers?

"For a price. Necromancers usually take things you need. Like lives or bodies or souls. I think you might want to keep those for yourself, wouldn't you?"

I didn't answer the question. Wasn't necessary. "Looks like we're out of choices." I looked at Logan. "When do you think they will allow us to see her?"

Logan sighed again. "Let me see what I can arrange." He got to his feet then paused to search my face. "Are you sure about this?"

"Yes. Greer needs rescuing as soon as possible. And after what Melisande and Nerina had to say, I think I've pretty much been convinced I made the right decision. We do whatever it takes to rescue Greer. Besides, I don't think my mother would be too impressed if I left her daughter in the Graylands to die a horrific death."

Logan nodded and rose to his feet. "Right, then. I'm off to HQ. Maybe Gunther can help me smooth Kira's feathers a bit, get her in a good mood before we see her. Jess?" He glanced at the Immortal.

She waved him off. "You go ahead. I have a few things I need to attend to."

Logan gave me a smile then hurried out of the apartment. I stared at the closed door for a moment. "He's really not happy about this, is he?"

"He knows we have to deal with paranormal red-tape as he calls it. He just doesn't like it very much when egos get in the way of him doing his job," Jess said, her voice holding a clear note of affection for Logan.

"I think I know exactly how he feels." I took a deep breath. The Graylands certainly didn't seem like a place I wanted to go. In fact, I would have thought nothing would get me to set foot in a place that sounded as dangerous as that. But here I was, putting things in motion, preparing to do exactly that.

I turned to Jess. "Is he okay? I mean in terms of your watching over and protecting him because of who he is?"

Jess nodded serenely. "I do what I can. The rest is up to Logan."

"So what is so all-fired important about him anyway?"

"I am afraid I cannot discuss the details of Logan's purpose with anyone."

I'd expected a similar response so I wasn't surprised. Just annoyed at being thwarted again. But I decided to press on. "Then can you discuss *me* with me?"

"What would you like to know?"

"What exactly is it I am supposed to be. This Ni'amh? What is it?"

"The Ni'amh is the Hunter."

Another cryptic answer. I gritted my teeth. "That doesn't tell me anything. It's what you told me the last time. I need more information than that."

"The last time we spoke, I told you about the prophecy. You are the ultimate Hunter—a Demon Hunter who will save the world."

I stared at Jess. "You're not going to tell me, are you?"

The Titan remained silent. I almost expected her to wind the magical threads of her Immortal power around me. To seduce me with her immortal allure and make me forget everything I wanted to ask her.

But she didn't.

"The prophecy is convoluted. What we do understand of the foretelling is that you will destroy the new Wraith army."

"What is this new army? Who are they and what do they want?" I frowned, not liking the thought of a potential Wraith revolution in the earth plane.

"They are a faction. Their intention is to break the treaty. And gain entry to our world again. They have been banished for a long time, and now there are certain groups within the Wraith realm that believe the punishment meted out for a few indiscretions so long ago were unfair and they want to avenge years of what they call *oppression*."

"Are they right?" I asked, wondering if they were justified in their belief.

"What do you mean?" Jess asked, frowning.

"Was the banishment really unfair? Was it only a few Wraiths who broke the rules?" I clarified, knowing what can happen when only a small group make the rules. It's not like the paranormals had a proper political system.

"From what I recall, the incidences were widespread enough to justify the ruling. Perhaps it was not the entire race of Wraiths who were guilty, but it was enough for them to be deemed dangerous. At the time, it was agreed among all the races that they be banished from entering this plane."

I stared at Jess but didn't really see her. It made a lot of sense why an entire race of people would be angered at being punished for the criminal activity of a small minority. But it didn't really matter right now. I needed to get my mother and Anjelo safely out of Wrythiin. And for that I needed to ensure I didn't accidentally bite the hand that fed me information.

Jess continued to speak. "I am here for your protection. But as for information, I can only tell you what you need to know."

I remembered the words of the prophecy:

'The Cat shall lead the fight and cut them to the quick, but without the help of the Mages and all earthbound Ethereals, her fight will be for naught.'

I needed them no matter how frustrating they may be. And I'd just have to find a way to get the information I wanted even if Jess refused to give it to me.

"Thank you, Jess. Please, is there anything else you can tell me?" I had to try. I was working on such meager crumbs of information that even one more piece would help.

"I wish there was, but the full prophecy cannot be trusted for its accuracy." I blinked and frowned. "There are things the prophecy predicts that are open to interpretation. I think it is best you are not told things that may possibly steer you off your course because of interpretation."

"What you mean is the part of the prophecy that says I will be the destroyer of the world?" I'd heard it from two sources in one day. I had a feeling there were more people who knew about it than Grams and the Fae.

Jess stiffened, her eyes turning hard. "Where did you hear that? I do not recall telling you that."

"Did you think I wouldn't find out? I know too many people and too many people know me to keep that kind of thing from me for too long," I said it without being caustic although that's how I felt.

"Kailin, you have to understand. It is just as I said. It is the individual interpretation that makes this prophecy dangerous. You have the right to know what the prophecy says, but you need to be aware that what it says is not necessarily what it means. Prophets have a nasty habit of being misleading. And one's fate is not something to be messed with."

"You think if I know the truth about the prophecy, I'll do something to prevent it from happening?" I frowned, shaking my head. Surely she knew I had more sense than that.

"Sometimes just knowing can set your fate on a different path." Jess shook her head, brooking no argument.

"And you don't want me to walk a different path, right? You want me to be the one to destroy the Wraith Army."

"Yes. It has to be you. You are our only hope." She spoke kindly, gently, but the weight of her words wasn't kind or gentle. They were a mantle I wasn't sure I wanted to bear right now.

"Even if it means the destruction of the world?" I asked.

"I do not interpret the words to mean that. It may be metaphorical. The destruction of darkness. Change is known to be destructive too. Perhaps all you will bring about is change. How do we know really? And we cannot sit here, hands bound by one interpretation of a prophecy written a thousand years ago."

"A thousand years?" I swallowed hard. "Someone wrote a prophecy about me a whole millennium ago?"

Jess nodded.

I raised my eyebrows and sat back. *What could a girl say to that?*

CHAPTER 12

IT WAS AFTER EIGHT WHEN Jess left, but I was restless. Sleep pulled at me, dulling my senses and weighing my eyelids down, but I couldn't rest. Couldn't stop thinking about prophecies and mirrored worlds in which the dead and the demons roamed.

A knock on the door roused me from a semi-sleep and I was not happy. The bedside clock claimed 9 p.m. and I believed it. It had been a long day.

Before I reached the door, I knew who it was.

Gone were the days when I let my guard down. I'd done exactly that when I'd visited my father not too long ago. I'd allowed my emotional baggage to dull my awareness, to let my guard down just long enough to enter the apartment without checking, to allow myself to be abducted by Niko's thugs.

Not happening again.

Lily stood on the threshold, holding a paper bag, grinning at me. Something I was slowly getting used to. Lily had changed. Her spiteful meanness, the hooded eyes, the coldness. They were all gone. She was taking the whole life-saving thing to a whole new level.

In the last two weeks, it had been Lily who'd run my errands, popped in every day to make sure I was eating, to nag me until I forced myself into the shower. Mostly I just did as she asked so she'd leave faster.

I never let her know how much she'd helped me. It was hard to mope when staring down this new, cheerful Lily. Not that I couldn't see the bleakness in her eyes when she thought I wasn't looking.

Anjelo was never far from either of our minds.

"So how has your day been?" she asked, a little too chipper.

"Lily, it's after nine at night." I folded my arms and raised an eyebrow. "I do need my rest you know."

"But I see you've been up and about." She looked me up and down and sauntered into the room. "You actually look pretty damn good for a half-dead panther."

I sighed and shut the door. Now that Lily was here, even the pull of sleep was gone. She was rummaging in the utensil drawer and soon withdrew two spoons.

"I have ice cream. Double Chocolate Chocolate-Chip Delight." She waved the spoons at me, giving me another toothy grin.

Now how could I say no to that?

I switched on the TV and let an old movie play softly in the background—one appropriately about ghosts, and the making of pottery, of all things.

It seemed so weird. Too normal, too mundane to be sitting here eating chocolate ice cream while Greer was stuck in a demon-filled dead land and my mother and Anjelo were waiting to be saved from a Wraith jail.

"So tell me what's been going on. I take it Logan's been by?"

"Huh?" I stared at her. How would she have known that? I was dressed for sleeping—pajama bottoms and a tank top. Then she flicked her eyebrows at my bare arm.

"Yeah. He came by last night. He'd been practicing and wanted to administer another dose of his poison-killing fire." I made a face.

"It sounds so clinical. As if he walked in here with a syringe and jabbed you in the butt."

I snorted. "That would have been the preferred method of administration had I had the choice."

"So now that you're feeling better, what are we going to do?"

"What do you mean?" I asked, digging into the ice-cream tub.

"Well, we have people to save, in case you forgot. Did Logan fry your brain cells while he was *administering* his treatment?" Lily leaned forward as if by looking into my eyes she could detect any fried brain cells.

"Of course I didn't forget." After a micro-moment of hesitation, I continued. "We found Greer. I have to go for her first."

"Really? That super-cold bitch?" For a second, Lily reverted to the Lily I'd known when Anjelo had been around.

I put my hand on her arm, but she held herself stiff. "I know, Lily. And you know how I feel about Greer. I wasn't going to go for her first. I'd honestly decided to go back to Wrythiin first. I even have the portal key."

"Then what happened to change your mind?" Her eyes spat fire.

"I decided to be smart about it, so Logan arranged a tracker to scry for Greer, and we found her. Logan made me promise to wait to make my final decision. I guess he wanted to be certain I wouldn't regret my decision. And maybe he was right. The tracker found Greer."

Lily's eyes lit up. "You were scrying for her? Did you have a witch and everything? How did they do it? A map and a crystal necklace I bet. How cool." I gave a wry smile. Lily and I apparently had the same taste in old movies.

"Lily, pay attention. I said we found Greer."

"I heard you the first time," she grumbled. "So where exactly is the ice princess?"

"She's in the Graylands." I dropped it on her and waited for her reaction.

"What?" Color drained from her face. "Oh, man. That's bad. How the hell did she end up there?"

Not so heartless after all, hey, Lily?

I hid a smile. "No idea. Must be something to do with the fact she jumped into the portal so suddenly. I think Widd'en may have moved the portal key, so maybe he changed the destination. I have no clue how it works."

"Typical." Lily sniffed. "She causes herself to end up in the land of the dead and now you have to go save her ice-maiden ass?"

I sighed and sat back, licking my spoon. "Something like that, I guess. It's bad enough she's there but the DeathTalker said she had to be saved and quickly. She's going insane."

"Not that she wasn't already." When I looked at Lily, she met my gaze all innocence as she stuck more ice cream into her mouth. "You know, insane I mean."

I shook my head, the pit of my stomach still unhappy with my new plans. "Yeah, well, I have to go get her."

"You won't be going alone."

"Unfortunately, I will," I replied, keeping my features neutral.

"No way. I'm coming with you," she insisted, moving to the edge of the sofa as if she were ready to battle it out with me.

"Lily, I told you already, this life-debt thing you keep going on about, it's silly. You don't owe me anything."

"It's not about that. You and I have been through a lot together, and sure I owe you my life, but I'm your friend too. I won't let you go to the land of the dead alone. Ailuros knows what you will find there." Lily's face lost all its humor as she contemplated the impending disaster that was my mission.

"Lily, I'll find demons and ghosts and Greer. Stop being so dramatic."

"Whatever. I'm still coming." Her chin jutted out and her eyes were sparking.

"No you're not."

"Why are you being so damned difficult?"

"Because you can't come. The portals won't allow you through."

"What do you mean?" Lily frowned. The look she gave me said she wasn't going to fall for it.

"The portals are magically protected. If you're not a demon or Dark Ethereal, you can't travel to any of the Dark Ethereal planes if you're alive."

"What? So you're going to kill yourself to save Greer?"

"Lily? Why would you...? Oh... Gosh, you are silly." I shook her hand, curbing the urge to grab her by the shoulders and give her a more thorough shake. On the other hand, I just wanted to have a good giggle. "I can cross through the portal while I'm still alive."

"How could you possibly do that?" Her eyes narrowed.

"Because I'm a Hunter."

"Because you're a Wraith Hunter you mean?"

"No. Because I am a Hunter. A Demon Hunter. Like my mother."

"Your mother is a Demon Hunter? But, Kai, Walkers aren't Mages."

"Of course there are Walkers who are Mages."

"That's not what our elders told us. As far as we knew, there were no known Walker Mages in existence."

"I'm sorry, Lily. Either your elders didn't know or they were keeping the truth from your people. Maybe they were trying to protect your clan, but the truth is Walker Mages exist. I am proof of that."

"And so is your mother."

"No, she isn't."

"Oh man, Kai. You're making my head spin. You just told me she was a Walker Mage." Lily rubbed her temples and scowled.

"No, I said she was a Demon Hunter. Not a Walker Mage. And not a Walker."

"Dear Ailuros, Kai. Your mother is a human?" Lily's jaw dropped and she stared at me.

I nodded, probing myself for feelings of shame or embarrassment. There were none. And there was no judgment in Lily's expression either. "So you're okay with this?" I asked her.

"Why shouldn't I be?"

" 'Cos not too long ago you didn't even want me anywhere near Anjelo, Alpha or not."

"That's 'cos you're too hot for your own damn good and I had dibs on Anjelo."

I snorted. "You were afraid I'd steal him from you? You're nuts."

"I guess I just didn't realize at the time what type of person you were or why Anjelo always had your back. Now I do. And you being a Demon Hunter and a Walker Mage makes no difference to me. I'm still here. By your side. Not going nowhere." Lily nodded more to herself than to me, asserting her status by my side.

"And what do you plan to do when I go to the Graylands?"

"I'll wait for you. And I do have school. Storm will kick my ass if I skipped without a good reason."

"How is Storm?" I hadn't seen the Immortal in ages.

"Worried about you. He asks way too many questions every time he sees me. He said to tell you to take care of yourself. I think there are many people who've wanted to see you but kept away so you could recuperate."

"Yeah, tell him I'm much better."

"I will." Lily placed the tub of ice cream on the coffee table and turned to face me. "Now, tell me for reals. Are you okay? You've been through so much in the last few weeks. Clancy. Niko. Finding your mother. And now this whole Demon Hunter thing."

"I'm fine. I'm dealing with it. Lots of time to think when you're too weak to do anything else but lie in bed all day."

"And the center? Have you thought about your job?"

I snorted. "Yeah, I can see Dr. Hyde just jumping up and down with excitement knowing I'll be back full-time." I shook my head. "I'm not sure I can go back. I'll have to think about it."

"I can understand that. So what about your studies?"

"That too. I'm still thinking about it, but I might take a year off. Find my feet with this whole Demon Hunter thing. I have a feeling I have some work to do to brush up on skills I never knew I had." I stabbed the ice cream with my spoon, suddenly feeling the weight of all my responsibility begin to suffocate me.

"So this demon killing stuff. Is it like the Wraith hunting?"

"I assume so. I could track the Wraiths because of the trail they left behind. It's like a residue, almost a dust. A pinky-coral color. They used to leave it everywhere, on the doors and the walls. And on the people they spent time with. I'm not sure how to track a demon, but I believe the Wraith tracking is part of my abilities since Wraiths are demons."

"Makes sense." Lily met my gaze but I hesitated. I wanted to tell her about the prophecy but I convinced myself I still needed to know more about it before I began sharing the information. "So what's your next move?"

"I wait on Logan to see if we get an appointment with the DeathTalker's High Priestess and then pray like crazy that she grants us the use of a key."

Lily's eyes widened. "Man, Kai. I can't believe you're actually going to go to the Graylands. There's only ghosts and demons there. How will you protect yourself?"

"I'm waiting on some weapons and ammo from Tara. Specialized demon-hunting stuff."

"Oh, good," she said, her stiff shoulders relaxing a little.

I looked at Lily with new eyes. Brave, strong, tenacious. She was no longer that lost, rebellious, stubborn girl I once knew. "Lily, how are you doing?" She knew what I meant.

"I'm fine. I haven't touched the Synthe since we got out of Niko's lab. I don't need it anymore. I know why I used. I was empty inside. Even though I had Anjelo, being Pariah made me feel hollow, like I was only a shell."

I understood what she meant. I'd been an Alpha but I'd never felt like it was a title I deserved. I'd felt empty too for a lot of reasons. But I let Lily talk. She needed it.

"But when I saw what Niko had done, and what your sister had become because they were just like me, I saw a future I didn't want. I knew I needed to deal with how inadequate I felt before it took any more control of me. And then there was you. No matter how nasty I'd been, you still helped me. You didn't care what I'd done. You just went ahead and saved my ass. Like you're doing now with your sister. Forgive me, but there's no way in hell she'd do the same for you, yet there you go, off to save her sorry ass too. And that's what made me wake up too. I lost Anjelo and I gained you, and I don't want anything to ever get between us." She paused, then turned to face me. She took my hands in hers and said, "I accept you as my Alpha."

That was not what I was expecting.

I cleared my throat, unsure what I was meant to say to her pledge. But Lily had already stuck her spoon into the ice-cream again and was busy eating. Saved me from concocting a response. "Right then. If you're going to be by my side, then you're going to need to get shooting."

"Huh?"

"Guns, Lily. You're going to need to practice your shooting. Now is as good a time as any. Let me just grab you a couple of my practice weapons. A gun, a crossbow, and a few different knives should do it. And a bunch of dead shots."

"Dead shots?"

"Yeah dead ammo. So you can shoot, but won't hurt anyone or anything."

"Okay, fabulous. That's just so cool." Lily bounced up and down on the couch a few times.

"Do you need to be anywhere tonight?"

When Lily frowned, I said, "We can start tonight if it's okay with you. I'm also going to teach you how to fight. Just a little. Just enough so if you're ever in a dangerous situation, you can debilitate someone long enough for you to get away."

I thought of Brand, then. For all my own ability to fight, I'd walked right into Brand's lair and got myself trussed up like a Thanksgiving turkey ready for carving. If not for Logan, I would have made a tasty snack for Brand.

"Oh thank you, Kai. You won't regret it. I'll be the best student you've ever had."

"Don't get ahead of yourself, Lily. You're the only student I've ever had." Then we both laughed.

CHAPTER 13

WHILE I PACKED UP, I had to deliberately zone Lily out. She buzzed with so much energy I wanted to tape her mouth shut, tie her up, and leave her in a dark corner. My head ached, my arm ached, my neck ached.

Purple and blue bruises darkened the skin around the healed ridge of the cut. And dark blue veins were beginning to spread throughout my body again. Sure didn't take long for the poison to reclaim its hold again. Would it be worse in the Graylands? Or better?

I tried to wipe it out of my mind. Pointless thinking about something I couldn't change. Logan would have to treat me before I left and we'd just have to hope for the best.

I packed my weapons into my rucksack and Lily and I headed out the door. It was easy to ignore her chirpiness as we strode deeper into the abandoned part of town, beyond the unspoken line between the good part of town and the part where you could lose your life in the blink of an eye. But there were worse things than dying and we had a mission.

The pace we set wasn't normal. I usually only used my panther speed in the really late parts of the night when the chances of being seen speeding around the streets were nearer to zero. But the part of town we headed for wasn't very populated. You only went there if you had to.

The abandoned factory entrance sat at the end of a long dark alley. We sped down the alley, which was unusual for what it was. It didn't have the usual rank odor of human waste and garbage. Abandoned long ago, nobody came around here long enough to use the stretch of empty concrete as a latrine.

"Here." I beckoned Lily to follow me toward a metal door.

Every inch of the door was rusted, so it looked more like bronze than steel. I cranked the handle and motioned for Lily to follow inside, wiping crusty flakes of rust and metal off my hands and onto my pants. I barred the door and followed Lily up a short flight of stairs.

I'd been here many times so the place was already set up with bull's-eyes pasted on many of the concrete pillars dotting the empty floor. An office building in a previous life, it was now abandoned. All the partitioning and interior decor had been removed leaving just bare concrete floors and pillars, and yards of electrical wiring hanging from the ceiling.

I knelt at my usual spot and began to empty my bag onto an old fold out table I'd brought over months ago. I glanced over my shoulder and met Lily's curious gaze. "Over here. I like to lay all my weapons out next to each other." Lily did as I did and then stepped away ready and waiting for the next instruction.

"We'll start with the gun. It's your standard revolver and it has a bit of recoil, so tense your muscles for it, or you could get hurt."

"Recoil?" Lily frowned.

"When the gun goes off, the power it takes to push the bullet out of the chamber is enough to generate a reverse power into the gun. And since you're holding it, that power goes into your hands and your body too."

"I see. Okay. Gotcha." She nodded, her eyes still sparkling with excitement.

I positioned Lily in line with the target, lifted her elbow, got her jaw and eye in line, and shifted her hips. Everything my siblings and I had been taught when we were growing up. I'd almost forgotten we'd all received the same military-style training. Made sense what with Dad and Mom and Grams all working for Sentinel.

My gut tightened. That, of course, meant Greer could look after herself to a certain extent. The only question is for how long?

I refocused my attention on Lily and asked, "Ready?" She jerked her head up and down in a stiff, nervous nod. "Okay. Fire when you're ready."

She stared the target down, an almost comical look of concentration on her oddly angled face. Her finger closed over the trigger. Then she pulled it.

And stumbled three feet backward, tripping and landing on her butt, a look of shock spreading slowly on her face.

I would have bet she was about to burst into tears.

Instead she giggled and said, "Cool."

It was near one in the morning when we packed up and left the abandoned building. I didn't want to go for too long. Lily had gotten a good feel for all the weapons and it was enough for her first session.

We hurried back through the dark streets. No streetlights worked in this part of town. It was as if the city council deliberately wanted to forget about the area and its people.

Our route took us through the edge of the darker red-light district. Both Lily and I were used to the sight of the working girls, garishly painted, barely clothed, pacing their spots until a client drew up beside them. But I stopped walking so suddenly that Lily continued for at least twenty feet before she realized she was alone. My heart thudded and I prayed I'd been wrong.

"What's wrong? You look like you've seen a ghost." The honey of Lily's lynx eyes glowed with worry. Even for a Pariah she still had some underlying feline instinct.

"Not a ghost." I breathed, gaze moving between Lily and the girl. "A Wraith. Or the trails of one at least."

"What? Where?" Lily tensed, searching the street as if she would see what I did.

"Across the street. The girl in the fishnets and red corset." I looked at Lily who stared over at the girl.

"Dear Ailuros. She doesn't look older than fourteen." Lily's face was barely visible, yet the set of her shoulders revealed her horror.

"Yeah. That's her."

"What do you see, Kai?" Lily whispered loudly as we both watched the girl. Heavy black liner shadowed her eyes, making the gaunt lines of her face deeper. The color of her lipstick matched the painfully bright red of her corset. The garment was meant for a more well-endowed woman. In the girl's case, it made her look even younger, as if she were playing dress-up in her mother's clothes.

But what drew my attention and held it was the coral trails encircling the girl's neck that ran from her shoulders down to her hands and twisted around her wrists.

I had to know who the Wraith had possessed, and just by looking at her, I knew who I'd start with. Her pimp. My gut insisted it would be him or one of the guards he would set to watch over the girls.

"I have to talk to her," I said, my voice a little shaky. I normally didn't get nervous, but the sight of the girl set me off kilter.

"Are you insane? Do you want to get yourself killed?" Lily asked, her tone ragged.

"I have to find him. And preferably tonight." Lily gave her head a sharp shake. She didn't like it but she didn't see what I saw. "Lily, if her pimp or someone close to her is possessed, it means there's more to these possessions than we thought. It's strategic. They are no longer taking bodies just for the power the souls give them. What if they want to control businesses? The darker seedier parts of town would be the best place to start."

"I know what you mean, but you can't just go barging in there and give the pimp the shakedown," Lily countered, her hands now firmly on her hips.

I nodded. "I know. That's why I have a plan."

"Kai?" Lily said warily. "What are you up to?"

"Just come with me." I grabbed her arm and dragged her around the corner and into the first wide doorway. "Keep watch."

Lily stood at the edge of the step, her eyes flitting up and down the street. "What are you doing?" she whispered loudly, sneaking glances in my direction.

"Preparing." I shimmied out of my jeans and dragged my racer tee down my hips, sending a thankful prayer to Ailuros that I'd decided to wear it. The hem of the cotton-top ended on the knee and I tried tugging it higher hoping it would stay. When I turned I shuddered at the hazy reflection in the abandoned store window, I knew it wouldn't look too out of place at all especially when I headed back around the corner.

The long, black tee and ankle-high goth boots would have to do. I grabbed a pen from my rucksack and twisted my hair up into an untidy knot, pulling a few tendrils free, then pushed the sleeves of my leather jacket up my arms. The bruise showed clearly but I knew what it would look like at first glance. A junkie's ravaged arm. And I could work with that.

A quick search in my rucksack and I loaded both the gun and the crossbow with live Wraith ammo. Even though the weapons were ones I used for practice, they were perfectly capable of completing the job.

"Right," I said, firmly trying to bolster my waning determination.

"Holy shit." Lily stared me up and down. She looked about to faint.

"What's wrong?" I asked, concerned she was about to be sick or something.

"You look hot," she said, although she didn't look particularly impressed. She just looked shocked. And horrified. "How the hell did you do that?"

I glared at her as I shoved my jeans to the bottom of the rucksack and laid the bow and gun at the top for easy reach. I considered giving the gun to Lily, but she wasn't trained enough and would just waste precious ammo.

I grabbed a dagger and flipped it over, handing it to her by the blade. Her eyes widened, the honey irises glowing stronger the more stressed she became. "What am I supposed to do with that?"

"You wanted to be my side-kick. We start now." I held her gaze not daring her to say no.

"Gee, you certainly don't give a girl time to get familiar with the job." She took the dagger and turned it over to examine the blade. Then she nodded and said, "Cool."

"Right, I need to know you have my back." It was a lot of pressure to put on her with so little training and experience. But at least she had me to show her the ropes. "Lily, you have more experience in this than I did when I started this job."

"What do you mean?" She stopped staring at the weapon and glanced up and down the street before meeting my gaze.

"I killed my first Wraith without even knowing what it was or how I was supposed to properly end its life. You've seen a Wraith. You know what they can do. And you've had some practice with weaponry." I tried to make it sound practical. Why was I even getting her involved in this?

She snorted. "That means nothing. You just happen to be a Demon Hunter. I'm nowhere near even being a hunter for dinner, let alone soul-sucking demons."

"You'll be fine." I patted her shoulder then bent to slip a dagger of my own into my boot. Better safe than sorry.

"Okay, hot stuff. Exactly what is it you want me to do?" Lily slid the dagger in one of her belt-loops at the front of her jeans and I glared at her.

"Certainly not that." I gave the dagger a pointed look and watched her grab for the handle as it cut through the fabric and began to fall.

"Oh, shit. Sorry. Man, this thing's sharp." She scowled and held tightly onto the handle.

"Yeah. Don't let it fall on your foot," I said dryly.

"I won't." She sounded determined.

"I'm going to go find the pimp. He shouldn't be too far and it will be easy enough to track him. But first, I want to talk to the kid."

"She isn't a kid, you know," Lily said, and edge to her voice.

"Lily, just look at her for Ailuros' sake."

"Kai, I do love you, you know, but for all your killing and tough-guy attitude, you're still a bit naive." I scowled. She had a nerve calling me naive. "No, don't look at me like that. You are. That kid has probably been working the streets since she was ten. A life like this hardens you. I can guarantee you there isn't a thread of child in that kid. Her childhood died when she started in this business."

I glared at Lily. When did she become so hard and practical? "That doesn't mean she can't be helped."

"I didn't say that. I know you want to help her out, but I'm just warning you. There is a good chance she won't want to be helped. And if that happens, you can't punish yourself. You can't save everyone." She leaned to me and grabbed my sleeve giving it a little shake. "Did you hear me?"

I nodded, the action a little jerky. Her words were so mature, so experienced and a little lacking in hope. But I knew where she was coming from. I also knew I'd do anything to help the girl get out of this life. I just had to get in and kill the Wraith first or she was going nowhere.

"Yeah, I heard. And I know what you mean. I do." She didn't

look convinced but I continued, "Now, let's get going. I need you in the alleyway behind the brothel. Find a fire escape and hide."

"How can I help you from there? Can't I come with you?" I raised an eyebrow and looked her up and down almost exactly the way she'd done to me a few minutes ago. She huffed. "Okay fine. Whatever. I'll wait outside."

"I'm going to try to get him into the alley then you can back me up in case I get into a difficult spot." She stared at me as if in a trance. "Ready?" She blinked and then nodded. "Then go. I'll wait until you are in position."

She headed off and crossed the empty street before disappearing into the shadows. She popped her head out and waved before being absorbed by the night.

CHAPTER 14

I SMEARED ON SOME LIPSTICK, tugged the hem back up my thighs again, and headed back around the corner, sauntering across the street as I made a beeline for the girl.

Her brown eyes narrowed when she saw me. "What do you want?" She glared at me, her eyes slightly dilated. "This is my spot. If you don't want that pretty face of yours pulverized, then you'd better take yourself elsewhere before Gus sees you." Her words were harsh, bitter as she sized me up.

I raised an eyebrow, haughtily looking her up and down. "I'm not here to sell. I need to see your boss."

"What? Aren't you looking for a john?" She sneered. "There's enough of us here working our asses off to make a buck. We don't need another girl on the job."

"Don't worry, kid. I'm not looking for work. Though it seems to me you'd be better off finding yourself another line of work."

Her lip curled as she looked me up and down again, her eyes narrowed, stopping on my hemline before giving me another once-over with a new gleam in her eye. Somehow I'd known knee-length was not short enough. "What are you? Some kind of save-the-prostitute social worker or something?

I opened my mouth, intending to tell her she had options, but she cut me off. "Look, this is my life. There's no changing the way it is. So leave me the fuck alone." She folded her arms stiffly, giving the building behind her a dark, almost fearful glare. "If you wanna see Gus, he's on the first floor, through there. Don't blame me if you don't come out alive." She pointed behind her then turned her head stiffly away from me.

"Don't worry. I can handle myself."

She snorted then looked back down the road. I reached into my jacket pocket for the card I'd kept ready. "If you ever want to get out of this life, get clean ... you can. My friend will help you, no questions asked. Here's a number." I waved the card in front of her and she took it hastily, looking around her to make sure nobody had seen the exchange.

She held it in her hand and glared at me, weaving a little unsteadily on her feet. "Don't hold your breath." She spat the words out, her pale blue eyes gleaming.

"It's up to you, kid," I said then walked past her to the entrance she'd pointed out. It reeked of urine and alcohol. I shoved the door open and headed up the thin flight of stairs. Two doors at the top. One left, one right and she hadn't said which one.

But it didn't matter. Only one door glowed with the threads of coral, announcing the Wraith within.

I slipped into a small sitting room complete with faded red love seat and fake potted plant. The trails of the Wraith covered the door opposite me. Clearly he didn't spend much time in his waiting room as the place was devoid of any trace of coral-colored residue.

I let my panther senses reach into the room for me. He was alone. And he stank of death.

Gripping the tarnished metal doorknob, I thrust it open and

leaned against the doorjamb, jutting one hip forward. I traced a finger along my cleavage as his eyes widened.

The human he'd taken would've been model-handsome a long time ago. Before drugs and alcohol abuse had taken its toll. Now he was dead, a Wraith looking back at me through Gus's haggard eyes. The Wraith had been using him for a while.

From the looks of the red-rimmed eyes, the empty nail beds, and eroding hair, his time would soon be up. I didn't care. I wasn't planning on leaving the soul-sucking bastard here to take advantage of these women anymore. What the hell was he doing here anyway? He was way too comfortable as a pimp.

"What do you want?" His gaze flitted over my shoulder. Probably checking if one of his lackeys had brought me up.

"One of those guys downstairs said you'd be up here." I kept my voice low and husky.

"Did they?" The skin at the corners of his eyes tightened. I didn't care. I wanted him just suspicious enough to follow me out.

"Yeah. I was hoping you'd be interested." I slipped a finger under the hem of my tee and drew it slowly up my thigh, stopping a few inches from danger.

"Is this a joke?" He stood. "There are enough girls out there. Why would I be interested in you?"

"They're used. Old meat." I sneered. Then pouted. "Me, on the other hand, I'm not like them. I haven't been around. Wouldn't that be something you might like?"

He remained on his feet. He opened his mouth to say something, but I could see I had him stumped. "So if you're interested, I'll be in the alley behind the building." I pushed off the doorjamb, gave him a red-hot, alluring smile—or what I hoped would pass for one—and spun on my heel.

My heart thudded as I headed out the door and down the stairs as fast as I could. I hurried to the alley, the shadows my friends as I drew my gun and dropped the rucksack beside a half-filled, stinking dumpster.

Halfway inside the alley, I leaned against the wall, gun hidden behind my back, one leg propped up behind me. Movement at the entrance of the alley drew my gaze.

Damn. He hadn't taken the bait. He'd sent one of his men. The big guy loped toward me. "What do you want? Gus is awful pissed so you better 'fess up. He don't like games."

He was human and I didn't kill humans, not unless they were threatening my life and even then, I sometimes let them go. Not necessarily undamaged though.

I let him come to me. "Aw, come on, honey. I was only wanting a good time."

"Gus has plenty of good times." He was big. Big shoulders, big thighs. His muscles bulged from the sleeves of his tee shirt as he set his hands on his hips.

"So how about you then?"

"Huh? Me?" He wasn't very bright. And he stank. I cringed but I'd gotten pretty darned close to those stinking Wraiths so a stinking human wasn't much different.

I swallowed the urge to throw up, disgusted by what I was doing. "Do you get any good times?" I asked softly, hoping he'd come closer, make it easy for me.

He did. He stepped closer, a twisted grin on his face. As soon as he was a foot from me, I punched him in the gut. He bent forward, sucking air. I slammed the gun hard into the back of his head. Hard enough to jolt the brain and knock him out. He dropped heavily to the concrete, slamming his forehead hard.

Dragging him to the end of the alley, I piled a few trash bags over him and returned to take up my previous position.

It didn't take long for the Gus-Wraith to come looking for his missing man. But when he stalked into the alley, he must have changed his mind. He turned to me, his Wraith eyes more interested than they should be.

I shuddered.

Killing a Wraith in cold blood was no problem for me. Killing one who was coming on to me was a whole other ballgame. I breathed in and his gaze traveled to my chest.

Scumbag.

Interesting that Wraiths were interested in sex. Disgusting, but interesting. I'd always thought they were just here for the power of the human souls. Something must definitely be up.

He walked forward two more paces. I drew the gun and pulled the trigger. The gun gave a soft pop as the bullet was expelled from the chamber. It slammed into his chest, splattering a little of the green goo as it entered his body.

He stared at me in surprise. And for a moment I thought he was going down.

He wasn't.

The Wraith came straight for me, slamming into me so hard my head hit the wall and I almost passed out. The gun slipped from my grasp. I made a grab for it, but I missed and the weapon clattered to the ground.

He grabbed for my neck, his claw-like fingers fitting around my throat like a murderous collar. A growl escaped his throat as he squeezed. And I recalled that weird golden glow on my hands when I'd attacked Todd's Wraith. I'd been desperate that night, almost passing out—desperate to save a boy from a Wraith possessing his father. Could I recreate that power?

Gus's nostrils flared as he pressed harder.

I tried to regenerate that glow, tried to see if it worked, but nothing happened. I kicked out at the Wraith, helpless without my gun. I lifted my leg to reach for the dagger.

Gus was focused on squeezing the life out of me. He didn't see me raise the dagger. I plunged it into his side and he grunted, moving back to hold a hand to his abdomen. He looked surprised and a little hurt. Gus's body was failing the Wraith. When he lunged toward me, I stabbed at him again, slicing across his gut. I expected a rush of warm entrails but Gus held his stomach closed and lunged forward once more. I was about to swipe at him again, aiming at his throat but he dropped hard.

And landed on his knees at my feet with a thud.

I looked up. Lily stood staring the Wraith down, a triumphant grin on her face as she held the dagger out in front of her.

"Good job, side-kick." I shot the words at her as I grabbed the gun from the ground a few feet from me. I put two shots into the Wraith's brain just to be certain he was on his way to being deader than dead.

The Wraith clutched his chest. His breath clattered in his throat, Adam's apple bouncing in tempo. His eyes bulged, his face caught in a horrible grimace. His muscles pulled taut in a gross parody of shock and agony. He crumpled to the unforgiving concrete.

Dark, wispy shadows spewed from his mouth. As we watched, shadows writhed and curled and twisted away from the body, smoky gray fingers reaching for the tiny rips in the Veil, seeking to escape to the questionable safety of the Wraith world. The body of Gus, the human host, lay discarded, a dried husk of the man. Desiccated skin lay sunken on bones, papery thin and fluttering in the breeze.

Lily gasped as the last bits of the Wraith disappeared. Her hand fell, and she held the dagger loosely at her side. Adrenaline must be pumping through her veins right now. I knew the feeling.

"Come on. We need to get out of here." I pulled on her stiff arm as the sound of a groan reached me. "The other guy's waking up. Let's go." I pulled her along, pausing only to grab my rucksack from beside the dumpster.

We hurried across the street. I glanced back at the girl. She stood on the sidewalk staring at the card I'd given her.

She looked up just before I took the corner. Her eyes met

mine but they were unreadable. I couldn't tell if I'd made a differ-ence. I hoped she'd call. Storm would be able to help her.

And then we turned the corner, hurrying to my apartment with Walker speed. I felt the pull of my panther stronger than ever. But I had to resist. I'd never change in front of Lily. Not unless I knew she'd be okay watching my transformation.

We reached the apartment, relieved and slowly coming off our adrenaline high, and stumbled inside. I glanced over at Lily, the exhilaration on her face. Her eyes shone. "That was so cool."

I shook my head. I certainly didn't think it was so cool. But Lily had been everything I could want in a partner. "I have to say you did really well. That took a lot of courage."

"I have no idea how I did it. One minute I was on the fire escape, the next I was pulling the knife out of that thing's body." Lily shuddered. "Man, I've never seen anything like that before. So creepy."

"Yeah. It's what happens when they die." I wasn't sure how to make her feel better. "You'll get used to it."

"Creepy but cool."

I glanced up at Lily and laughed.

She was grinning from ear to ear. What had made me think she needed to feel better?

CHAPTER 15

I HAD TO CHASE LILY home with threats of never training her again if she didn't leave. She'd loved the hunt way too much but that was a good thing. And she had good enough aim that some solid practice would make her an ace shot.

I sank into bed and managed to fall asleep almost immediately.

When the phone rang, I barely heard it at first and I had to force myself to answer it.

"Hello." I grunted into the phone. What I really meant was "Who the hell is bugging me this early in the morning?"

"Hey, Kai." Logan's voice filtered through the phone and my stomach did a little somersault. I'd missed him.

"Hi." I tried to clear the sleep from my throat. "You got any news for me?"

"We're still waiting to hear back from Nerina. It's looking good to get her to see us. The rest is up to her I guess." He sounded tired.

"Thanks for doing this." I rolled over and stared at the ceiling, blinking against the sunlight streaming through the window.

The other end of the line was silent for a moment. "Kai, do

you want to get out and get some air? You must be getting claus-
trophobic by now."

I snorted. "I've been out most of the night with Lily. But sure.
What's up?"

"There's someone I want you to meet." His voice sounded
guarded.

"Where?"

"O'Hagan's? How about one?"

I glanced at my cell for the time. "Sure. I'll be there."

Logan rang off and I squinted at the phone, deathly curious
now. I stowed the weapons and neatened up the apartment a bit.
Grams' door was open a tiny crack and I peeped in to see if I
could disturb her. She lay flat on her stomach, a hand at the side
of her face, serenely, deeply asleep. I smiled and pulled the door
shut softly.

I left her a message taped to the kettle "Don't leave without
speaking to me!!"

O'HAGAN'S WAS dark and cozy. I hurried inside and chose a
secluded booth. With another half hour to go before Logan
arrived, I ordered a burger and chips to sate my hunger, watching
the door for Logan.

Logan entered on time. Alone.

So much for meeting someone.

He grinned as he sat across from me, ordering a drink with
the waitress before shucking off his jacket and heaving a
great sigh.

"You sound like you have the weight of the world on your
shoulders." As I spoke the words I realized how much better they
suited me and my predicament. How much did Logan know
about the Ni'amh anyway?

"You look like you're on your way back to being bedridden," he said in answer.

"Yeah, I know. The poison's taking over again. Pretty powerful stuff I'd say." When he rubbed his temples and pressed his fingers to his skull I asked, "Are you okay? When did you sleep last?"

"I'm fine. And I think that was on your sofa."

"You need your rest, you know. How can you help me if you're exhausted?" He glanced at me sharply as if the thought hadn't occurred to him. "So who is this you want me to meet? I noticed you're alone. Did they bail?"

He shook his head. "He'll be here soon. Just don't freak out."

"Okay," I answered slowly, warily. Who or what was he trying to spring on me?

Just as I answered him the air beside Logan twisted and shimmered. We were hidden safely within the dark corner of the booth, watching the moving shadows spin and coalesce with a spark of orange embers into a grinning man.

Dark-haired, olive-skinned, black-eyed, Arabic-style tattoos covering much of his visible skin. He leaned forward, grabbed a chip from my basket, dunked it in the bowl of ketchup and proceeded to munch on it in the silence that followed.

I raised an eyebrow at him, then moved my attention to Logan who looked a little sheepish and just shrugged his shoulders. "This is Saleem."

"Nice entrance," I said to Saleem.

"Thank you. It's what I do," he said, giving me a quick wink.

I wanted to giggle. There was a quiet sensuality about him, quite overrun by a playfulness that gleamed in his black eyes.

Logan cut in. "Saleem is a djinn. And because the djinn are of the shadows, they are able to enter the Graylands. Unlike the trackers and DeathTalkers, the djinn can enter in a corporeal state just like you."

"Ah. I see." I leaned back and grabbed a chip. It finally made sense. "You want Saleem to come with me?"

"Yes. I think it would be wise for you to have some sort of protection. And he was the only person I could think of capable of doing the job."

"What can he do to protect me?" I asked, sounding like I was interviewing a potential employee.

"He is right here," Saleem offered but neither Logan nor I paid him much attention.

"He's an excellent fighter, excellent with weapons. As far as being good company goes, I'm not so sure but he'll do."

"I'm still right here." Saleem pouted then stole another chip, which didn't work well with the pouting.

Logan and I turned to look at Saleem. I was silent for a moment. I wasn't stupid and it would be stupid to pass up the opportunity to have someone with me, someone able to fight with me and get through the mission alive. It was just that he was an Omega operative that worried me. But then, so was Logan and he knew almost everything there was to know about what I was or was not doing.

"Fine. You can come."

Saleem inclined his head in thanks. "I won't let you down." A shadow of seriousness wiped away the humor for a moment. "I know you don't know me, but you can trust me."

My gaze narrowed. "I trust Logan, and if he trusts you, then I guess I can give you the benefit of the doubt." Saleem grinned. "But, just one thing. If you ever cross me. Even once. You're out. No second chances."

Saleem glanced at Logan and his eyebrows moved up a little. "I see what you mean about her."

"What did he say about me?" I glanced between the two men, very interested in the answer to my question.

"He said you were strong, determined, feisty, don't take any shit and are a pain in the ass."

I laughed. "And he's right." I looked at Logan, who grinned back at me. My heart soared for a moment and I hoped I didn't look lovesick. "So what do you need in terms of weaponry? Are you kitted out well enough or do we need to get some weapons made for you?"

"I have my own djinn-forged weapons that have been designed for combat on any of the demonic planes." He inclined his head, an enigmatic smile on his face. "Thank you for the offer, though."

"So your weapons aren't from Omega?" I asked, curious.

"No. Omega has obeyed the High Council and has never breached the Veil. This is the first time they are sending an operative to one of the demonic planes."

"Well, there's a first time for everything, isn't there?" I said, watching as Saleem and Logan exchanged an odd look.

CHAPTER 16

S ALEEM, WITH HIS QUICK WIT and penchant for the funny, reminded me of Anjelo and I spent a few moments missing him terribly. Assuming he and Mom had each other for company in whatever Wrythiin jail they've been stuck in was a reach for me.

I didn't believe for a moment that either of them would be well treated. The New Army of Wrythiin sounded ominous. I just hoped my family wouldn't end up in the middle of their battle.

Right now, I hated Uncle Niko with a passion. The fault was his. Anjelo would never have been careless and gotten caught if he hadn't been desperate to find me. Of course, he'd been rash and a little naive to think he'd make it in and out of Niko's hideout without detection. But his heart had been in the right place as always, and he'd gotten caught, drugged, beaten up, imprisoned, and possibly tortured because of it.

I shuddered at the thought of torture.

Mom was there too, at the mercy of the Wraiths. Torture was something they wouldn't shy away from given Mom's reputation for killing them.

I blinked away hot tears. Thinking of Mom made me want to

see my family. And maybe that was exactly what I needed right now.

THE WIND TUGGED at my hair, scraped at my face as I ran.

I'd wanted to transform and run through the forest on my way to see my father, but Logan's warning and my increasing weakness stopped me. My panther was constantly wanting out these days. A different sort of problem to the days when the last thing I'd wanted was to change.

I released my panther ears and sight to better assist me as I ran. It didn't take me long to reach the colony, and by then, I was reasonably refreshed and not in the least tense.

The last time I'd come home was to see my father, a time filled with tension and anger and blame. Today was different. He'd called me regularly to check how I was doing. Acted more like a father than he ever had. The negative side of me thought it was a pity it took my mother's imprisonment in a demon plane to bring him around.

But he had come around. He was trying and I couldn't fault him for it.

I broke through the tree line and headed for my old house. My father still lived in our old home, as did Iain. Made sense since all the women in the family had deserted them.

Now that I was done being so angry with Dad, I worried about him a lot. How did he manage without Mom? Especially after Grams' explanation of what had happened to make Mom leave us.

I entered using my key and strolled through the house to his study, but the room sat empty and silent.

I found him in the kitchen with Iain. Both fair heads bobbed up as I entered, and Iain grinned. "Cappuccino double shot please."

Dad looked at him funny and then something clicked because he too smiled and said, "Make that two."

"You're both hilarious, you know that?" I shook my head and headed for the coffee machine, setting about making their orders. "Why is it that every time I come home I end up making coffee?"

" 'Cos you're the only one who can tame that stupid ancient piece of crap."

"Shush. Be nice or you'll get sand in your coffee."

Iain laughed and Dad smiled, the sun streaming in the window and giving his hair a kind of halo glow.

"You look tired," he said.

"I am. Logan did his fire magic treatment on me the night before last but it's already fading."

"Why? Is it not working?" My father frowned.

"I'm not sure. I suspect the poison is stronger than we ever expected."

"At least you're up and about." Iain gave me an inquiring glance.

"You could say that," I said dryly.

"What have you been up to?" he asked.

"I had an interesting visit with Grams." I looked pointedly at Dad, who scowled.

"What did she say?" Dad's scowl didn't budge.

"Oh, not much." I paused, keeping my voice neutral and my eyes on the coffee. "Just a little trip down memory lane with Corin and Celeste and Sentinel." I raised an eyebrow and he paled. "You should have told me, you know. It would have been so much easier if you had."

He sighed and scrubbed a hand through his hair. "Sometimes people take the more difficult path in life. And even when the going gets too tough to move ahead anymore, we still don't turn back. Perhaps it's pride, or ego, or pigheadedness, but we end up stuck."

I knew what he meant, but his omissions had affected me in

too many ways. Affected my actions, my behavior, my emotions. "But I said so many things I shouldn't have."

"Who says you shouldn't have said those things? Perhaps I needed to hear them," he said. The silence was awkward as Dad smiled at Iain and me concentrated on his sandwich, looking very guilty about something.

"And what's the matter with you?" I asked as I placed his mug of coffee in front of him.

He cleared his throat. "So what exactly did Grams say?" I went over our conversation only leaving out the part about the Ni'amh. "Is that it?"

"What do you mean? What more did you want her to tell me?" I stared at him, my eyes narrowing. Something was up with Iain and it had to do with Grams' revelations about Mom and Dad and about Sentinel. As I stared at his face, now reddening so much even his ears were pink, the last piece of the puzzle fell into place. "I get it. You also work for Sentinel, don't you?"

Iain spluttered as he took a sip of the coffee. "No. What gave you that idea?" His splutters turned into a bout of choked coughing that had Dad pounding Iain's back until my brother was even redder in the face than before.

"Son, perhaps it's time we stopped lying to each other in this family." Dad gave him one last thump in the middle of his back and I had a feeling that was not for his coughing fit. I hid a grin.

"But I wasn't—"

"It's a lie by omission and it still counts." Dad faced me. "We both still work for Sentinel. But I do much less field work these days."

"How do you manage with all your Alpha work?"

"It's called delegation," Iain said, putting on a haughty air.

I snorted. "You must be an awful boss."

"Why?" He was serious. As if he really wanted to know.

" 'Cos you're a pain in the ass."

Dad laughed loudly. "She's got you there, son."

Iain just shook his head, scowling.

"So there's something else I need to ask you. I'm going to check with Grams too, but I thought the more information I have the better."

"What is it?"

"It's about hunting. Can you remember anything about when Mom used to hunt? Did you ever see her work or did you ever go with her?"

"Yes. I went with her on her hunts for almost as long as she hunted." There was a reminiscent look on his face that told me he missed the old days.

"So did you ever see Mom's hands glow?"

"A golden, shimmering light you mean?"

I nodded.

"Yes. It was a power she used against the demons if they ever got too close or she couldn't use her weapons. I preferred she killed from a distance, so did she, but there were times when things didn't go according to plan and she had to use the glow."

"So what did the glow do?"

"It killed the demons, whatever they were, Wraiths, spirits."

"Do you know how it works? I need to train myself but I have no idea where to start."

"I don't recall your mother doing any practicing. I have a feeling the glow only ever happened when she was physically touching a demon. There wasn't much opportunity to practice."

"Damn." My shoulders slumped.

"What happened?"

"I fought a Wraith last night. Killed him. But there was a moment when I needed to use the glow and I had no idea how to call it."

"It has happened before?" Dad leaned forward.

"Only once, and then it happened when the Wraith had me by the throat and was very close to killing me."

Dad paled, but to his credit, he didn't argue against my job.

"The power is probably too young and weak. You might need more time and you most likely need practice using it."

"Ugh. You mean I need to get more up close and personal with those things." I made a face.

"Not what you want to hear, but I got nothing else."

I sighed. "Yeah. I guess I knew that already. I'll have plenty of practice soon enough."

"Why? What are you planning?" I got Dad and Iain up to speed on Greer and her location and our plans to retrieve her and by their expressions they were none too happy. "Kailin, that sounds too dangerous."

"I don't really have a choice."

"There must be another way," he insisted.

"There isn't. We've explored every possible option. And this is the only viable one. As long as the DeathTalker High Priestess will give me a portal key, we are good to go."

"I hate the thought of you going there alone." Dad said the words but his expression told me he knew he had no choice.

"I won't be alone. I have a djinn coming with me."

"Is that one of Logan's people?" Iain broke in, frowning. I nodded. "How do you know you can trust him?"

"I've met him but I can't know if I can trust him. I will just have to trust Logan's judgment." I scanned Iain's face. It made so much sense now why he'd been so suspicious of Logan. Did the operatives within each organization take sides? Would they fight each other in the name of their employers? Hopefully we'd never find out.

"I guess that's all you can do." Iain scratched his chin. "Have you been practicing?"

I nodded, slightly amused. All this time I'd been hunting Wraiths, practicing alone with guns, knives, and my crossbow, and here was Iain acting all responsible and bossy. Almost as if he wanted to train me or something. I didn't say anything though. It was nice to have both him and Dad around in a non-confrontational way.

And when I looked at them, I realized too why a hasty decision to join Omega would probably be a bad idea. Sentinel seemed to be a family thing, and if the agencies were really in opposition to each other, would I just be asking for trouble going with Omega?

I put it out of my mind and soaked up the midday sunshine in our family kitchen.

CHAPTER 17

MY PHONE RANG AS I walked to my apartment door just before seven that evening.

Logan. "What's up?" I answered.

"Nerina called. We have an appointment with Kira. At eight tonight at their estate." His response was curt, as if he really didn't want me to be doing this

"Estate?" The DeathTalkers had an estate.

"Yeah. They have a secluded place a few miles out of the city. I'll pick you up in ten minutes."

"I'm ready already," I said as I shoved my key into the lock and rang off.

Ready as I'll ever be.

THE DRIVE out of town was serenely beautiful. Oaks, maples and elms flitted by and the colors of fall, the reds and golds and rusts blanketed the landscape as the sunset repeated the russet and bronze tones high on the horizon. But I barely registered the view. My mind was still on the Wraith I'd killed and the golden glow that was useless to me until I figured out how to use it. I glanced at Logan out of the corner of my eye. Dark shadows circled his eyes, confirming he'd also had trouble sleeping. He looked haggard.

I chose not to tell him about my encounter with the Gus-Wraith. He'd probably warn me about the dangers of doing missions alone. Something I didn't want to hear. Dad had restrained himself from nagging, but I wasn't sure Logan would have the strength to stop himself.

Forty-five minutes later, we turned onto a dirt road and followed it deep into the forest. Five minutes later, the road ended in front of a set of tall, imposing iron gates.

Logan braked and I searched for a speakerphone somewhere on the wall beside the entrance but found nothing. Instead, the gates creaked open of their own accord. A security camera swiveled as we drove into the grounds.

The drive passed well-manicured lawns and led to a large fountain set before a gigantic stone mansion, complete with dark, eerie windows and three turrets that would give most people the shivers.

Logan parked and headed up the slate steps. I felt the weight of the building pressing down on my shoulders and my gut screamed to be very careful. I didn't see Nerina as being danger-ous, but that didn't mean the High Priestess or her guards weren't.

But there were no guards. The grounds seemed empty and the entrance remained unguarded. Logan knocked and a Death-Talker answered, her eyes downcast, thin, pale-gray hair hanging down either side of her pearly white face.

Her eyes flitted from Logan to me and she didn't move.

Logan cleared his throat, meeting my eyes, unsure of what to do next. "Logan Westin and Kailin Odel to see the High Priestess Kira."

The DeathTalker tipped her head and allowed the door to

swing open. She led us down the hall and took the left wood-paneled passage to a small waiting room furnished with dark mahogany coffee and side tables and chocolate-brown leather sofas.

"Please wait here. Someone will be with you shortly." She inclined her head and glided away.

I sighed and leaned against the sofa. My arm throbbed beneath the sleeve of my jacket, and I made a mental note to speak to Logan about it once we were done here. I needed another round of treatment.

"You okay?" Logan looked at me, frowning.

I shook my head. No point in lying. "The poison's taking over again. I might need a blast of your fiery magic very soon. Preferably before I keel over."

He patted my hand. "Sure. Let's get this over with and I'll do another round. I'm so close to perfecting it, Kai. I'm nearly there."

I nodded, suddenly feeling far too exhausted to face down the head of the DeathTalker clan. I breathed deep. *Just got to get through it and get home.*

Someone walked up the passage toward us and Nerina came into view. She smiled and came to stand before us, her hands clasped before her, a look of serenity on her face.

"Greetings. I trust you have not been waiting long."

Logan shook his head. "Just a few minutes."

Nerina tilted her head. "Logan, please do not take offense, but Kira has left instructions that she will only receive Kailin into the meeting."

Logan stiffened. "But she knew I was coming too."

"Kira is aware that you have accompanied the Hunter. But she wishes to only see Kailin. And Kira is not to be trifled with." A shadow darkened Nerina's pale face for a moment before she forced a smile to her lips. "And you need not worry. Kailin will not be far and she will be safe. I will stay with her."

Logan sat back, scowling. He gave me a resigned glance.

I had assumed she was here to announce us, but Nerina glided to the seat beside me and sank into the leather, seemingly content to wait for her mistress to call on us.

Twenty excruciating minutes later, the door opened. Making us wait could have been strategic on Kira's part. Show us who's boss. It worked. Logan had been sufficiently pissed off and waiting had eaten away at more of my energy.

"The Lady Kira will see you now," said a tiny DeathTalker who exited the room as if she floated on air. She was as pale as the others with one significant difference—she didn't look any older than twelve. Even her voice had the high pitch of a pre-teen. She smiled at me and inclined her head, stepping aside to free the doorway for Nerina and me.

Nerina rose and walked ahead for which I was grateful. Kira sounded like a force to be reckoned with and having Nerina guide me inside made me feel a little less intimidated.

I wanted to laugh. I'd been through so much, yet I was intimidated by someone I hadn't even met. I took one last glance at Logan. He scowled, his face dark with anger.

Nerina held the door open for me. As soon as I entered, she shut it with an ominous click.

The room was cathedral-like, high glass ceilings, bookcases that seemed to go on forever and plush seating dotting the carpet. It was more a library than anything else. An impressively large library.

I didn't let the grandeur of the room distract me. After a cursory scan of the room, my gaze fell on a woman who stood before a large, arched window. A book sat on a podium in front of her and she stood silently as if waiting for me to speak. I didn't. She had summoned me. So I waited in silence.

One thing stood out clearly as I waited. Her hair was the inkiest black possible, so unlike the gray non-color of the rest of the DeathTalkers. Did that bode well for her when she performed callings? Or perhaps as the High Priestess she no longer did mundane work like Callings.

Minutes ticked by as the high priestess stood with her back to me, as if she wanted to extend my wait just that bit longer.

At last she turned, staring at me with glittering, dark eyes. "State your name and the reason you are here." Her words were cold and arrogant. Why did she need me to state my name and purpose? She knew it already from her contact with Nerina.

But I was here for her help. No sense in pissing her off. "I am Kailin Odel and I'm here to respectfully request a portal key to allow me entry to the Graylands." I kept my tone neutral, hoping none of my irritation slipped through.

"And do you not understand that only the demons and the dead can walk the plane of the In-Between?" She looked me up and down, her tone cutting into me as she questioned me.

I forced myself to continue. "I am able to travel within the Graylands."

"And pray tell how that is possible." She moved closer to me, studying me, a cold sneer lifting her lip making her look deadly dangerous.

"Because I am the Hunter." I left it there, hoping she wouldn't want to talk about the Ni'amh.

"That is a wild claim. I know the Hunter. And you are not her." Kira snapped, her eyes flashing.

"If you mean Celeste, she is my mother."

"So the daughter deigns to think she can be as powerful as her mother. Quite presumptuous aren't you, little cat?"

A cat jibe. How very mature. I felt anger rise. My panther didn't like this woman either and she clawed for release, but I tamped her down. I was not going to allow Kira to get a rise out of me. Taking a slow deep breath, I let it out just as slowly, urging my heart rate down. "I am not trying to take her place. She isn't able to save my sister from the Graylands. I really have no choice."

"Ah yes, the reason for your travel to the Graylands. You wish to save your sister?" Her voice was still cold even though her words hinted at a little empathy. But I could be wrong about her having any feelings. Her face was pinched. Emotionless. And she looked at me with cold derision. "How very heroic of you."

"I don't really have a choice. If I leave her there, she will die or go insane."

"I am well aware of what can happen should a living soul be trapped within the Graylands." She attacked as if I'd intended to insult her, but before I could even think of apologizing, she said, "So what will you be willing to pay for the portal key?"

I hid my surprise. Nobody had mentioned a price, but it was naive to think I would get it for nothing. Everything had a price. "What is the cost? What do you wish me to pay?" I was sure I could raise whatever amount of money she wanted. My father was a very wealthy Alpha.

"Oh, don't you worry your little feline head about money. It's not money I want." There she went again with the cat insults. This woman was really rubbing me the wrong way. But I kept my cool and waited. From her expression, she was frustrated that she wasn't getting a rise out of me. I liked that. "But tell me first. Why should I help the likes of you?"

She looked at me from head to toe as if I lived in a garbage dump. Even her lip curled as if she couldn't stand the smell of me. My panther growled, wanting release and probably wanting to rip the High Priestess's face open. I wasn't sure how to answer her, but she didn't really want a response. She just enjoyed playing her little games, so I let her, despite my rising fury.

She paced before the book. "What is it to me that a foolish Walker gets herself trapped in the Graylands? She deserves to die there for her stupidity."

I hid a smile. Kira didn't know I wasn't falling over myself feeling sorry for Greer. How sisterly of me, but that was just the way it was. "I think my mother would prefer for her daughter to survive her trip to the Graylands."

"Ah, yes. Celeste. Foolish choice she made. Children are a burden a woman like her should never have taken on. It has made her weak, vulnerable." Kira's skin gleamed in the fading evening light. "Very well. I will give you the portal key on one condition."

Her about-face was so sudden I blinked, then schooled my features, hoping my surprise didn't show. I wasn't keen on revealing my feelings to her. "What would you have me do, Lady Kira?"

"I will have you swear a blood promise to me. You will get the portal key in return for a promise to do my bidding whensoever I should ask it."

MY CHEST TIGHTENED. THAT WAS a huge favor. There were any number of things she could ask me to do that there would be no way in hell I would do. I opened my mouth but she cut me off. "There shall be no bargaining with my offer. It is . . . how do you say . . . take it or leave it." She smiled, her lips curling coldly.

I clamped my jaw shut and chewed on my lip. She hadn't left me a choice. It was the blood promise or Greer dies. I hoped my sister appreciated what I was about to do for her.

"I agree to the blood promise." Kira arched an eyebrow, the skin at her eyes tightening in surprise. A sough of breath behind me told me that Nerina was also shocked that I'd agreed.

"Good." Kira moved to a table a few feet from the podium. "Nerina, bring me the ceremonial goblet."

Behind me, Nerina's skirts swished and the door opened and shut. The younger DeathTalker passed me, giving me a worried glance before handing Kira a drinking vessel made of gleaming white stone streaked with gray. She placed the goblet on the table and moved away.

Kira bent and drew up her flowing gray gown to remove a

vicious-looking dagger from a sheath on her pale thigh. These DeathTalkers weren't as unassuming as they looked. The high priestess placed the dagger beside the goblet and took her place on the other side of the table. She motioned for me to come forward and I stood opposite her.

"To seal the blood promise, I need your blood. Any objections?" She raised an eyebrow in question. I shook my head. She handed me the dagger and said, "Cut. Wherever you want, I don't really care. I just need a few drops of your blood in the goblet."

Taking the knife, I made a thin incision across my palm and held my hand over the vessel, allowing blood to drip steadily onto the bowl. I looked up at Kira. She just stood there, watching as drop after drop of ruby red splashed onto the white stone.

"Enough. My dagger please." She held out her hand. I gave it to her, still red at its tip from releasing my blood. She didn't bother to wipe the blade clean, just punctured her palm and dripped her own blood into the goblet. Red mixed with red and swam around each other as if even our blood refused to associate with each other.

She took the dagger and mixed the blood together, the scrape of the metal against the stone sending shivers down my spine. What had I just gotten myself into? I gritted my teeth. *No time for looking back. Just get on with it.*

Kira grasped the goblet then spoke a few words over it, the gray in her eyes growing cloudy, swirling with shadows and light. She closed her eyes for a moment, then snapped them open. They both flashed black for a split second before they returned to normal.

Then she raised the goblet to her mouth and tilted it to sip at the bloody contents. My panther pushed for release again, the blood calling to her most basic need. I tamped her down, using all my strength. *Ailuros, help me keep her at bay.*

I sucked in a soft breath as Kira handed me the goblet, her lips tinged red from our blood. I wanted to gag at the thought of having to swallow her blood. But I grasped the goblet within steady hands and swallowed the rest of the blood.

Kira nodded and took the goblet, setting it on the table again. "Good. It is done then. Sometime in the future, I will call for you to uphold your promise, Hunter. And you will do whatever I ask. Oh, and there is what you call fine print." My gaze narrowed on her face. "Oh, don't worry. It is just a rights handover, if you will. In case of my death. The blood promise will remain in effect until the oath is completed. If I should die before claiming that promise, the rights shall be transferred to the next High Priestess."

I nodded. "So when do I get the portal key?"

"Oh, you don't waste time I see."

"It is what I came here for."

"Very well. Nerina, please hand me a key." Nerina hurried to a large wooden chest that sat in front of the podium holding the enormous book. She dug inside for a moment and rushed back to Kira with a metal disk in her hand. It was identical to the bronze, donut-shaped key Grams had given me to use to enter Wrythiin. My stomach tightened. Was this where Mom had obtained her key? Is that how Kira knew her?

Kira raised the knife again and beckoned to me. More of my blood? I didn't protest, just stepped back to the table and watched as Kira sliced into my palm again. Despite her cold attitude toward me, her movement was gentle and careful as she slit the skin open and let the blood flow. She held my hand over the metal disk and blood dripped onto it, running it along the carvings and filling the tiny crevices.

At last satisfied, she pressed a thumb to the cut and held onto my arm, motioning for my other hand. I gave it and she held onto both my arms tightly. She began to chant—strings of words woven together like an unearthly melody.

A breeze stirred through the room, lifting our hair and moving our garments. Kira chanted louder, and my ears began to ring with the strange words of her chants echoing in my mind.

The air moved and a gust of wind ripped through the room. I glanced about for an open window even though I sensed the wind was coming from nowhere else but between Kira and me.

Air spun around us as Kira chanted louder, almost shouting to be heard above the rushing wind. The metal disk rose between us and began to spin so fast I could barely see it anymore. The portal key had been drenched with blood but strangely I wasn't spattered with any droplets.

Kira managed a last shouted chant and a blast of air hit us from the spinning key, sending our hair flying out behind us, flattening our clothing to our bodies and making my eyes burn. The disk slowed its crazy spinning and gradually descended to the table, laying itself flat as if an unseen hand placed it there with deliberate care.

Kira sighed and reached for the portal key, raising it, then turning it over and over in her hand. She gave it a thorough inspection and nodded, a satisfied gleam in her eye. Then she thrust the key at me as if she couldn't get it out of her hands fast enough.

"The key is now yours. Only you can use it to open the portal to the Graylands. Of course you may bring your sister back with you as long as you are the one opening the portal."

I frowned, thinking of the other portal key I'd used to enter Wrythiin. I cleared my throat. "If the keys were coded with the blood of the user, how was I able to use my mother's portal key to enter the Wraith realm?"

"Surely you have worked that out already, my dear. You do seem smart enough." There was that bite back again. I frowned. The blood of the user enabled the opening of the portal but the key would have been coded to Mom's blood, which meant we had at least part of our blood in common. "The blood. My mom's blood and mine."

"Yes, little cat. You must have had enough blood in common to allow the portal to open."

"So would my portal key open for Greer?" The possibility was worrying.

"No. This particular one may work for your mother but not your sister. Your combination of blood would be too different."

"But Greer could use Mom's portal key to enter Wrythiin."

Kira nodded. "It's possible. But not certain. You will only know if you try. I'd be very careful with those keys if I were you. You do not want them to fall into the wrong hands. The failsafe is that it is coded to your blood, but there are those out there who would do anything for power. One can never be sure what another person is capable of." The words hung in the room, a cloying warning.

I swallowed and turned the key over in my hands. "So dark water again, I take it?"

Kira nodded. Then she turned her attention to the book and spoke no more.

I was dismissed.

I hesitated a moment, then looked at Nerina. She turned to the door and beckoned me to follow. I slipped the key into my jacket pocket as she opened the door.

Logan was already standing. He was agitated, his hair sticking up on end. He must have been pacing and he didn't look happy. "What took you so long?"

"What do you mean?" I looked from Logan to Nerina, frowning.

"You were in there almost two hours." I glanced at Nerina again and she gave a small nod.

"Really? Two hours?" I asked, hardly believing it.

"Yes. Rituals can take more time than we realize. And we did perform two of them."

"Rituals?" Logan looked from Nerina to me and back again.

I spoke quickly. "The rituals were to get the portal key to work." Nerina glanced at me, a small question in her eyes, although she seemed to understand and said nothing further.

"So was it really necessary to leave me outside?" He was still angry.

I laughed. "Unless you were offering your blood to the portal key, then I think so."

"Blood? What did you offer your blood for?" I explained how the portal key was coded to the user and Logan nodded as if it made sense but he didn't look satisfied. Then he stared at me. "Blood means your energy levels will be lower than ever. We have to get you home fast."

"She didn't drain me of every last drop, Logan." I smiled at him. "I'm fine. No ill effects from blood loss, although I will readily admit to being strangely exhausted."

"Fine. Let's get going then. I'm not going to be carrying you up all those stairs to your apartment." He began to walk off down the passage. I looked at Nerina and rolled my eyes and she giggled.

We followed Logan in silence until we were almost at the door. Nerina put a hand on my injured arm and I had to force myself not to flinch. "Kailin, you must be careful. Keep the portal key very safe, and if you ever need any help or advice, please call me. When you arrive, try to blend in. It's best you not talk to anyone, demon or ghost. That way they will think you are also a ghost, and hopefully, they will leave you alone. And don't tell anyone your name. Don't address each other by your names. You do not want anyone to overhear your names. And, Kailin, you really must take care. You can die within the Graylands. I am very concerned because your sister lives in darkness. Her heart is hard and slowly blackening. It is possible she may be possessed or under the control of some kind of evil. It is not impossible for an evil entity or spirit to possess a person in the Graylands. So please be very, very careful."

I nodded and looked up to face the worry in Logan's eyes. He'd heard every word and the reality of it was sinking in. I looked away. Nothing he said would change my mind and he knew it. I held Nerina's hand. "Thank you, Nerina. And please, if you ever need anything, you must promise to come and see me."

She smiled her serene smile and nodded. "I will." And I believed her.

She led us to the door and opened it. The skies were already inky black with night, reminding me of how long we'd been there. Hurrying to the car, I jumped in, feeling more sure of myself now that I had the key in my possession. I waved at Nerina and she shut the heavy door.

Logan gunned the engine and took off in a flurry of gravel. His anger had faded but he was still pretty annoyed. I stole a glance at his profile.

He'd be way more than annoyed if he found out about the blood promise.

Not that I planned on letting him know.

CHAPTER 19

THE DRIVE BACK WAS LONG and I nodded off, surprised at the toll the rituals had taken on my energy. Logan was silent for much of the drive. Thankfully it was more a thoughtful silence than a sullen one.

He remained quiet until we were inside the apartment. All he said was, "Lie on the bed. I'll be there in a minute." Then fixed his gaze on his phone.

"I'd like to shower first. I feel a little contaminated. Mistress Kira isn't the nicest of people." I made a face.

Logan glanced up at me, giving me a thoughtful stare. "Sure. I didn't think of that. Yell when you're ready."

I nodded and headed for the shower. Although I wanted to stay under the hot spray, I hurried, thinking of how tired Logan looked. He really needed to take better care of himself.

Comfortable in yoga pants and a tank top, I went to the door to call him only to find him sprawled on the sofa, fast asleep. I smiled. He looked so endearing, phone in his hand, mouth a little open. Even the soft snore that emanated from his mouth failed to annoy me. I tiptoed to him, saved the phone from his relaxed fingers and threw a blanket over him.

A second night on my sofa. This was becoming a habit.

~

I'D FALLEN into an exhausted sleep, awakening only when a light footstep made the floorboard at my door creak. I sprang from the bed, claws already lengthening when the door swung open and Logan stuck his head into the room. He grinned to see my face inches from him.

His grin faded when he caught sight of my extended claws. "I think you can put those away," he said, giving me a wry smile.

"Right," I said and put them away. "Did you sleep well? You look rested."

"Why did you let me sleep?" He scowled, mussing his hair. "I had work to do."

"You had fire healing to do. Probably not a good thing to do when exhausted. Besides, you looked so adorable." I gave him a little sexy smile.

"Adorable?" He laughed. "I'll show you adorable." He grabbed my good arm and pulled me to him, giving me a thorough, toe-curling kiss before letting me go. "Get on the bed."

"Ooh, now you're talking." I skipped to the bed.

"Behave. I'm going to be working," he said, his tone dry.

I laughed and got comfortable on the bed. A glance at the clock said it was just after six in the morning. Logan rounded the bed and took up his cross-legged position beside me. It was then I noticed the small black bag he held toward me.

"Ooh, you come bearing gifts." I grinned.

"I think you'll like this." I took it from him and began to unzip it. "I wasn't sure it would work, but it did. Needless to say, we were all pretty surprised."

I flipped open the top of the zip-up bag to reveal a row of six syringes. A fiery golden liquid swirled within the barrel of each one.

"Don't tell me you managed to bottle your fire."

"That's exactly what I did. With Jess's magical help, of course." Logan nodded. "I don't think it would be possible without Jess's power."

I nodded, suspecting that Titan power would have something to do with transforming simple Fire Mage power into something as amazing as this. "Wow." I nodded. "This is going to be so helpful."

"So use two to three at a time on the original wound. That should be enough of a treatment. Unfortunately, half a dozen was all I could manage to create with the time we had."

"That's great. Six is probably all I need. I'm not staying there a minute longer than is totally necessary—don't you worry." I smiled and his shoulders relaxed a little. Leaving the case safe on the nightstand, I gave him my arm and said, "You may begin."

He looked at my arm and then at me, shocked. "I didn't realize it had gotten so bad so quickly." He stared at the blue and purple and yellow bruises covering my forearm around the scar. He narrowed his gaze. "What have you been up to? You must have done something to drain yourself of energy for this to happen so quickly."

I shrugged. "Just a little Wraith hunting." I winced, expecting the backlash.

"What? Kai are you insane? You are supposed to be resting. And when did you find time to hunt a Wraith anyway?"

"Last night. It was a now-or-never kind of thing." He glared and I just shrugged. "Something is happening, though."

"What do you mean?"

"This Wraith was methodical, businesslike. He'd taken over a pimp's body, down in the red-light district. I haven't seen this type of behavior with the Wraiths before. It used to be just the power of the soul they wanted. Now it seems businesses are playing a role in their choices. Not to mention the fact that this Wraith was interested in sex." It was out before I realized it.

"What?" Logan stared at me. Then he asked warily, "What do you mean by that? How do you know he wanted sex?"

No point in holding back. I told him the story and was half amused and half worried at his reaction. His face was black with fury.

"You shouldn't have gone in without backup. Why didn't you call me?" he demanded, his fist curling, tendons taut.

"Logan, I was hunting Wraiths long before you came on the scene. You can't go all knight-in-shining-armor on me now. I can take care of myself. I can do my job and I can do it very well." I spoke firmly but kindly.

"Yeah, but you've never had Wraith poison flowing thick in your blood before, have you?" He glared at me, shaking his head slowly. "You have no idea what this poison can do to you. It could weaken you so badly a Wraith could kill you because you couldn't react fast enough."

I knew that but I didn't say anything except, "I had backup."

"What do you mean backup?"

"Lily. I'm training her. She did pretty well. Kind of came to the rescue too." I was still proud of Lily. She really had guts.

He snorted. "Great. A poisoned panther and a kid lynx. You make a fine fighting team."

I snorted back. He decided that line of conversation was over and bent his head over my arm. I didn't resist. But a rush of warmth filled me at the thought he cared so deeply for me, and for my safety. I liked the feeling very much. Although I wasn't sure I liked the idea I had to keep calling on Logan for his treatment so I could remain active and healthy. I liked that he cared for me, but I didn't like that I was becoming dependent on him. And it didn't matter who he was really. I'd hate being dependent on him even if I didn't like him so much.

"How far off are you from perfecting the technique?"

"Not very far. I'm hoping I can do one more treatment before you leave." He glanced up at me. "Any idea when that is?"

"As soon as Tara and Gracie give me my weapons, I'll be good to go."

"Fine. Whenever that is, even if it's tomorrow, I want to do a full treatment before you leave. It may not fully resolve the poison, but at least it should give you enough poison-free time in the Graylands. I'm just worried how being in the dead plane will affect you and your wound and the poison."

"I'll have to deal with that when I come to it. No point in stressing about it now." I shrugged. It was true. We knew nothing about how things would pan out in the Graylands. What was the point in stressing over something we couldn't even imagine, much less prepare for?

I watched as he repeated his fire treatment process, hands covering my arm top and bottom, sending flashes of first soothing, then searing heat into my body. I watched as the skin on the parts of my hand that were mottled with purple slowly faded to a less-angry color. He spent a while bent low over my arm, frowning and concentrating while my hand burned beneath his touch.

At times I wanted to hiss with the pain, but I let him do his job unhindered by my agony. This time the treatment took much longer, draining both Logan and myself of almost all our energy. I felt a stab of guilt knowing it had been my hunt that had depleted my energy.

But I couldn't just sit around and do nothing. There were Wraiths out there. Ones with more serious agendas. Knowing that, I definitely couldn't waste time lying in bed all day.

And now that I had the portal key, I could stop wasting more time and get Greer.

CHAPTER 20

I woke at lunchtime to find Logan already gone. I'd passed out just after he had completed his treatment, so I had no idea what time he'd left. I limped to the bathroom, brushed the fuzz from my teeth and headed to the kitchen to get coffee.

And found Grams making chicken salad sandwiches.

"Hello, darling." She patted my cheek. "You do look tired. What have you been up to?"

"Oh, you know, training sidekicks, killing Wraiths, bleeding all over portal keys and getting supercharged fire straight into the bloodstream. So yeah, not much. How about you?"

Grams smiled and pointed a finger at the other side of the kitchen counter. I went dutifully and sat on the nearest stool, still a little unsteady on my feet. She slid a plate with a sandwich on it, and soon joined it with a mug of fresh coffee.

"Eat, miss smart mouth."

"That's miss smart mouth destroyer of the world to you." Grams' face fell, and the look of worry she gave me made me want to eat my words. "I'm sorry. I'm just teasing. Don't look so worried."

"It's my job to worry about you, silly girl."

"Why does everyone want to worry about me?" I complained.

Grams glared at me and I turned my attention to my food. Too soon my plate and mug were both empty and I sat back patting my stomach, hoping I wouldn't burp too loudly.

"I got the portal key by the way." I dropped the bomb nonchalantly.

Grams' gaze shot up from her sandwich, which she was already having trouble eating. "You saw Kira?"

I nodded. "What's the deal with that woman? She's one cold-hearted b—"

"Kai," Grams admonished.

"Grams," I whined. "I'm old enough to swear. I'm eighteen, soon to be nineteen, for Ailuros' sake."

"I don't care. Don't let me catch you swearing in front of me, young lady."

I just shook my head. She was impossible. "So you get any more information for me on the prophecy?"

"Still working on it."

"Well, I have the portal key, and as soon as I get my weapons sorted—which should be confirmed today—I'll be leaving. Could be as soon as tomorrow if we're lucky."

Grams glared at her sandwich, still half eaten. "Things are moving along quite fast." What she meant was things were moving too fast for her.

"The faster the better, don't you think? You wouldn't want Greer to be lounging around in that death trap for too long. Nerina mentioned a darkness taking her over so I think we do need to get a move on and get her out of there."

"I understand, Kai. I'm just worried you won't be ready for what you see there."

"Can anyone really be ready for the Graylands? From what I hear it's not exactly Miami Beach in the summertime."

"You are right of course. I'm just—" She stopped speaking.

"Worried. I know. And I can't stop you from worrying. I'm worried too, but we just have to deal with one thing at a time." Then I remembered. "And I have to ask you something about Mom's power."

"Go for it." She tackled the sandwich with renewed vigor.

"Did Mom ever mention the gold glow she got when fighting a demon?"

Grams nodded. "Yes. It's the mark of the Hunter. The ability to kill a demon with one's bare hands."

"Does that mean any demon?" This could help me for sure.

"Yes. Any demon," Grams answered around her mouthful.

"Good. Okay. So what about the glow? Did Mom have a way of practicing with it? Dad said she didn't, but I wanted to see if you knew something he didn't since you've been in contact with her all these years."

Grams glanced at me, but there was no judgment or accusation in either my words or my tone and she relaxed her tense shoulders. She shook her head. "No. Your dad was right. Celeste could never practice that ability. I do know that she would deliberately not use her weapons sometimes so she could practice the power in a fight. She only ever did that when she knew her weapons were handy or if she knew she had backup."

I stared off into space for a moment, thinking again about the Wraith pimp. "I guess I'll have to do the same the next time I come face-to-face with a demon."

"Would it make a difference if I suggested you stay away from demons for a while?" she asked hopefully.

"Nope." Then I remembered I'd told Logan about the Wraith. "I think you need to know something. I killed a Wraith the night before last." She looked shocked and about to reproach me but I rattled on. "They seem more planned, more business-oriented. Their focus seems to have changed."

That got her attention. "That's unusual."

"You could say that again." I glanced at her face. "And there is one more thing. The one I killed, he was interested in sex. Isn't that something that never happens?"

"Where did you find this one?"

"Downtown red-light district. He took a pimp's body. And he was running the show."

"Maybe he got a taste for it from the girls working for him?"

"Maybe. I just don't like it at all." I paused. "And he seemed stronger than the others. Maybe Niko really did help them to use their human suits better while still retaining their strength from their true form."

"I bloody well hope not."

I cringed. It was so easy to forget that Uncle Niko was Gram's son. Too easy. "I'm sorry, Grams."

"Nothing to be sorry about, dear. Niko was . . ." She sighed, sadness coming off her in waves as she stared off into nothing. "I miss my boy, no doubt about it. But I've been missing him for a long, long time. He chose his path. Yes, he had a problem. Nobody wants to be Pariah, but he made so many wrong choices. I only hope that now he has achieved a state of peace for himself... So let me know when you're ready to leave for the Graylands."

Grams looked away. Neither of us wanted to mention the more likely possibility of Niko enjoying the hospitality of a hell he more than truly deserved.

CHAPTER 21

I HEADED TO SEE TARA as soon as Grams left. She was worried but there wasn't anything I could do about that. Everyone was worried about me. I didn't need the pressure of their concern.

I turned onto Tara's street to see a couple exiting a pawn shop. They didn't look like they belonged in this part of town. I almost passed them, but then the woman hissed. I glanced at the pair. He held tightly onto her wrist. Too tightly.

Maybe I would have left them be. Domestic quarrels were not my business. Not unless it involved a demon. And the coral trails around the woman's wrist, along her arm, and around her neck were enough for me.

I watched him tug her toward a waiting Bentley and fling the door open. The driver stared ahead, his eyes flitting back and forth across the street. He wasn't immune to the woman's abuse, but he was powerless.

The man waited until the woman slid inside, then got in and shut the door. The driver took off and I didn't spend a moment thinking about it. I followed, watching the streets, watching the car, speeding through the city until the concrete landscape faded into upper-class domestic bliss.

Double stories, large gardens, great big oaks and winding driveways. I hung back beneath the widespread branches of a tree as the car turned into one of the properties with large, oak front doors, entryways covered in peach tendrils.

The couple entered while the driver parked and went around the house. Servants' entrance? I followed him, hanging back among the bushes. I let my panther hearing and smell loose, allowing my senses to travel through the house in search of the couple.

Words filtered back to me. Heated words.

"Do not think you can leave me." The husband growled. "Not now. Not ever."

The woman said nothing.

"Did you really think you could run without me knowing, without me catching you?"

"You don't want me anymore." She hiccupped. "What's happened to you, James? You just want the money." The woman's tone changed, pleading. "If that's what you want, take it. I don't need the money. Just let me go."

"And how will it look to my constituents when my wife leaves me?"

Constituents? The man was a politician. And the Wraiths were upping their game. Lucrative and influential positions. That's what they were looking for now. There was a greater scheme at work here. But I didn't plan on allowing them more of a foothold than they already had.

I listened but the conversation seemed over. I had a sense of the room they were in and hurried around the house to find the window. Fortunately, I quickly found a downstairs room with an easy-to-jimmy sliding window. I slipped inside, closing it behind me.

The woman sat on a small love seat against a far wall. She held a letter opener in hand, the dull light of the room reflecting off the deceivingly blunt edge. I moved toward the door, hoping she'd pay more attention to her thoughts of suicide but she glanced up and her eyes widened when she saw me.

I put a finger to my lips and prayed she would remain silent. She stared at me, an uncaring, uninterested expression on her face. Yet she spoke automatically. "What do you want?"

"I'm here to kill him. Stay out of the way and you'll be fine."

The woman laughed. "You can't kill him. I tried." A look of fear filled her face. When she spoke again, her words were a desperate whisper. "I tried."

"You tried to kill him?" I asked, more to keep her occupied as I withdrew both my gun and daggers, slipping each into a boot. Then I drew the bow and checked the cartridges.

"Yes. I stabbed him. But he just pulled the knife out and hit me. He didn't even bleed." Her eyes fell on my bow and widened for a second as if she could see the possibility. "Will that work?"

"This one will. Not an ordinary bow." I kept my voice low.

"What's wrong with him?" She asked the question and I glanced at her. What was wrong with her? But I was unfair. Did I really expect her to be stronger? She'd said she had tried to kill him. She had acted. But she had no idea what she was dealing with.

"Don't worry about it. I'll deal with him." She nodded. "Where is he now?"

"In the study two doors down on the left. I'm going upstairs to my room."

"Stay there until the police come."

She nodded on her way out, then turned back to look at me. "Who are you?"

"It's best you know as little about me as possible. For your own good. Just know I'll deal with him." She gave me one last hopeful, yet hopeless look and left the room. I watched her climb the curved staircase, waiting only until she disappeared down the upstairs hall.

I sensed he was alone. His breathing was low, shallow and calm. I gave the driver a moment's thought and hoped he wouldn't try to intervene. I'd be forced to shoot him with Wraith ammo. Not something I wanted to do as it meant leaving the traces of poison on his body.

Moving down the passage, I walked along the opposite wall, bow at the ready, watching the doorway as the Wraith slowly came into view. I ducked back before he could see me. I moved again to get him within my sights but he was gone.

Where had he gone? I dialed up my hearing. He was still in the room. Was walking across the carpet to look out the window. I got him in my sights. Aiming for the middle of his back, I pulled the trigger.

It hit him square in the back. The bullets were packed tight with microscopic needles filled with a lethal poison. The vial was designed to split on impact and enter the body in a fine spray.

He slumped forward with a grunt, holding onto the window pane. He left a coral handprint on the clear glass. Then he turned, still strong, as if unaffected by the bullet and the poison it contained.

He reached for a chair back and I gave silent thanks. The poison was working, but only enough to weaken him. I still had the problem of killing him. He hadn't yet noticed me in the shadows of the passage.

He hobbled toward the door, his eyes widening as he finally saw me. I stepped into the room, crossbow held to my cheek at the ready. His eyes widened, hand going inside his jacket, the butt of a gun revealing itself slowly.

I didn't give him the satisfaction. Just pulled the trigger again. This time he fell, lying on the carpet, staring at me, disbelief written all over his face. "You have ruined it all."

"No need to thank me."

"You don't know what you've done." He struggled to sit up and managed to rise, supporting his body with one hand. "You will pay. This is not over."

"Maybe not, but it's over for you."

I grabbed the gun from him and threw the weapon away. It went skittering under the enormous mahogany desk. He lifted his hand, groping for my neck. But he was weak, the poison doing its job.

This was my opportunity. I had to try. I glanced at the door again just in case, but the coast was still clear. I placed my hand on his chest and concentrated. I tried to channel the fear I'd felt when Todd's Wraith/Father had held my neck in his grip and almost squeezed the life right out of me.

My heartbeat sped up, my breath increasing to a shuddering. My fingers warmed and a soft glow grew around each digit as I held it against his chest. He shivered, then gurgled as if he wanted to scream but couldn't get the sound out. The glow strengthened, grew brighter around my hand until heat began to spread from my palm.

I was so focused on the heat I almost didn't see the effect it had on the Wraith. I flinched. The skin of the human began to shrivel, little slashes opening in the flesh all over his body. Scraps of shadow escaped from the slits, disconnected parts of the Wraith discarding the host. The body sank inward like a slowly deflating balloon and I shuddered. No matter how many times I saw it, I still hated what the Wraiths did to the bodies they took.

The shadows sped from the body and I could hear a soft but high-pitched screaming as if the shadows were furious at having to be banished again. The pressure changed and the air shimmered. The hundreds of circling shadows began to disappear into what looked like little cracks in the thin air.

And then they were all gone. The pressure subsided and I got to my feet. The shriveled, desiccated corpse of the man remained on the floor. I hefted my bow and left the house, quick and silent.

The woman would do what she had to. Say what she had to.

I'd bet she would just be happy to be free of the Wraith.

CHAPTER 22

I headed back to Tara's adding one more thing to the list of strange when it came to recent Wraith activity. Politics. Influential positions. That made my gut twist. Could it get any worse? What were they planning? It all seemed too strategic to be random possessions.

Tara sat at the front counter, packing away a sword in a long, velvet-lined box. "Hey," she said, barely looking up at me. Her hands moved swiftly as she sealed, wrapped, and labeled the box, setting it next to the register, ready for mailing. Then she came around and locked the door, putting out the closed sign. "Come. Your stuff is inside."

I followed her into the apartment behind the shop and entered their dining room. The table seemed weighed down with an array of weapons and ammunition. "All this for me?" I stared.

She nodded and led me to inspect the spread. "We can begin here." She pointed to a range of bullets and vials filled with colored liquid. She placed a finger on a red vial. "These poisons have been adapted for demonic entities." She moved a finger to the blue vials. "These are meant for the undead or ghostly entities. Mother managed to have them consecrated and blessed by various shamans and Mages to increase their power."

"How can I be sure they will work?"

Tara raised an eyebrow. "Mother has had both potions field tested." What could I possibly say to that?

"Thanks." I turned my attention to the weapons. There were only two of them. One a double-barreled gun that looked like a sawed-off shotgun, and the other a short, wider blade with a jagged edge.

Tara picked up the sheath of the sword and handed it to me. "What do you see?"

I turned it over in my hand. "A metal sheath to house that blade." I pointed.

"Anything else?"

I looked closer, then noticed a tiny lid covering one end of the sheath. I removed the lid to find it attached by a thin metal chain. "What's this?"

Tara picked up a fat bottle filled with blue liquid. "That allows you to keep the knife's edge seasoned with the poison at all times. Just pour a little poison into the hole and run the blade in and out of the sheath. Then you're ready. Just killed a demon and need to kill another? Wipe off the demon blood and stick the knife into the sheath to re-poison the edge. Unfortunately, you will still need to go through the process of cleaning the blade. We couldn't find a way around it. The blood will just dilute the power of the poison."

I nodded and took the sword in my hand, sliding it into the sheath to get the feel of the weapon, to balance the weight of both pieces in my hands. "I like it."

"Right, so the other one is just a gun with two chambers to allow you to reload less. It's your choice though as I've made ammunition for all your guns and for your crossbow as well."

I couldn't believe the extent that Tara and Gracie had gone to. "Thank you! I really owe you. Put it on my tab and I'll sort you out when I get back." Then I stopped and stared at her. "Or maybe I should pay you before I leave."

"Why?" she asked absently as she began to pack away the vials into long thin boxes. Then she stacked them at the bottom of a sturdy rucksack, topping them with the weapons.

"In case I don't make it out alive." I smiled wryly at her.

"Stop being stupid. You'll be fine." Tara glared at me. "Besides, I don't think Mother wants payment."

"No way. She did too much for me not to reimburse her." I shook my head firmly. No way I was taking charity.

"You can have it out with her when you get back. She isn't here right now." She held the bag out to me.

"Fine, I will." I took the rucksack by the strap and hefted it onto my unoccupied shoulder.

Tara gave me a small smile as she walked with me to the front of the store. "So when will you leave?"

"Now that the weapons are sorted, probably tomorrow." There wasn't anything stopping me now except one more round of fire treatment. My gut twisted. It won't be long before I entered the Graylands to bring Greer home. And hopefully I got there before she went totally insane.

"And how are you feeling?" Tara scanned my face with her knowing, dark eyes

"There is that. Right now I feel fine, but that's because Logan's just treated me with the fire. He needs to give me another treatment before I leave, so I'm hoping it will last long enough to get Greer back home. Otherwise I'm in deep shit."

Tara frowned. "I'm worried about you. Are you going to be okay alone?"

"I won't be alone. Logan's sending an Omega operative with me. He's a djinn. So at least I'll have company and a little protection."

"Good." Then she threw her arms around me. I squeezed her

back. "Please take care, Kailin. And please come back." She smiled sadly at me as I pulled away and unlocked the door.

"I'll try. But that's all I can do. What will happen will happen." I kept moving and glanced over my shoulder as I walked out the door. I didn't want to make any promises just in case something did happen and I didn't make it out alive.

$\mathcal{A}$ FEW QUICK PHONE CALLS updated my father, Iain, Grams and Logan on when I was leaving. Lily was waiting at my door when I got back home, so she sat and studied the weapons while I spoke on the phone.

She remained silent even after I came to stand beside her. "What's wrong?" She continued to stare at the weapon-laden table for a moment.

"I just realized this is dangerous. More likely deadly." Her voice grew softer. "What if something happens to you?"

I wanted to tell her that nothing was going to happen, but why would I want to lie to Lily? Not when she was prepared to lay her life down for me. "To be honest, I can't be sure I'll come out of this alive. Nothing is certain. Only that I'll do my best to stay alive because I have my mother and Anjelo waiting for me." I touched Lily's hand and she met my eyes. "If I don't make it, promise me you will choose action. I don't want you to mourn and mope around. You need to do something with your life. Take action. Make a difference. You hear me?"

Lily worried me.

As much as she put on a strong front, she'd succumbed once

to the call of a drug to ease her pain. I didn't want her to repeat that if I didn't make it out of the Graylands alive. When Lily nodded and gave me a weak smile, I hid a sigh of relief.

"Yeah. I hear you."

"Promise me." My voice didn't give her any choice.

"I promise, Kai. I won't let you down." She spoke firmly and sounded determined. I just hoped that strength would hold out if I didn't come back.

A knock sounded on the door and Logan entered, his face a study of emotion. Worry, impatience, frustration. "What's wrong?"

"Nothing. It's just Omega stuff." Logan waved me off and winked at Lily, who smiled and gave him a small wave before turning back to study the weapons.

Logan turned to me. "Do you want me to treat you now? How long before you leave?"

"Now is good. I'm just waiting on Grams. She'll tell me where the nearest dark water is. And then there's just your djinn friend."

"Okay then, let's get started." He headed off to the bedroom and I followed, giving Lily a small grin. This time I sat on the edge of the bed. He'd done the last treatment only yesterday and I was fairly sure that neither of us would be as taxed by the procedure this time. When I removed my jacket, I was reassured. My arm was only lightly flecked by the poison's purple and blue mottling.

The treatment took a fraction of the usual time and I remained silent for the most part. Logan seemed preoccupied and not much in the mood to talk, which was fine with me. I couldn't find anything to talk about, either. My mind buzzed with nervous energy, which I couldn't direct anywhere just yet.

I toyed with telling Logan about the second Wraith but decided he seemed too edgy to throw more stuff at him. It wouldn't make any difference anyway.

When we were done, we walked back into the living room to find Grams and Lily talking in the kitchen.

"I take it no introductions are necessary?" They both smiled.

"Are you ready, dear?" Grams got down to business.

"As I'll ever be." I began to pack away my ammunition and weapons and ended up with a rucksack and a satchel, one for each shoulder. The weight of the two bags worried me—they would hamper any progress I might make. But I had to draw up a plan once I got there, stow the gear someplace where I'd have easy access. Otherwise, I'd be asking for trouble.

Grams nodded and Lily shifted from one foot to the other.

Logan joined us. "Saleem?" I asked with a raised eyebrow. He was late as far as I was concerned. Had he gotten cold feet?

As if in answer, the air beside me thickened, spinning slowly, shimmering as a small whirlwind of color became a spinning image of a person. Then the spinning ceased, the colors settled, and Saleem stood there with a cheeky grin.

"It's about time you got here," I said, eyes narrowed.

"Apologies. I had to account for my weapons." His shrug drew my gaze to his shoulder. A black, military-style rucksack weighed him down.

"Right. You ready?" He nodded. "Oh, and one thing. Since you are coming with me, I need to know you understand the situation. I'm in charge. I won't have us off in the Graylands fighting for control of this mission."

Saleem looked at Logan. Then I looked at Logan and frowned. "Are we going to have a problem here?" Logan looked at me. "Neither Omega nor you are in charge of the mission. I'm making that clear now. If you don't agree, then don't come." I directed the last sentence at Saleem whose eyebrows were very close to his hairline. Dark curls fell to his frown-creased brow.

He glanced at Logan again and whatever had gone on unsaid between them seemed to be over. He looked at me and nodded. "I'm good with that."

"You better be sure, because if you give me any shit, I won't hesitate to incapacitate you and leave you behind." I turned away and grabbed my bags, glancing at Grams and Lily who both raised their eyes.

From Grams' expression, she understood completely where I was coming from. I didn't want any split in authority while I was on the dead plane. Omega needed to be aware that they had no authority over me or my mission. And that I wouldn't waste any time should they decide to assert themselves while we were on the mission.

I turned back to Logan, who held out a hand for one of the backpacks. Handing one over I headed for the door. "Where to, Grams?"

"Lockwood Lake. It's deserted and the dark water is the deepest in this area."

"The pier not good enough?" I recalled the dock I'd used to enter Wrythiin. It was secluded enough. And Lockwood was a mile away.

"Lockwood is better, more secluded, and the water is deeper, older." Grams answered, brooking no argument. I had no problem submitting to her authority and I didn't care that Logan and Saleem could see that.

CHAPTER 24

THE DRIVE TO LOCKWOOD LAKE was silent. Just Logan, Lily, Grams and me. Saleem had done his djinn thing and disappeared from the apartment. We found him waiting in the gravel parking lot when we arrived.

Darkness had settled over the mountainside and my stomach clenched a little. We followed the signs, taking the trail into the trees. It took a few minutes of hiking carefully along the winding pathways until the trail opened out onto a small pebbled beach that led us down to a large, dark lake.

The water rippled and small waves hit the shore softly, crashing onto the stones on the water's edge. The lake felt secluded, surrounded by dense forest, old oak trees reaching up into the night sky.

Someone had constructed a handful of wooden piers along the water's edge, each about twenty feet apart from each other. I walked to the edge of the stone beach and stepped onto the nearest pier, hearing the wood squeak beneath my weight.

This was it.

Once I took that leap into the dark water, there was no turning back.

I'd done this before, so I wasn't nervous or worried. I just wanted to get it over with, get on with saving Greer.

I glanced at Saleem who had come up beside me. "You ready?"

He nodded, hitching his backpack higher on his shoulder. "So how does this work? You coming with me through the portal or do you arrive there on your own?"

Saleem inclined his head in what felt like a tiny bow. "I'll make my own way there. I'll track you, so I'll be waiting for you on the other side."

"Track me?" I frowned.

"Djinn have the ability to sense a person's aura, so we can track that person wherever they are."

"Like a tracker?"

"Something like that, but trackers usually work with items belonging to the missing person. Djinn can only use the person's actual aura. So it would be much harder for me to find you if I had to use your belt or your knife or some other possession."

I nodded, still unsure how I felt about Omega's djinn having the equivalent of a GPS tracker on me. Too late to refuse Saleem now. Besides I needed the backup. I'd be stupid to decline him.

"Okay, then." I faced the group, ready to leave.

Grams held out her arms for a quick hug. I was keenly aware of the possibility it would be our last. "Take care of yourself, dear, and be careful at all times."

"Yes, Grams." I smiled, shifting my gaze a little too quickly from my grandmother's face.

Lily gave me a small wave and an even smaller smile.

Then they both looked at me and at Logan, who moved to my side.

Saleem shifted beside us. "I'll meet you there then?" I nodded and he shimmered and disintegrated.

Logan came closer, taking my hand in his. "Please be careful." His voice was soft. So soft I almost didn't hear the fear lacing his words.

I placed a palm on his cheek. "You know I will."

He laughed, then wrapped me in his arms. "That's just the thing. I know you won't be careful. You are rash, and you run headlong into every challenge as soon as one presents itself." I smiled into his shoulder. He knew me well. "And as much as I know you are capable, I still worry about you. I just wish I could come with you."

His hand at the back of my neck made my skin tingle. His cheek grazed mine as he moved back slightly to trail a few kisses along my chin. Heat rose in the pit of my stomach and somehow, I didn't care that my grandmother stood a few feet away.

When his lips closed over mine, the world melted away. I couldn't get enough, and he deepened the kiss for the briefest moment, his tongue caressing mine and sending shivers through my body, making me ache for more. Then he released me and placed his forehead on mine, breathing hard against my lips.

No more words were needed.

I smiled and drew the rucksack higher onto my shoulder and faced the water. I walked slowly across the length of the pier until I came to the edge of it. The water was black as pitch.

I pulled the portal key from my pocket and held it in my palm. Everything rode on whether or not this key would open the Veil and allow me to pass through. The disk had grown heavy, weighing my hand down more now than a few seconds ago.

I tossed it over the water. If it fell and sank into the lake, I'd probably wring Kira's neck with my own hands.

But Kira was safe. The disk hovered above the surface of the water, and before I could enjoy the relief that it worked, a column of light shot from it. The pillar of brightness stood ten feet high and just a handspan wide. It thinned and disappeared into the hole in the middle of the key.

I took a deep breath then glanced over my shoulder at the waiting group. I threw them a quick wave and jumped straight into the light. It seemed impossible even though I'd done this before. The light held me, compressed me, and sucked me into the center of the key. A whoosh of air blasted my ears and I landed on my feet. I'd remembered to keep my stance soft and my knees bent to ease the jarring force of my landing.

The light disappeared and the disk clattered to the pier below me. I quickly grabbed the key and stowed it in my pocket.

My way out. I had to keep it safe.

Then I stood and took in my surroundings.

I'd arrived in the Graylands.

CHAPTER 25

CLOTHING RUSTLED BESIDE ME. SALEEM shifted into solidity at my right. His eyes gleamed a red, golden fire as he examined our surroundings. Everything was gray. Every possible shade of colorlessness.

Lockwood Lake was every shade of gray imaginable. So weird.

I shrugged my pack higher up my shoulder. "So could you maybe take my heavy pack to the city and I'll meet you there?"

"Sure thing." Saleem nodded. "Give me a second to get there and look for a good place to hide my stuff. I'll be back in a moment to fetch your stuff. I'll take both your packs and tell you where to meet me." He disappeared almost as soon as he finished his sentence.

It wasn't long before he returned and I handed my packs over. I felt a slight twinge of worry about the weapons and ammo, but I did have a few knives and guns on me. I'd have to be satisfied with that in case the djinn decided to betray me. He directed me to an alleyway near the address Nerina had given me and left in a cloud of amber dust.

I set off at Panther speed and met Saleem in the alley in less than fifteen minutes.

The world was in reverse. The streets of Chicago were mirrored here in the dead world. We'd arrived around the corner from Tara's shop.

The streets were deserted.

I almost expected tumbleweeds and litter to come rolling along on an errant breeze, but that would be wrong. The Graylands were dead. Nerina had said that nothing grew here. That ruled out tumbleweeds.

A street sign on the corner said "teertS htuoS" and went in the opposite direction to the street I was familiar with. It was a little disorienting and more than a little disconcerting but we had to get moving.

"Come. I have an address we need to go to." I glanced over my shoulder at Saleem who was staring up the street, frowning. "What's wrong?"

"I don't know. I think I saw something."

"You probably did." I was about to walk off when I thought of something. "Have you ever been here before?"

"The Graylands? Nope. Not exactly my kind of place." He grinned at me and tiny little flames flickered in his eyes.

"Omega never sent you here?"

"No. Never had a mission in the dead lands." He stared at me thoughtfully. "Besides. I wouldn't be allowed to tell you even if I had."

I snorted. "Let's get going."

"Where's the address?"

"It's up here, 256 South St., around the corner at the end of the street." I took the turn up Tara's street and headed past her shop. My steps slowed and I peered inside to find the shelves empty and lights off. Nothing stirred. I sighed. "This is so freaking weird."

"Tell me about it." Saleem shuddered as affected by the strange place as I was. Then he cupped a hand and stared inside the shop as well. "What's this place?"

"My friend's shop. So weird seeing it empty."

"Well, clearly the demons from around here take whatever they need whenever something appears."

Made sense. From what I understood, when something new is placed somewhere in the normal world it appears in the Graylands. Stood to reason anything Tara created would appear here. Which meant all her weapons that never left her shop were somewhere here in this land. It made me shiver to think of that kind of firepower readily available to these demons. But most of the rounds were meant for ghosts or demons. A reassuring thought, if only a momentary one.

I looked up and shivered. The cloudless, gray sky was a flat ceiling above us, not even high enough to be called a sky. I looked back at the shop and made a decision.

Withdrawing my scimitar from its sheath at my back I slid it into the space between the door and the jamb. I moved it down until it touched the lock, then raised it and hit the metal pin hard. It shattered beneath the blade and the door swung open. I had expected to hear the little doorbell, but the only sound that echoed around the room was a strange dull clanging, as if the bell was muffled somehow.

A slight push sent the door swinging inward and I entered, listening for the usual tap of my boot heels on the old wood floor. As I suspected the sound was muffled, deadened with no echo and no density to it.

Saleem followed close behind me. I let him pass, then grabbed a stool and shoved it against the door to hold it closed. "I hope the things we do in the Graylands don't have a flow-on effect in the real world."

"I don't think so. Not from what I've heard at least."

"How much do you know about this place?" I asked him.

"Not a whole lot. Just what my father used to tell me." He

shrugged and turned to study the room. I suspected he was avoiding my gaze, but I didn't have time to interrogate him just yet.

I returned the scimitar to its sheath and led him inside the apartment and into the kitchen, dropping my rucksack and satchel on the table. I turned to the lower cupboard and opened the doors, half expecting to see food. Shaking my head, I began to stack our canned food into the farthest, darkest corner of the cupboard.

Saleem came around to pass tins of tuna and bottles of water and crackers. I sat on my heels, looking around the kitchen and frowned.

"What are you looking for?" asked Saleem.

"Something to block the food off. Just in case somebody comes by and decides to steal our stuff."

He nodded his approval and got up to look.

"Check the broom closet."

He rummaged inside for a few seconds, then returned triumphantly with an old box filled with gray rags.

"Perfect." I ripped a piece off the side of the box before angling it to hide our loot and shut the doors. I got to my feet and dusted my hands on the seat of my pants. "So now that's done, we need to figure out what next."

"That address. Whose place is it?"

I shrugged. "No idea. Nerina gave me the address while she was trying to call Greer. I'm assuming it's where Greer is." I stared out the window which overlooked the alley behind the shop. "But wouldn't that be too easy."

Saleem nodded. "Way too easy." Then he stood. "So let's go check it out."

I rose and grabbed my bags, watching Saleem from the corner of my eye. He did the same with his bag. Good. I liked that he wanted his weapons close. Meant he wanted to be ready for anything. Still, it didn't mean I trusted him completely.

"So, tell me about the djinn. I had always thought they were actually demons. No offense." I sent him an apologetic smile.

"None taken." He grinned and followed me out the door, waiting while I turned back to fold a piece of cardboard and hold it against the door jamb as I closed the door. It held and I was relieved. As soon as we started walking again, Saleem continued. "Djinn are technically Dark Ethereals or demons. But our form is human and we live among the humans. We have done so for centuries, so it's not surprising that the High Council has never thought to ward the portals against our kind."

"So your kind can move through the portals at will?" Saleem nodded. "Convenient for Omega, isn't it?"

Saleem curled his lip. "Not really. Omega is bound by the laws as well as the next person. If we ever needed to enter one of the forbidden planes, we have to obtain the permission of the High Council first."

"So you got permission to be here?" A nod. "So they know I'm here too?"

"Yes, they were given a full rundown of the mission and who it involved." After we'd crossed the street, he looked at me. "Have you decided either way what you will choose to do?"

"What do you mean?"

"Logan mentioned that Omega wants you on board."

"No secrets among you boys, is there?" I raised an eyebrow.

"No secrets among our team, Kailin. Jess is our supervising officer and Logan is our team leader. When we are on team missions, that is. When we go solo, we still answer to Logan but we get to make our own calls in terms of the specific needs of the job." I glanced at the djinn and said nothing. Why was he being so informative about their team dynamic? Was he also on a recruitment drive?

"Here." I stopped on the corner and looked at the building. Two stories of solid, gray brick and off-white mortar. "Let's go around back." I led him to the alley behind the building and we entered an odor-free, garbage-free back alley complete with an empty dumpster and a neatly closed row of clean garbage cans.

"Wow. Back home this would put the garbage disposal companies out of business in the blink of an eye."

I hurried to the closest of the back entrances and jimmied the lock with my dagger. The old lock didn't hold up to the sharp twist of my Fae metal blade. We scurried inside and the door swung shut, heavy on its hinges. We were in some sort of commercial kitchen, maybe a restaurant. Skirting the wide metal tables, we went to the swinging doors and peeped through the porthole windows.

Nothing moved inside so we entered, crossing an expanse of bare carpet. Tables and chairs edged the room in disorder and the place had an abandoned, yet occupied air. I shook my head. That was so silly.

Farther inside was another room, larger. A ballroom or a conference hall. Then it clicked. "The Fenton."

"What?" Saleem asked, his eyes scanning the high-ceilinged room.

"I'd forgotten. This is the Fenton Hotel. It's a small place. About thirty rooms. Reasonable rates. The working girls with special higher-paying clients use these rooms."

Saleem's face darkened, nostrils flaring a little. Guess he didn't like the thought of prostitution. He'd just moved up a notch in my estimation.

We headed across the floor of the shadowy room and were halfway across when a cold breeze grazed my skin and raised goosebumps. We'd dressed warmly as we'd known the Graylands to be cold, but this rush of air was Arctic.

And strange.

I stopped dead in my tracks and Saleem almost bumped into me. "Did you feel that too?" he whispered.

"Yes. Any ideas?"

"Ghost?" he offered.

I went with it. "Is anyone there?"

No answer.

"Hello. We're not here to hurt you. Can you tell us who you are?"

"He won't do that."

"Won't do what?" I asked, my voice rising. I'd forgotten to whisper.

"Tell you his name," Saleem answered, all attempts at keeping our voices soft were gone.

"Why not?" I frowned, remembering Nerina's words but wanting to get Saleem's version.

"When people die and they pass through the Graylands on the way to their ever after, they never utter their names."

"Why not?"

"Because a name is power. It can give a demon power over you if you're no longer alive. A demon can enslave the recently dead here in the Graylands for eternity."

"If only I had known that when I first arrived in this place," a soft voice said from the shadows.

CHAPTER 26

A GHOST.

I FLINCHED BUT managed to remain relatively still. I wasn't allowed to go screaming and running off at the first sign of a ghost. "How long have you been here?"

"I don't know." His voice wavered and sadness shadowed his eerie, almost-not-there face.

"Do you remember anything about your life?" I watched the air in front of me and it was like watching an image from a projector that was aimed at a dark wall. The form of a teenage boy could be seen hovering in front of us.

Hi-tops, jeans, a baggy sweatshirt, and cap with the peak turned to the side. All he was missing was a skateboard.

"How old are you?" He looked about fifteen, but I just wanted to engage him. Get him comfortable enough to talk. There must have been a reason Nerina sent us here and I suspected the reason was this ghost boy.

"I'm sixteen. I just turned sixteen, I mean. It was my birthday when it happened." There was a short, awkward silence in which I wanted to say I was sorry, but bit my tongue because I realized how stupid that would sound.

"Do you know this place well?" I decided to keep my questions to the Graylands. This boy's past and life weren't our concern unless we could help him. And he was dead.

Nothing we could do about that.

"Yes. I know it like the back of my hand." His confident voice fell as he stared off into the distance as if listening for someone. "I just wish they would let me use my skateboard here." A look of fear passed across his face. A face which didn't seem so hazy for some reason. I blinked, but I wasn't imagining things.

I focused my attention on my questions. "Are you okay?"

"Yeah. I'm okay." He looked at me again as if seeing me for the first time. "Did Nerina send you?"

I did a double take. "You know Nerina?"

"Of course, I know her. She came to see me as soon as I arrived here. I couldn't leave after a while, so she visits me now and again. She is such a nice lady. Are you the people Nerina sent?"

We nodded. It felt odd looking at a ghost who now seemed as solid as I was.

"Nerina said she'd be sending some people who would need my help." But something else he'd said was bothering me.

"How long did you say you've been here?"

"I don't really know. I can't recall. Too much time has passed."

I frowned. "You're possessed by a demon, right?"

"Not possessed." He scrunched up his nose as if the word stank. "In service. I've been roped into the service of a low-level demon."

"How can we trust you then? Won't you just go running to your master and tell him we are here?" What had Nerina been thinking? Had she set us up?

"No. Low-level demons have less power over their . . . *servants*. He has no mental link with me, and sometimes, if I concentrate to block him, he can't sense where I am. I'm more or less free to do as I please." He looked sad. "Plus he's in trouble with his own boss anyway so he's more interested in keeping his own ass alive than worrying about me."

"Why is he in trouble?"

The boy shrugged. "I don't really know the details. I think he tried to leave and go back to the demon realm. Something about him wanting a higher position and being tired of answering to his boss. But someone ratted on him—which is no surprise really 'cos demons aren't known for their loyalty. His boss was furious, beat him within an inch of his life, made him swear his loyalty again, but he doesn't do loyalty very well. I know for a fact his time's up. He's been working with someone else again to over-throw his boss, but his boss knows—you see Lester's not very blessed in the brains or the luck department. I try to stay as far away from him as possible. Don't want to get caught in the cross-fire you know."

The boy sighed after his little monologue, then fell into a little contemplative silence. It was a lot to think about. An extended "life" here at the beck and call of an incompetent nasty demon, caught in the messy crossfire of demon politics.

To change the subject I asked, "What does he make you do?" Then I felt a little bad for him, for what his death had meant. Hardly a good end to a young boy's life.

"Hauntings mostly. He tries to use me to take possession of people. Most times it doesn't work. He's not very smart."

"Isn't there a way for you to get free?" Saleem asked, frowning. He was as affected by the boy's predicament as I was.

"Only one way and that's when and if he ever dies."

Saleem and I exchanged a glance. Now it made a lot more sense why the DeathTalker sent us to the ghost boy. But that couldn't have been her only reason.

"Have you seen a girl around here? A living girl?" I asked.

"You mean the white-haired chick?" When I nodded, he continued. "Yeah she's been here a few weeks. She's a strange one though."

"Why is that?" I asked, curious what his take would be on my very unique sister.

"Doesn't act like a normal person would. When she arrived, she lashed out at everyone. Even the ghosts who recognized she was alive and tried to warn her of the dangers. We were very confused, though. How did a living person end up in the Gray-lands?" He was frowning, staring at my face, a strange look in his eyes.

"She was accidentally thrown through a portal from the Wraith world." I gave him the short and sweet version. No need for details.

"Doesn't explain how she's alive. She didn't come with anyone."

I tamped down a breath. I hadn't thought about it too much, but after what skater boy said, I had to wonder how exactly had Greer come through the portal. She'd come through using Widd'en's key, not Mom's. Had his key been special in some way? Or had it somehow been coded to Greer's blood? The only possibility that came to my mind was that if Niko had allowed the Wraith Lord to use Greer's body as a vessel at some point.

I shuddered at the thought. I wouldn't put it past my crazed uncle to do such a thing either. Swallowing hard, I refocused my attention on the ghost boy as he continued. "So she arrived here, screeching mad, and we're trying to calm her down so the demons don't find her, but it doesn't help. It looked like she'd lost it, so we kinda left her there. We didn't want the demons to find us, so we had to make a choice."

"You left her?" I knew it sounded like a judgment, but I didn't mean it that way.

He nodded sadly. "I'm sorry. She didn't want to stop scream-ing. And that's exactly what happened. She made so much noise they found her."

"Who found her?" I asked.

"The demons. Yanuk. He's a high level. Very powerful."

I continued. "What kind of demon is he?"

"A Shedu demon. He's large, red, and super ugly." Skater boy shuddered. "I'm just glad he's not my master."

"Did he bind her to him?" I had a sinking feeling the demon had possessed her.

"Yes. And Yanuk is well-known for being vicious." Skater boy went quiet for a moment. "He hurt her."

"What did he do to her?" I hoped the injury hadn't been serious. If it had, it meant she'd be weak and more in need of our help than we expected.

"He has this whip." Skater boy cringed. "It's got a little spike on the end of it." He didn't need to say anything more. My gut twisted.

"How bad was it?"

"It was really bad at first. She was bleeding all over the place. But he eased up when she stopped screaming, and I guess she realized it was in her best interests to stop too."

"What did he do to her? How does the possession work with her being alive?" I suppressed a shudder at the images my mind created of Greer being whipped.

"Well, that's the thing. Nobody's really sure the possession is working the way it does with the ghosts. It's almost as if she is crazy and he just knows how to manipulate her. She doesn't behave like his slave—which is basically what ghosts are once they are possessed." Skater Boy was lost in thought for a moment.

"How is she behaving?" I asked.

"Like she's his right-hand man or his consort or something. And Yanuk, he just lets her walk around acting like she's his boss. All he does is smile that stupid smile of his. I'm not sure how to explain it, but it's almost as if she sometimes thinks she's actually in charge."

"In charge?" This was getting more complicated.

"So what's the hierarchy like? Do the other demons defer to Yanuk? Or do they all do their own thing?"

"Yeah. Yanuk is the head honcho around here. Most demons come and go, but Yanuk has stayed. He's been here long enough that most demons and spirits defer to him if they know what's good for them."

"So he's like a demon overlord?" This was getting worse and worse. Greer in the service of a powerful demon? And liking it? This didn't bode well for breaking her out of here.

Skater boy nodded. "In a sense they answer to him, but only to a certain extent. Like he can't take any of the other demons' slaves from them, but he can give them orders, which they probably won't ignore. He'd make life a living hell here. It's bad enough this place is like a big slice of nowhere, but Yanuk has his own special way of punishing his slaves and sometimes his own demons too."

"What does he do?" I asked, frowning. More torture?

Skater boy looked distracted. His gaze went to the doorway behind me. "He puts them in the black hole." The ghost answered, his attention still trained over my shoulder.

"What's wrong?" I asked, all thoughts of the mysterious black hole gone the moment the boy's expression took on one of taut fear.

"He's coming. I can feel it." The ghost boy looked scared.

"Who is it?" asked Saleem softly.

"My master." He shivered. Then he moved his gaze from the door and met my eyes. "Go. Hide. He won't be able to find you."

Saleem touched my arm and we hurried off across the ball-room to a set of doors that led into a bar area. We ducked down behind the bar just as a demon walked into the ballroom. His pale, almost gray-white skin fitted naturally with the rest of the Graylands.

Except for his red eyes.

I watched him through a small space in the paneling at the bottom of the bar. Skater boy had disappeared and the demon couldn't see him either. He looked around the room, exasperated.

Then the ghost boy appeared behind him, hovering above the ground a little out of the demon's reach. I wasn't sure what he would do to punish a non-corporeal being and was relieved that the boy would be relatively safe.

"Get down here now." The demon sank a hand into his pocket —his jacket incongruously modern, black and shiny leather. He retrieved something and held his hand out. The boy cringed, looking like he was about to run. Whatever the demon held in his hand terrified him. "You know it's best for you to come down now."

Despite the fear on his face, the boy floated to the ground and stood in front of the demon. He had his back to us now, and I couldn't see his face. It made me uncomfortable. The demon opened his palm and a blue stone shimmered, letting off tiny sparks of yellow light. What the hell was going on with all these colors in the Graylands?

Beside me, Saleem stiffened and I glanced at him. He didn't seem to notice, all his attention remained focused on the demon and the boy.

The red-eyed demon tilted the stone toward the boy, and a flash of blue light arced toward the ghost. It struck him and spread over him in a wave of spattering sparks. As soon as the sparking receded, the demon stepped forward and grabbed the ghost boy by the arm.

Saleem and I glanced at each other, but although I reeled in shock, Saleem seemed to be taking it in his stride. Was it a dude thing? Don't show the chick any emotion? Or was there something I needed to know about this stone? I shook the thought from my head. No time to think about it this minute.

For now the fact that the demon had just made the ghost solid was enough of a shock. He twisted the boy's arm, a look of pleasure on his sneering face. I flinched and Saleem put a hand on my arm. Already he seemed to know me too well. I met Saleem's eyes, my glare clear of my intentions. He merely shrugged and removed his hand unarmed.

The boy moaned and I gritted my teeth. The demon growled. "Who are they?"

The ghost shook his head. "I don't know what you mean."

"Who are the two who came into this building earlier?"

"I don't know." The boy shook his head again. "I didn't see anyone."

"Do not lie to me." The demon growled close to the boy's ear. "You know what will happen when you lie to me."

"I'm not lying. I promise. I didn't see anyone." The boy shuddered as the demon traced a nail across his cheek. The vicious nail slid across skin, splitting it open to reveal the boy's cheekbone. No blood. The boy screamed, a low, painful sound that made me shiver. I wanted to kill that demon so badly. A glance at Saleem's corded neck showed he was equally affected.

"You know how I enjoy our little games. You know I can continue this for a long time."

The boy shook his head. "But I don't know anything about anyone."

The demon studied the boy's face, a look of uncertainty clear in his eyes. "That had better be the case because if I find out that you lied to me, I will enjoy much more than this little injury." The demon leaned forward and ran his tongue along the open wound. A white, forked tongue that glistened as it moved against the boy's cheek.

I shivered again, wanting desperately to separate his head from his shoulders, but Saleem again placed a steadying arm on mine and I breathed, shrugging him off. It wouldn't be long before he left, and what if we needed the ghost boy's master to get to Yanuk?

The demon laughed, the sound hollow and flat, as with all sounds here in the Graylands. He gave the ghost boy a hard shove, then put the stone back into his pocket. The boy fell to the carpet and sparks shifted and rippled through his body as the demon turned and walked out of the ballroom. It wasn't long before an outer door slammed and the demon was gone.

I was about to rise and go back to the boy when he turned to look in the direction of the bar, shaking his head almost imperceptibly. A sound at the door confirmed the return of the demon. He stood at the entrance and examined the room, suspicion still strong on his face.

The ghost boy looked up at him, a hand on his cheek. The demon sneered then turned and stalked off. This time the slam of the door was harder and louder, yet still oddly hollow.

Saleem and I rose from our hiding place and hurried to the boy's side. He still held his cheek. "Does it hurt?"

"Only while he held me with the stone."

"What was that thing?" I asked, as I stared at the exit door.

"It's the way the demons control us. They use it to torture us. Make us hurt so we won't rebel." He let go of his cheek and I blinked. The wound was gone. "Whatever happens to us while the stone is working is only temporary. The main purpose is that we feel the pain as a living person would. So every time they break a bone or cut into our skin, it hurts like we are alive."

"And when they take the stone away, you go back to normal and the wounds disappear?"

He nodded. "Yeah, all gone like nothing ever happened, but you remember the pain for a long time."

"I'm sorry you had to go through that for us." He was a means to an end, but I still felt bad he'd suffered on our account.

"It's okay. I've been through worse." He opened his mouth to speak but whatever he was about to say was cut off by a high-pitched shriek emanating from the corridor.

Nobody had a chance to move before we heard someone yell, "What the fuck!"

Skates whispered, "That's Lester."

I couldn't help but grin at the incongruity of a demon using human profanity in the land of the dead.

Saleem moved toward the door, and although I gave him an are-you-insane glare, he went anyway. He cracked the swing door open a little and peered through the opening.

An oomph sound filtered toward us, like someone being punched in the gut. Lester screamed, making me smile and wish I'd been the one doing the punching. "What the hell was that for?" he spluttered.

"That's for making things difficult for us," a guttural voice said. He sounded like he was enjoying administering Lester's punishments. "Yanuk wants to see you so you'd better come quietly."

"What does he want?" Lester asked, his voice quite petulant.

"Huh? You really think he tells us his business? You stupid or something?" The demon laughed. "You must be in deep shit if you're already this scared."

"Don't worry, Lester," another voice said with a cruel laugh. "I'm sure he won't make you suffer too long."

After a few shuffling and dragging sounds, Lester and his entourage left the building. Saleem waited at the door until he was sure they'd gone before coming back to us.

"They're gone."

"Why would Yanuk want Lester?" I asked, frowning.

" 'Cos Yanuk is Lester's master," Skates said, raising his eyebrows as if I should have already deduced this. I looked over at Saleem, who also seemed to have missed this vital piece of info. Skates looked from Saleem to me and shrugged. "Oh. Did I forget to tell you that? Sorry I do forget stuff sometimes."

A moment of silence passed in which I wondered if coming here was maybe my worst idea ever. Then Skates snorted. "Poor Lester," he said, grinning.

I shuddered to think how that could have been worse if they had found us. "I so want to kill that sucker," I said through gritted teeth. The ghost boy looked at me, startled. It seemed as if the possibility had never occurred to him. I felt a rush of pity for him. Willing to help us because of Nerina, yet expecting nothing in return.

"You will need him alive so he can lead you to Yanuk," the boy said, then he grinned. "Once he's served his purpose, you can kill him."

"Why do we need him anyway? Can't *you* lead us to Yanuk?"

The boy shook his head. "My connection is to *my* master. I can usually tell where he is at all times."

"But he can't always sense you?"

He shook his head. "Nope. I don't think he's smart enough. Or maybe he has some kind of block to his ability, but we've been connected since he made me his slave. I've always been able to find him, but he's a bit useless himself."

"So. Lester?" I asked, already feeling like I wanted to pulverize the freaking demon and needing to burn up some of the buildup of energy.

"Yup."

I snorted. "Nice demon name for a nice demon. What is he anyway?"

"Type of demon?" he asked and I nodded. "Lester is a lamia."

"Not very powerful for a lamia." I scowled.

"Why do you think he wants me? He needs me to lure the young girls for him to possess." Skate's face darkened and I knew I saw guilt in his eyes. It didn't serve anyone's purpose to broach the issue of his guilt in obtaining the lamia demon's souls. I just wanted to find Yanuk so we could save Greer and now kill Lester the lamia.

"So, where to now?" I asked the kid.

"Now we track him. Follow him and we'll find Yanuk. If you are ready, that is." He looked at me, a question in his eyes.

A glance at Saleem confirmed he was just as ready as I was to get on with it.

Follow the lamia, find Yanuk, save Greer.

CHAPTER 27

WE HEADED THROUGH THE BALLROOM with Skates going ahead to check the place out. All was clear and we made it to the alley exit without a hitch. Again the alley was clear and we headed outside, taking South Street and heading away from Tara's shop. The Graylands had no sense of time; the sky remained gray all the time. No change. Not even a lightening of the sky to imply daylight. Not an easy life to live if you're stuck in a place like this. My chest tightened at the thought of Greer living here all these weeks. No surprise that both Melisande and Nerina said she was going a little insane.

It didn't take long to realize that Skates was taking us into the abandoned part of town, where back home I would find the red-light district where I'd killed the Gus-wraith, and the warehouse where leopard Walker Brand had almost eaten me alive. Fitting that the demons would congregate in the unoccupied zone. Not that the entire Graylands didn't seem empty anyway.

Skates stopped so suddenly that I knocked my rucksack into his shoulder. It went right through him but I still felt bad.

"What's wrong?" I asked.

"I think we're being followed," he whispered, ducking into a nearby alley.

"I didn't hear anything." Not that that meant anything.

"You wouldn't if it was a ghost or even a demon. You wouldn't know until it was too late." He looked worried then moved slowly toward the corner, his back pasted against the wall, or rather almost through the wall. He peered around the edge then slammed himself back against the gray brick. "Yes, we were being followed. Two low-level demons. May even be working for Lester. You guys hide. I'll try to head them off across the street."

"Wait." I almost reached for him before realized I wouldn't be able to touch him. "Are they dangerous?"

"They might be." He looked worried.

"If they even look like they'll hurt you, I'm going to take a shot, okay?" I raised my eyebrows looking for his agreement.

"Sure. As long as you shoot to kill. Whatever you do, don't miss. Or I will be in deep shit if they survive."

"Okay, go." Despite my reluctance, I let him go.

Saleem and I ducked behind a large dumpster and peered out as Skates headed into the street again. He was about to cross the street when a shout sounded from one of the demons.

Skates stopped and turned to face them. Both the demons came into view. One a lamia who seemed thinner and weaker and a little more spineless than Lester. I didn't recognize the other demon's species. Not surprising as my experience with demons was pretty much limited to Wraiths.

"Hey, ghost boy. Who were those people with you?" the lamia asked, prodding his finger into the air in front of Skate's chest.

"Who?"

I cringed. *Bad move, Skates.* He should have owned up straight away and then created a cover story. Now he'd have to backtrack.

"Those two. Guy and girl. With you not long ago," the lamia asked while the other purple-skinned demon looked up and down the street, giving his grape-purple horns a cursory scratch.

Skates shrugged. "No idea. Just a couple of ghosts wanting to know where they were. You know, the whole new ghost shit." He shoved his hands into his pockets. Probably knew they were giving away his nerves.

"Don't lie to us, boy. Lester said you were up to something, and sure enough, you're down here cavorting with those two. Ghosts? My ass. They looked very alive to me. Just like that blonde girlfriend of Yanuk's."

"Girlfriend? You mean more like his new boss." The other demon snorted, and the lamia shoved an elbow into his chest, making him cough up a wad of green phlegm. It struck me again that demons weren't colorless in the Graylands. Both the demons now confronting a very gray Skates were dressed in painful shades of orange and yellow. They probably looked much worse surrounded as they were by shades of dull gray. The wad of phlegm on the sidewalk glowed a sickly green.

"What do you mean? I thought Yanuk was in charge?" Skates asked, feigning curiosity.

"See what you did? You and your big mouth." The lamia back-handed the purple-horned demon, who held his hand to his mouth in utter shock

"What did you do that for?" he grumbled through his fingers.

"For having a big mouth. Going and telling the ghost boy that the girl is the boss and not Yanuk."

"Well, it's not as if that's a lie," the demon whined.

The lamia growled. "Will you just shut the fuck up?"

"Fine." Purple Horns pouted and crossed his arms, refusing to look at the lamia again. That was good for me. I pulled my crossbow from my satchel and took aim. Things were heating up and the lamia looked unpredictable.

The lamia took a step toward Skates, who took a step backward, bringing them in a good line of sight. "Now, tell me who those two were and I might let you live."

"You can't kill me. I belong to Lester," Skates answered, lifting his chin. That was all the defiance he was up for.

"Not for long you don't," the lamia sneered.

"What do you mean?" Skates pretended to look worried. He seemed to be a pretty good actor. Must need the skills around here.

"You know the rules. When one demon kills another, their slaves go to the killer." The lamia's lip curled.

"So?" Skates jeered. "Lester is still alive. I just saw him a few moments ago."

The lamia grinned. "Not for long," he said again.

This wasn't looking good. Why would the demon tell Skates that and then let him live to tell his master? Skates gaze flickered across the street as if he was forcing himself not to look in our direction. Smart boy. The lamia followed his gaze.

"Where are they hiding?" He got nose-to-nose with Skates, his voice raised to what must have been threatening to him, but which only sounded flat and as unscary as a puppet show. "Are they in there? The old video store?"

"I don't know. They walked off in that direction so maybe they went in there. I have no idea." Skates shrugged.

"Don't lie to me, you little creep."

"I'm not lying," Skates whined and leaned away from the demon.

"Well, I have one way to find out, don't I?" The lamia grinned, the row of sharp vampiric teeth gleaming in the bleak light. He drew a blue stone from his pocket and I knew there was no turning back.

I turned to nod at Saleem whose expression darkened. He wasn't even looking at me. His attention was focused on the lamia. Hoping he'd move on instinct with me, I rose to my knees, letting a poisoned demon arrow fly. It struck the lamia through his left rib cage and would have pierced his heart. Assuming he had one. I'd missed Demon Physiology 101, so I had no idea.

I felt Saleem move at the same time and heard his shot leave his weapon. The bullet struck Purple Horns in the back and he threw his arms forward as the momentum of the shot dropped him on his face. I glanced down to confirm—a pistol with a nice big silencer. I nodded at Saleem and slung my bow over my shoulder using the strap. I raced for Skates, who nodded in appreciation at the two dead demons at his feet. As I got there, he kicked at the lamia. Of course he didn't land the blow. His foot just went right through the demon's body but Skates seemed satisfied enough.

"Where can we leave them?" Saleem asked.

"The dumpster can finally serve its purpose. Even if it's only to get them out of sight for a few minutes." Skates jerked his head in the direction of the alley behind us. I grinned.

Quite appropriate. I hauled the lamia up and dragged him to the garbage bin. Skates followed close on our heels. Just before I tossed the lamia inside, I slipped a hand into his purple coat pocket and retrieved the blue stone. Never know when I might need that.

He made a loud thud when he landed, followed by a similar hollow sound as Saleem threw Purple Horns in.

I turned to Saleem. "Nice pistol."

"I told you I was well supplied in the weapons department."

"What kind of ammo?"

"High-level demon poison," he said nodding and winking as if he were a petrol-head proudly referring to engine parts or something.

I just shook my head and grinned. They probably used the same people Gracie had used. No surprises there.

"Right. What now?" I faced Skates.

"I can still feel Lester. But now I'm worried. After what that lamia said, I'm a bit concerned about my status. I'd rather be dead than have Yanuk as my master." Skates shuddered.

When I raised an eyebrow, he snickered. "I mean dead-dead. Lester is a skate-in-the-park compared to some of the other second- and third-level creeps out there. Seriously, if they kill him, I'm dead meat. What you saw Lester do with the stone? That was nothing compared to the kind of torture some of these guys think up. I'd like my body parts to remain attached to my body thank you very much."

I shuddered at the thought. "I can't promise anything, but we'll try to not let that happen, okay?"

"There isn't anything you can do, really. If they kill him, I'll just disappear and reappear before my new master. I get my new orders and a little speech... yada yada... and then he'll torture me a little just so I know who is boss. You'd have to find him and kill him and that depends on how strong he is compared to Lester."

"Then, let's get moving. The less time we spend talking, the quicker we can track Lester down and free you," I said firmly.

Skates nodded and rose as I stashed my bow and Saleem did the same. A flash of something flew across his face. Worry? Fear? I wasn't sure. "What's the matter?" I hung back a bit to ask him.

"Nothing, really. I just hope we can trust this kid."

"He's our only lead," I said, frowning. I was beginning to feel a little too protective of our ghost guide. "And it's not that I'm not wary of him too. We can't let our guards down for a single second."

"Yes, but it would've been good to get the stone just in case." He paused to look at me. "The one the lamia wanted to use on the boy. You go on ahead. I'll go back for it and catch up with you."

I wasn't sure why, but I hesitated to tell him I had the stone. Then, in a split second, decided not to say anything. "No. We can't afford to lose you. We can check the dumpster on our way back. It's too late now."

"But—"

"Saleem, leave it for now. We can't delay any further. What if we lose the boy? What if I need you to cover my back?"

He relented but doubt still darkened his face. "Fine. I'll check the dumpster on the way back."

CHAPTER 28

SKATES HAD GONE ON AHEAD, then paused to wait for us to catch up. "What's wrong?" He also looked worried.

"Nothing. We were just comparing ammo stock," I said, not looking at Saleem for corroboration.

Skates nodded. "We're not far away. It's a warehouse a couple of blocks away."

I still felt a little disoriented to see buildings on the wrong side of the streets. But I was getting used to it. The ghost boy led us past Brand's warehouse and I shivered as I walked by the building. Memories of how close I'd been to death had haunted me since Logan had saved my ass from being Brand's dinner.

I had unfinished business with Brand.

We checked the crossroads, not a sign of life or movement on any of the streets. Something twisted in my gut. This was too easy. "Be alert, guys. This is too easy. Why are there no guards?"

"There will be. They're just hiding, waiting for the right moment to pounce." Skates' voice was ominous and I hoped not self-prophesying.

The blackened panes of the glass fronting warehouse stared

gloomily at us as we approached. A million black eyes glaring at us for encroaching on their territory. A metal door barred our way and we headed around the block to the alley at the back. Another metal door stopped our entry, barred tightly without even a handle to force the door open.

I stared up at the fire escape and the face of the building. All the downpipes and ducting would serve as footholds if I needed to scale the building. It wouldn't be hard if I shifted into panther form a little.

At this point I just allowed my panther hearing and vision through a little bit. Heat singed my ears and eyes as the tops of my earlobes extended and the shape of my eyes elongated. Hollow sounds around me became clearer. I placed my ear near the metal door and listened.

At first, I heard nothing, no movement, no sign of life. And then footsteps pattered toward the door. The footsteps came down the stairs then turned and headed into the back of the building. A voice sounded in the distance. A male from the depth of the timbre.

"Two people are in there now. One guy definitely," I whispered to the others.

I listened again. Another voice filtered through to me, still clear despite the metal in the way. "What do you want to do with him?"

"Who? Lester?" the gravelly voice asked.

"Yes, sir."

"Well, Lester has served his purpose. We can dispense with his services soon." He paused, more footsteps. "Where is he?"

"First floor. First room on the left. He's ready for you."

"I don't think he has any idea what he is in for." He chuckled and the second demon gave a strangled laugh. "I will attend to Lester when I am ready. I do appreciate the idea of him waiting for me, terrified as he looks down the barrel of his future. Has anyone told him what's in store for him?"

"No, sir. Except for when we picked him up, we haven't spoken to him directly at all."

"Good. Keep it that way." The gravelly voiced demon cleared his throat. "Now, leave me."

The second demon scurried away further into the depths of the ground floor and the room fell into silence.

I turned to the djinn and the ghost. "We need to get inside. Lester is being held upstairs, And I think his days are numbered. No scratch that. His hours are numbered. Seems he is of no use to them any longer."

"Why don't I check how many people there are around?" offered Skates.

"Won't that be dangerous for you?" I asked.

Skates just shook his head. Then he said, "Not when I go invisible." He flashed out of sight.

I snorted. "Okay. Do your thing."

I couldn't tell where he'd gone, so neither Saleem nor I spoke while Skates was off doing recon.

The ghost boy returned a few minutes later, semi-transparent now. "Done one round of the building. We got two demons on the ground floor, opposite end. There's Yanuk also on the ground floor. Lester and one guard on the first floor. They've got Lester all tied up with no place to go. Not going to be easy to get him out."

"Is the girl around?" I asked.

"No. No sign of her, which isn't unusual. She likes to do her own thing. She's probably gathering her own set of demons and sending them off to do her dirty work."

"What do you mean?" He didn't seem to be describing Greer.

"That white-haired chick. The one you're looking for. She's into the whole demon-control shit. A lot of them answer to her especially since she acts like Yanuk's right hand almost. You heard those demons. Many people here wonder who is really in charge these days."

I shivered. The thought of Greer becoming the overlord of the Graylands didn't sit well with me. What if she liked the power too much and didn't want to return with us?

"Right, so we need to put Greer on the back burner for now. First, we have to free Lester and squeeze him for info. Then we can figure out what to do about Yanuk and Greer." Saleem nodded.

Skates nodded too, then his eyes widened as he stared at the alley behind us. Scuffed footsteps announced we had company at the entrance of the alley. Four demons sauntered toward us, all painfully brightly clothed, and they moved toward us with a confidence I didn't like.

"Go invisible. They wouldn't have seen you from that distance." Before I'd finished the sentence, he was gone.

"I'll hang around."

"You do that," I said as I dragged my crossbow from the backpack and threw the strap over my shoulder. I let off an arrow and one demon fell to the ground, unmoving, his orange sunglasses cracking into pieces on the concrete.

I sent another arrow flying but they were too close. I let the crossbow fall to my back and grabbed a scimitar and Tara's special sword. Both blades sang as they left the scabbards on my back and I danced on the balls of my feet.

Let them come to us.

Saleem had the same idea, holding a sword and a pistol out in front of him. The three remaining demons drew their own weapons and laughed incongruously as if the sight of their weapons would still our blood. When they received no reaction, they looked at each other and then came flying at us.

Saleem took the one on the extreme left down, but from the scuffling, the pink-jacketed demon was far from out. The one nearest me grinned, his yellowed, chipped teeth gleaming in the gray light. He slashed with his jagged-edged sword and I spun out of the way, coming back around with a blow to his shoulder with the poisoned blade. He leaked green goo and yelled as he grabbed his arm.

The third demon was close on his tail, and I swiped at him with my scimitar, happy to try to add to the horrible scar that patterned his cheek. He dodged then returned with a blow to my arm. The armband sang, taking the brunt of the blow and leaving my wounded hand burning with pain. I tried to block out the pain, and sliced the scimitar at the demon's hand as he retracted it. Scarface moved much slower than he realized.

I sliced his forearm open.

He stared at it and didn't make a sound. He slashed at me again with his gory-looking sword that looked like a cross between a spear and an antler.

Just then, movement distracted me from the ground behind Scarface. Sunglasses' corpse began to deflate with a hiss, green goo bubbling up from the empty sack of what used to be alive.

So that's what Skates meant when he said the dumpster won't be needed for too long. Gross.

Scarface and Yellow Teeth stared at him in horror. It took mere moments for them to process the reality of their dead friend, and they turned and ran at us, fury spurring them on.

Yellow Teeth closed on me, a short dagger in his hand. He held his injured, poisoned hand loosely at his side. Sweat beaded his forehead and his pupils were dilated.

Good, the poison was working.

I jumped and gave him a full kick in the ribs that sent him backpedaling until he hit the opposite wall of the alley. He slid to the ground in a cloud of gray dust and sat there, looking at me, a hurt expression on his face.

What did these demons think they were? Invincible?

A spike of pain went up my ribs and I glanced down to see Scarface had taken advantage of my lack of attention, plunging a dagger deep into my side.

Stupid thing to do, Kai. Real stupid.

I tugged the dagger out and flung it away. It went skittering across the ground where it stopped near a manhole cover.

Blood gushed from the mouth of the wound and I pressed at it with the heel of my hand as I circled Scarface. Scuffling sounds confirmed Saleem was having a tough time with Pink Jacket.

I tried to put the pain out of my mind and concentrate on him. Another lamia. He grinned, clearly triumphant at the damage he'd done. He licked his lips. "Ooh, I'm going to enjoy drinking all that delicious blood, little girl."

"You can certainly try." I smiled at him.

He blinked then recovered. "Oh, you can bet I will. I can smell it, so strong, so potent, and so delicious."

I ignored him and continued to circle him. Moving my fingers, I felt the wound pulse again. His eyes fell to my blood-drenched fingers and he licked his lips again. I spun the scimitar around and hit him full force in the neck. His head went spinning across the alley floor. His body fell to its knees and then tilted sideways until it collapsed in an ungainly heap.

I heard a grunt a few feet away. Saleem's battle with Pink Jacket just ended. I stared at the pile of two bodies then grimaced as Yellow Teeth turned to green goo. Poor Saleem. He was in for another surprise when he goes dumpster diving for the ghost stone.

He pushed himself up. "You could give me a hand you know." He glared at me.

"No, I couldn't." I made a face at the goo then stumbled back a few paces feeling a little lightheaded.

"You're hurt," Saleem cried as he tried to wipe off some of the sticky residue.

"Thanks for the tip." I answered with a raised eyebrow.

"Is it bad?"

"I think I've lost quite a bit of blood." A popping sound drew my gaze and I watched as Scarface's headless body began to shrivel, as did the head a few feet away. It whitened and reduced to a desiccated heap. I nudged it with my toe and it burst into a shower of ashes.

Almost at the same time, Pink Jacket melted into a pile of black ash.

Okay then.

Skates reappeared beside us moving my attention off my wound and onto the matter at hand. "Well that was four demons you guys killed. And I think they were the outside guard."

"That's all they have? Seems a bit stupid to have such a light guard." I shook my head.

"Yanuk thinks everyone likes him as their leader. He doesn't foresee any sort of uprising or coup. He's wrong, but as long as he doesn't know, it's good for those who do want to get rid of him."

"Are there any interested parties?" I asked, curious about Graylands demon politics.

"Various factions. No one in particular that I know of." He shrugged.

"It doesn't really matter. Not for what we need to do." I glanced at the now empty alley and at the flecks of green goo on Saleem's jacket. "Now we go get Lester out alive."

I stepped forward and lost my balance, almost falling to my knees, the alley and the door spinning crazily around my head. I blinked as Saleem caught me, nausea gripping my throat.

"What's wrong? You've lost way too much blood," he said, frowning and scanning my wound.

I shook my head. "No, it's not that." I paused and swallowed hard. "I feel strange."

"Maybe poison?" Skates offered.

"Poison?" Saleem almost roared the question and Skates flinched.

"Yeah, sometimes the demons poison their swords. It may be what's affecting her."

"You could have warned us," Saleem snapped.

"Leave the boy alone." I waved a hand at Saleem. "He's done a lot to help us so far."

"He could have warned us," Saleem repeated, his face dark with annoyance. "And now you're hurt. We have to go back to base."

"No. We need to get Lester first. We can't let this opportunity slip by," I insisted, glaring at Saleem. I knew he meant well, but I was fine.

"Don't be stupid, Kailin. You'll probably bleed to death before we find this demon."

Who gave him permission to boss me around?

Skates cleared his throat. "I know where he is. I peeked in while I went to check the place out."

"Fine. Let's go get this done before she dies on us." Saleem pointed a thumb in my direction and then helped me to get back on my feet. "You have bandages?" he asked me.

I nodded. Grams had packed a first aid kit just in case. Saleem dug around in my satchel and withdrew the kit. I lifted my shirt as he grabbed a swab and pressed it to the wound. I held it there while he unraveled the bandage and began to wind it around my waist.

"That will have to do for now." He sighed looking more worried than before.

"What's wrong now?" I asked, keeping my voice neutral.

"The poison. It looks like it's spreading. And it's spreading fast. Your skin is changing color and the veins look black."

"Shit. That's not the demon's poison. That's from my Wraith-sword wound." I looked at the armband but didn't want to even think about peeking at the wound. We didn't have time. "Okay, we'd better get moving. If the poison is spreading, it means I won't have too much time to hang around here."

I leaned an ear against the metal door again and shook my head. "Two people walking up and down this floor. I'm going to have to scale the wall."

"You're insane." Saleem shook his head and just gazed at me.

"I *am* a Walker, you know."

"And I *am* a djinn, you know," he imitated me and grinned.

"Oh." I scratched my head for a moment then gave him a crooked grin. "I'd forgotten."

He smiled brighter and then said, "Right, I'm going in. You wait right here. I'll open the lock from the other side."

Then he disappeared.

CHAPTER 29

I HOPED THAT WHEN SALEEM appeared on the other side of the metal door, he wouldn't be greeted by a horde of feral demons.

Apparently he hadn't been. The lock clicked softly and the iron door sighed open. Saleem held it just wide enough for me to slide through, then turned the handle quietly to shut the door.

We tiptoed up the staircase immediately to our right, keeping as close to the wall as possible. My panther senses told me we were safe to proceed around the corner. No heartbeats or breathing or movement of clothing to indicate anybody coming up the hall.

First door on the left was right there at the top of the stairs. Skates appeared so suddenly beside me I almost jumped out of my skin.

"Is it safe to go in?" I asked the ghost boy. His face was strained as if he didn't want to go in. "You don't have to go in if you don't want to." I offered him the out but he shook his head.

"No. I made this bed." I did a small double take at the odd words but returned my concentration to the door when he popped his head through the wood and pulled it back out smoothly. I had to admit it was too weird seeing Skates headless for a second. "It's clear."

My hand touched the doorknob and Saleem spoke in my ear. "What do we plan to do with him?"

"I'm happy to kill him on the spot because he's a danger to the boy, but we do need to get information from him first. Maybe we can take him back to base and get our info there. The less time we spend here, the better."

I freed my demon sword from its sheath and leaned against the doorjamb for a moment. I didn't dare touch my wound, but I felt the moist heat of it, knew the bleeding hadn't stopped. I swallowed against the nausea that crawled up my throat, turned the handle slowly, and slid into the room. Saleem and Skates followed in silence. The demon sat in the middle of the empty room safely encased within a pentagram protection spell drawn on the floor. He looked up as we entered and his eyes popped wide.

"What are you doing here?" Lester's voice was a growl with a hint of sharp.

"These two wanted to talk to you." Skates tipped his head in our direction, appearing nonchalant, as if bringing two strangers to see his trapped demon master was a normal, everyday thing to do.

"Who are you?" Lester asked us, smiling, his shark-like lamia teeth gleaming dully in the light of the single bare bulb that lit the room.

Lester thought he was too smart. Saleem and I exchanged a glance. "Don't you worry about who we are, Lester." I emphasized his name. "We're here for information. We'll be gone as soon as you tell us where to find the person we are looking for."

"Who do you want to find?" He scrambled to his knees careful not to touch the ring of salt keeping him prisoner.

"We're looking for a girl."

"Aren't we all," he said, smacking his lips, then he looked me up and down, making me want to relieve him of his bloodshot eyeballs immediately.

I grunted and curled my fingers around the sword handle. Lester watched me closely, his hand sparing a worried glance for my stiffened fingers and the weapon I held. If he was affected, he didn't show it despite being caught within the magical ward.

The magic also meant there was no getting him out of the room, let alone the warehouse. If Yanuk saw fit to bind his own flunky, then I didn't trust him to stay with me long enough for us to get back to base.

I tried something else. "You do know you're next on the list, right?"

"What list?" He grinned.

"Oh, not the list to take over Yanuk's role." The grin faded fast. "The list of demons to have their existences terminated."

He blinked and his face darkened. He wore a bright orange suit complete with multi-shaded orange tie and looked like a skinny pumpkin, his pale face at odds with the garish brightness of his clothing. "What do you mean? Who said that?"

"Oh, just a couple of demons. A lamia who liked to wear purple and another demon—I wasn't sure what he was, but he's dead now so I guess it doesn't really matter, does it?" I walked around the pentagram. He glared at me, more angry than disbelieving. He was fairly easy to convince. "Why do you think you are here within this little magical circle?" I asked, waving a finger at the salt ring.

"My master is just punishing me because I came back without information about the two of you. You are the two newest inhabitants of our dead world, are you not?" He grinned, his eyes flashing a shower of orange.

"Your master?" I stared at the lamia. "Who is your master?"

"Yanuk, of course. You aren't very bright, are you?" Lester smiled and I was getting pretty tired of his toothy grin. But I let him think he had the upper hand.

"So you're not a man of your own making."

"Who said I ever was? That little traitor there?" Lester glared at Skates who took a step back.

"You leave him alone." I stepped in front of the boy. "So since Yanuk is your master, I assume you can sense him?"

"Yeah. All his slaves know where he is all the time. That's not new news. Just like I know he was downstairs and now he isn't there any longer."

"Mmh. I'm not so sure about that. It's probably just the magic of the circle that's blocking your connection." The lamia lost his grin and stared around him. "We can help you, you know."

"Why would I need your help?" His words were defiant, but they didn't match his expression.

"Because you are caught here in this little magical salt circle and maybe, just maybe—" I toed the edge of one portion of the salt ring. "I can get you out."

He nodded eagerly, his grin widening.

"For a price," I said.

The grin disappeared. "What do you want?"

"We want information on the blonde girl. Help us find her and we'll set you free."

The lamia rubbed his hands together. "Sure. Let's go. I can take you to her."

"Nope. That's not how it's going to work, Lester." I wagged a finger at him. "You see my friend over here? He's a demon too. And he has this neat power to go wherever he wants. So you tell us where the girl is, he goes to check it out and comes back here. If it all checks out, then you get to go free. And everybody is happy."

His eyes narrowed as he glared balefully at me. He was stuck and he knew it. "Fine. I'll tell you where she is."

"Good. So talk."

He cleared his throat and rattled off an address that almost had me choking.

"What? Say that again?" I couldn't believe my ears. Of all the places in upside-down Chicago, Greer chooses to live in my apartment. Anger gripped my gut in a twisted fist. She certainly wasn't staying there out of nostalgia for home. The demon repeated my address, but I ignored him and tapped my sword against my boot. My ribs throbbed and my head hurt. We had to move.

"Fine." I looked at Saleem. "Go make sure she's there." Just as he was about to disappear, I stopped him. "Wait. Use the fire-escape. It goes right up to the window in the living room. You should be able to see her if she's walking around."

Saleem nodded then disappeared.

"What kind of demon is he?" Lester asked, sounding a little too haughty for my liking.

I almost flinched, but held it together. For a moment, I'd forgotten that the demon and even Skates were still in the room. "None of your business. Just shut up and hope he comes back and fast. I'm just waiting for a reason to gut you."

"Whoa. You sound just like her."

"Who?"

"That blonde bitch. She's controlling and manipulative. No surprise she's practically running the whole place. Plus it helps she's a little psycho too." He sneered.

"What do you mean? Who is she controlling?"

"Yanuk, of course. She's barely been here a few weeks and she's running the whole show. You want her, I ain't stopping you from finding her. You'll just be walking straight to your death."

Those words chilled me. "Is she killing anyone?"

"No, she leaves the dirty work to her slaves."

"She's got slaves?" I asked, pressing my fingers against my forehead. I was beginning to feel more than a little lightheaded.

"Sure. She tells all of us what to do."

At that moment Saleem appeared out of thin air in sparks and tiny little flames. "She is there. He was right."

"Good. Then he gets what's coming to him." I met Saleem's eyes and he nodded. It wasn't as if I needed his permission, but we were kind of a team. I turned on my heel, drawing my sword at my left hip and ended off wide to my right-hand side. The movement was smooth and Lester had risen to stand straight expecting me to mess up the salt circle and free him. His expectant grin never left his face. Not when his head began to slide off his neck, and not even when it hit the floor with a hollow thud.

"So he's served his purpose. Let's get out of here." I glanced at Skates who nodded while his eyes remained on Lester's head as it rocked back and forth until it stopped, Lester's eyes wide open and staring at nothing. My body stilled as the adrenaline surged away, fleeing my veins and making way for the pain and the weakness. My knees shook for a moment and I clenched my thighs, holding myself as stiff as possible, praying I would stay upright.

Saleem stepped toward the circle. "What are you doing?" I snapped.

"I want to see if he has a stone."

"Are you forgetting something?"

"What?

"You're a demon and that's a demon containment circle."

"Oh." Saleem stopped in his tracks. "Right."

I shook my head and turned to the boy. "You're safe now."

He nodded, a little hesitant. An odd look crossed his face and he opened his mouth to speak, then stopped and just nodded again.

"And you're free." I smiled at him. "How does it feel? Lester is no longer your master."

"Doesn't feel any different, I guess." The ghost boy shrugged and turned away.

I stared at him a moment, but we didn't have any time for me to have a heart to heart with him. Maybe later. "Will you stay with us or do you need to be somewhere?"

"I'll stay if you don't mind." He smiled but it didn't reach his eyes.

"Let's get out of here," I said to Saleem before putting an ear to the door.

One last glance at the body confirmed what I'd expected. The head began to shrivel and whiten and soon it was just a pile of ash. The rest of his body remained within the protective circle.

Whole.

Saleem grunted at the body then said, "I'll check it out for you." Before I could even nod, he disappeared. Then returned in a few moments. "All clear."

I opened the door carefully despite his assurance but the hall was clear. We hurried out and I followed him, moving gingerly down the stairwell favoring my injured side. My panther ears confirmed Yanuk was still within the warehouse along with a couple of guards.

We reached the exit and Saleem turned the handle. It barely squeaked and the metal door cracked open. A quick glance outside. All clear. We hurried out and shut the door softly behind us, then ran as fast as we could back out of the abandoned part of town.

As we neared the dumpster that would by now contain the melted, gunky remains of the two demons, I glanced at Saleem. He already had a bead on the alley and ran straight for it. We were far enough to know that Yanuk and his guards hadn't sensed us so slowing down for Saleem was safe enough.

He rushed to the dumpster, which still sat open to the gray day. Or night or whatever it was. He hoisted himself up and leaned on the edge with his stomach. "Shit."

"What?"

"They've melted and disappeared," he said disgruntled, his face dark and almost angry.

"As demons do." I raised an eyebrow.

"But there's no stone."

"Maybe their possessions melt with them?" I suggested.

Saleem dropped back to the ground and looked disgusted. "We don't have the stone."

"What's so important about the stone?" I asked, feeling the weight of the blue rock burning a hole in my pocket. Was that what he'd been focused on all along? Even in the hotel when Lester had first pulled it from his pocket?

"If we can get a hold of one, we can control the spirits."

"Why would we need to do that when they are helping us of their own free will?" I nodded at Skates, who looked worried as he stared at Saleem. Probably worried he'd find the stone and control him too. "Come. We don't need it. And I'm really tired."

"Fine. But keep an eye out. We've missed out on two so far." He sounded resigned but I didn't trust him. He was giving up way too easily.

We hurried back to Tara's shop and I went straight to the kitchen and pulled out the first aid kit and a small black bag filled with the syringes Logan had given me. I set about tending to the demon-inflicted wound in my side, first cleaning it with alcohol then covering it with gauze. I used the syringe of swirling heat and injected directly into the visible edges of the wound. Heat spread like living fire through my flesh and I wanted to scream with the pain of it. I bit down on my lip not caring that it bled.

"Damn it, K—sorry, you should have called me to help," Saleem said as he hurried into the kitchen.

"I'm fine." I spoke through gritted teeth and he just snorted. I shrugged out of my jacket and untied the buckles on my armband. Saleem gasped when he saw my wound, which had gotten as bad as it ever was. "There must be something about this place. Seems to be multiplying the power of the poison."

"That makes sense. It is a demon plane, isn't it?" I gasped with pain as I spoke.

After the worst of the pain had receded, I took a second syringe and injected into the skin around the Wraith-sword wound. Again, heat flooded into my flesh spreading agonizing pain into my flesh and bone. I gritted my teeth while perspiration dotted my forehead. I had to endure the pain. There was no other choice, so I bit down and breathed through it.

I stared at the case of syringes. I couldn't use pain as an excuse. I needed a successful dose and Logan had said two to three if the poison had spread badly. I reached for a third syringe and Saleem held onto my wrist.

"So you really think it's wise? You're in so much pain."

I nodded. "Logan said two to three, and this is technically only two for the original wound. No pain no gain, hey?" I jammed the needle into my flesh and depressed the plunger, sending more agonizingly flaming heat into my body. I slid down in the chair a little, the pain and the exhaustion taking over. I was barely aware as Saleem zipped up the bag of syringes, closed the first aid kit, and returned everything to my satchel.

Then he lifted me off the chair as if I weighed nothing and took me down the hall into Tara's room. I smiled, a little drunk on pain. I thought that Tara would like to know she'd helped me more than she'd expected.

He pulled down the covers and tucked me in, leaving my satchel and rucksack on the bed between me and the door. He understood. "Thank you."

"I should be thanking you. I haven't been much of a protector, have I?" He gave me a slightly self-deprecating grin.

"You've done enough." I swallowed, my throat beginning to tighten.

He snorted. "I get what Logan meant about you." I stiffened. What had Logan been discussing about me? "No nonsense, take it by the horns and don't mess with me. That's you in a nutshell."

I laughed softly. "I guess you could say that."

CHAPTER 30

I DOZED RESTLESSLY AND DIDN'T allow myself to lie there for too long. Eventually, I sat up and checked the wounds, all of which seemed to have recovered well enough to not be excruciatingly painful to touch. I got to my feet, put my jacket on to ward against the chill in the air and strapped on my swords just in case. Thinking of Tara, I bent to make the bed then realized I didn't really need to bother. It wasn't as if Tara was going to be walking in here anytime soon.

Heading for the kitchen, I rummaged inside the cupboard for some tuna and crackers and prepared a small meal. I was sitting at the kitchen table washing the tuna down with water when Saleem walked in.

"You're awake already?" Saleem frowned.

"I didn't want to waste any more time sleeping. Besides, I feel much better now. Those syringes pack a bit of a punch." Saleem just glared at me. "Hey. I promise, I'm fine. I won't slow you down."

He snorted and shook his head, then proceeded to prepare his own meal. He'd polished off most of it and was swallowing the last of the crackers when the door in the storefront crashed open and footsteps thundered through the room toward the kitchen.

I ran to the room, my first thought for the weapons. Dashing in, I kicked the bag and satchel under the bed and pulled the covers to hang it over the side, hiding them. I turned around to see three lamia and another strange-looking, horned demon enter the room, their faces flushed and angry.

I didn't fight them off. Wasn't a point. I was surrounded.

I just hoped they wouldn't think to take my weapons away.

They grabbed my arms and hauled me into the kitchen where a dark, stone-faced demon stood with a blade to Saleem's throat.

"Who are you? What do you want?" I yelled as I glared at Saleem, knowing he could blink out of there in an instant but he just stared back serenely.

What was he up to?

"Shut up. You don't get to know anything." One of the lamias sneered. He seemed to be the one in charge.

I stared around the tiny demon-filled kitchen and had to wonder how they had found us. How had they known where we were hiding out?

"You can't just barge in here and grab us like this."

"Of course we can. And if you have a problem with it, then take it up with the boss." The lamia grinned and his putrid teeth shone.

I shuddered, still glaring at Saleem. When I looked around for Skates, he was nowhere to be seen and I felt a knot of suspicion grow within my gut.

Skates was gone and that made perfect sense. He was the only one who knew where we were. Had he found a way to tell someone our location while I was asleep? Whose control was he under now that Lester was dead? Wouldn't that be Yanuk? Had he gotten to Skates? Or had someone gotten to him before we even arrived, so he could have been setting us up all along.

"What did you do with the boy?" I asked through gritted teeth.

"What boy? I don't see any boy." The lamia just shook his head. I couldn't deny I was disappointed in Skates. I'd trusted the ghost, but bigger things were going on right now. More specifically, how we were supposed to get away from these sulfur-exuding creeps.

"Tie her up and let's get going." The lamia shot the instruction off and the horned demon nearest the door growled and spun on his heel. He left the kitchen and the others rushed to follow his instructions. I counted while another lamia tied a rope around my wrists so tight it would have cut off the blood supply had I not fisted my hands and created a little space between the rope and my skin.

"Where are you taking us?" I asked, hoping to distract him and succeeding as he glanced up from his bad knot job.

"Shut up. You'll know when we get there," he answered, nostrils flaring.

I glanced around me, doing a quick headcount: three lamia, one horned demon, and the one holding the knife to Saleem that looked so much like a stone gargoyle I had to force myself not to stare. Only five. I could take them.

As we left the kitchen and entered the tiny hallway, I realized how fruitless escape was. The front room contained three more unidentifiable demons with weapons trained on me. Weapons I recognized from this very shop. Tara would be more than pissed.

I glanced at the weapons. I wasn't stupid enough to assume the ammo they contained wouldn't hurt me.

I couldn't fight bullets.

We passed through the store and I gritted my teeth as I scanned what remained of the front door. They'd smashed it to smithereens. The demons hustled me outside and the other group followed closely with Saleem. They hurried along the deserted roads and herded us back to the abandoned part of town.

I walked stiffly, tugging my arm away from the hard fingers

digging into my flesh. I glared at the demon, who just glared back. They were all so confident and cocky. What did they know that we didn't? What made them so sure of themselves?

We stopped abruptly, right outside the warehouse where we'd killed a bunch of their friends, and where I'd killed Lester too.

They were taking us to see Yanuk.

They shoved me over the threshold of the back door and I heard scuffling behind me as they did the same to Saleem. We passed the stairwell and entered the first floor to find only one corner furnished to an acceptable degree. And occupied.

A desk and a high-backed leather office chair sat to our left, back to the wall along a row of blacked-out windows. There was even a carpet in a lovely shade of gray. The demons pushed me to the front of the desk. One of them, the lamia whose throat I planned to slit, gave me a hard shove in the middle of my back that sent me stumbling forward with only the desk to stop me from falling flat on my face.

"Tie her to the radiator," came a familiar gravelly voice.

"You must be Yanuk." I said, enjoying the look on his hideous bull-like face. Something flapped behind him as if his annoyance fed through to some part of his body. The lamia grabbed my hands and pulled so I had to walk backward until I reached the wall. He tied my ropes tightly to the radiator pipe and took a sharp step back as if the thought of being near me revolted him.

The feeling is so mutual, dude.

I sat on the radiator and faced the demon king of the Graylands. Yanuk. He'd turned to face his desk and I saw what had flapped at his back. A pair of gigantic bat wings. Dark and crinkly looking, and very vampiric.

Lifting my chin, I waited for him to turn to face me, wondering again why none of them had bothered to take my weapons. Were they not afraid I would escape the ties and relieve them of their heads? Or were they way too confident for their own good?

Underestimating me was not a good thing.

I glanced around at Saleem, who stood calmly held tight between the gargoyle and another lamia. He met my eyes and wiggled an eyebrow. I knew before he disappeared in a flash of orange sparks and tiny flames that he was ready to go. He'd cased the place out, seen the weapons, counted the demons.

He'd better be back soon though or it might be his head I relieve from his body.

CHAPTER 31

AS SOON AS SALEEM DISAPPEARED, the room went silent. The demons looked from one to the other avoiding the gaze of their master.

Yanuk cleared his throat. "Did anyone of you imbeciles think to ensure he wasn't also a demon?"

"Boss, we had no idea he was a demon too. What the heck is he?"

"He's a djinn, you idiot." Yanuk bit the words out like bullets and the demon flinched as if he'd felt the impact of each one.

"I'm sorry, boss. I haven't seen a djinn before." He turned to the gargoyle. "Have you?"

The gargoyle shook his head and stared at Yanuk.

"Very well, he is gone. He'd be stupid to return to save her. And the odds are stacked against him." Then he turned to me, his amber eyes swilling in his bullish face. Here too, among these demons, color was rampant but Yanuk was all red. Skin and clothing and even what should have been the whites of his eyes.

He walked to me, glanced back at the demons gathered behind him, and backhanded his fist into my cheek. I was sure I heard my neck crack as my head snapped back so hard I saw stars and smelled blood.

The demons snickered amongst them as I brought my head slowly back down, hoping he hadn't broken my neck. Pain flamed at the base of my skull, but everything seemed to be intact.

"Now, tell me, girl, what is it you are doing here in the Graylands? Alive of all things," he asked almost kindly, his voice softening a little. As if that made a difference to me.

"None of your business." I didn't plan on making things easy for him. Besides, I wanted to play for time until Saleem got back.

He slammed his beefy fist into my other cheek and my jaw spasmed. My eye throbbed and my vision blurred. He'd burst a blood vessel in my eye, the bastard. "What do you want? This is my land, and as far as I can see, you are trespassing. What with you being alive and all."

"I heard this wasn't really your land anymore."

He slammed his fist into my gut and I doubled over. I felt the stab wound in my side split open and gush, wet and sticky. I hacked for breath and tasted blood again. More this time. My head spun with the pain and I tried to right myself. If I fell over, I'd probably break both my arms.

"Now, who would be telling you such tall tales, my dear?" he asked, smiling ever so sweetly, revealing spiky little white teeth.

"Your little lackey, Lester." I spat blood as I spoke.

"Ah yes, Lester. I take it you were the one who dispatched him for me?"

"He deserved it." Another punch to my gut. It felt like he hit me with fists of iron. The blood began to seep further into my clothing, and when he took his fist away, he smiled to see his red knuckles moist.

He stared at me, then began to slowly lick each knuckle clean. I shuddered. "Lester was mine to kill, girl. And you spoiled my fun."

"Sorry. Had I known . . ." I trailed off thinking maybe I would be better off shutting up.

Yanuk came closer, grabbed my chin, and lifted it until I stared right into his ruby red eyes. "You will talk or I will have to make this very, very painful for you." I was tempted to transform my jaws and teeth and clamp my canines around Yanuk's filthy throat, but I swallowed and controlled the urge.

What I did allow myself was to release my panther claws. Hidden behind my back my deadly sharp nails sprouted and I began scraping away at the ropes thread by thread. It was slow work as the ropes were oily and a little slippery, but I kept at it while I maintained eye-contact with the bull-demon.

I swallowed, my throat growing taut as he kept my neck bent. "I'm looking for someone." I got the words out and punctuated the sentence with a cough. It happened to be a cough right in Yanuk's face, but I wasn't that concerned with manners or propriety. Seemed he wasn't either. He let go of me and just wiped the spatter of blood off his face. Then he smiled. "Now, was that so hard. So tell me who are you looking for?" He paused then took a short sharp breath. "You know you remind me so much of another living girl I met recently in the Graylands."

For Ailuros' sake, not another person finding a resemblance between Greer and me. "Really?" I coughed again to hide the dryness in my tone. He looked at me sharply, his fists tightening. Then he must have decided I hadn't meant it as he moved away, settled himself on the edge of his desk and folded his arms over his generously bulked-up chest.

"So are you going to tell me who she is or do I have to beat it out of you?"

I stared at him, my head spinning. I was feeling far too faint to be messing about with a bull-demon as powerful as Yanuk. A dull throbbing in my arm teased me with the knowledge that the poison was taking its toll again. Where the hell was Saleem already? "Just a girl I know."

"Ah. A mighty fine coincidence. A living female arriving here in the Graylands not too long after another living female arrives. So you have come to save her, haven't you?"

I shook my head. "I just needed to know where she was. I have no idea who she is. I'm just doing my job."

"So tell me . . ." Yanuk came to stand beside me. He bent to my cheek and drew in a deep breath, sniffing my skin all the way from chin to temple. The susurration of air was long and ominous. "Walker, tell me really who you are?"

He knew what I was. My heart thudded against my ribs. "I'm a tracker. They sent me to find her."

"They sent a Walker to find another Walker?" He nodded to himself. "I suppose that makes sense. But I'm not so sure I believe that you don't know my little friend Greer. Now that I think about it, you bear a little resemblance to her."

I flinched. I'd never thought I looked like Greer at all. And nobody had ever remarked on such a thing. I'd been happy without any resemblance to her. Ever.

"Probably a Walker thing. I know from her file and the scent patterns they gave me that she's a panther like me." I offered that piece of information hoping it would waylay his suspicions. Or at least give him something to think about.

Yanuk shrugged. "Whatever the case may be, it makes little difference to me and my needs. As for Greer, her days on this plane are numbered. She may have entered the Graylands alive, but she will be leaving it very dead. She has taken more than she is entitled to. She has swooped in on our territory and has taken advantage of our hospitality and soon she will understand that we will not accept it any longer." Yanuk spoke as if he was reciting a speech. I wasn't convinced that he believed all of his own words. Something was off. But he did seem to have a plan. But whatever Yanuk was planning, he was also going to get what was coming to him. "Anyway, who you are is of little consequence to me. You are trespassing and you will, of course, pay the price. We, here in the Graylands, have upheld the laws of the High Council for centuries. No living person passes through the Veil."

"But the High Council is who sent me." That got me a startled look.

If a red-skinned demon's face could pale his would have. He couldn't know for sure. I could see it in his eyes. The doubt, the fear of the possibility I was telling the truth. He decided to hedge his bets and nodded with a small grin. "Ah, then see, we are on the same side. Perhaps we can come to a mutual understanding?"

"One which does not include you using me as a punching bag?" My ropes were almost free but I left the last hard tug for a better moment.

"You must understand I do what I have to do to maintain the status quo. It would have been much easier had you told us why you were here in the first place." He smiled but there was a hesitation in his voice, a tinge of fear, of worry.

"The High Council does not hire fools." I bit back, thinking I needed to be a bit more firm. And it worked. He turned his gaze away, chastised.

"Fine. If you came for Greer, I could help you get her out. We both have the same goal in mind. Of course, my aim was to make her stay here a legitimate one, but if the High Council wants her alive, then who am I to challenge that?" He stood up and looked at me. "They do want her alive, don't they?"

I nodded. Yanuk must not be very bright to be so ready to offer me his help and a truce at that. For all I knew, it was a grand setup with the goal being to get me killed. But I smiled and inclined my head. Let him think I agreed to his deal.

Yanuk clapped his hands together and stepped to me.

A flash of orange fire disturbed the air to my right and Saleem arrived bearing gifts. I tugged hard at my ropes and my hands came free.

I didn't miss the look of shock in Yanuk's eyes as he noticed my lack of bindings. Saleem tossed me my bow and pistol and the throng of shocked demons came to life.

Yanuk backtracked a little, giving his men first dibs to die. I shot the first demon who came at me—the lamia. Too bad. I'd wanted to behead him.

The gargoyle approached Saleem, who had his back turned, fighting off a horned demon who'd captured him by the throat with his meaty paws.

The gargoyle raised a hideous-looking, jagged-edged creation. I shot him between the eyes and the sword went clattering to the ground. The lamia lay crumbling to dust on his boss's carpet.

A shout of anger beside me and a flash of light in my peripheral vision confirmed that Saleem had done a disappearing act. I turned to the horned fiend and shot him in the head too. The gun was proving worth its while.

Saleem appeared on the other side of two demons I couldn't identify and he stabbed both in the back at the same time. They fell against each other, slamming their heads together as they dropped.

The two remaining lamia approached me, both twirling evil-looking swords of their own. The gun didn't seem to be bothering them too much considering how fast it was dispatching their friends. I aimed at the nearest demon and the gun clicked—out of ammo. Sinking to the ground, I grabbed my scimitar in one hand and the demon sword in the other, then made a quick sweep at knee height.

One demon stepped back in time, the other suffered two severed legs. The scimitar could still slice through bone like butter.

Thank you, Tara.

Saleem had his hands full with one last demon, so I concentrated on the one heading straight at me. He growled as he glanced around at his fallen comrades, as he probably realized he should have run while he had the chance. Like his coward boss.

Too late.

I slashed the demon blade in a tight curve as the lamia ran at me. His head came tumbling off and rolled under the desk while his body kept running toward the window behind me. I stepped aside and he crashed into the glass, shattering the lowest panes.

All around us demons were disintegrating and disappearing in lumps of green goo or piles of dust.

"What the heck was that?" I asked, toeing the horned demon.

"He's an oni demon." I glared at the horns and the hairy blue face of the human-looking creature as it disintegrated. Saleem continued, "And that was a gargoyle."

"Yeah, I had the feeling I knew that one." I thought of Yanuk. "And their boss with the horns. He's not oni."

"Nope, He is a shedu, a winged bull-demon."

I shuddered. "Yes, I saw those wings. Can he fly with them?"

"No reason why he can't." Saleem shrugged. Then held me by the arm as I began to slip. I'd ignored the lightheadedness and the bleeding for too long. "You're hurt."

"Well, it took you long enough to get back here." I touched my side and my fingers came away soaked red. "I took a few blows to the gut. Probably a few blows too many considering . . ." I slipped again.

"Easy, I got you. Just try to stay awake."

"Pity you can't transport me back to Tara's place," I complained.

"Who said we had to have it easy?" Saleem snorted and supported me as we both shuffled slowly out of the warehouse and down the street.

The journey back was long and tiring. As we walked, we watched out for lurking demons but we weren't followed or attacked.

I wasn't sure I was relieved by that.

CHAPTER 32

W HEN WE ENTERED TARA'S HOUSE, I knew immediately the place was occupied. I sensed it in my gut the way I'd first sensed that Skates had been around.

"Wait." I held the back of my hand to Saleem's chest, preventing him from walking farther into the store. "There's someone here."

"It's empty. You're just paranoid. Or hallucinating from loss of blood." Saleem brushed it off and walked farther into the store only to stop in his tracks and suck in a breath.

I stepped around him to see a line of ghosts hovering within the inner portion of the store, out of sight of the main windows. I scanned the group for Skates. He wasn't there.

"What do you people want?" Saleem held out his gun and waved it at them. None of them moved. I guess none of them knew that both Saleem and I carried ghost-killing ammo as well.

"What do you all want?" I asked a little less threateningly than Saleem.

A movement at the entrance to the inner apartment drew my eye and a man walked toward me. A ghost, but someone with a fair amount of strength. He wore a hooded leather jacket and his face remained in shadows, yet there was something so familiar about him that I took a step toward him.

I felt Saleem's palm on my chest and looked down at it. *Not the best time for groping me, Saleem.* I took his hand off my breast and threw it off me.

"Sorry," he said, his voice sheepish.

"I'll survive," I answered but my gaze remained on the hooded man. I stepped closer. "Who are you?"

Saleem stiffened behind me as the man dropped the hood. I could see his features clearly now, sharp ridges, strong jawline, high forehead and piercing blue eyes. So familiar.

"Do I know you?" I asked softly, a shiver running up my spine.

"Yes. We met once. Only for a brief moment, but you saved me."

"I didn't do much good if you ended up here, did I?" I looked around at the sad bunch of ghosts and then stared back at the man.

He stood out from the rest. He was more than just familiar to me. "You're a Walker?"

He nodded. "A Walker who owes you a debt. You gave me peace." And then it clicked into place. He was the skinned Walker I'd found in the community garden. The Cougar Walker Jeremy Ryan. My heart stilled.

"I found you on the side of the road." He nodded. "But you died. I didn't save you."

"But you did give me peace. You found my killers."

"If I gave you peace, then why are you still here?"

"I experienced a terrible trauma. It's still here . . ." He pointed at his heart and then his head. "And here. I can't forget as easily as that. Nerina helped me. She guided me to the light, but I couldn't go. The experience was too fresh, hurt too much. Maybe in time." He gave me a reassuring smile. "In the meantime, I can do something to help you."

"Thank you. We'd love your help. Only, how can we trust

you?" Jeremy looked hurt. "Sorry, but we were betrayed not too long ago by another ghost. One that Nerina sent us to."

"The boy is weak. He is needy, looking for affection. His death is perpetually his curse."

"What do you mean?" I frowned.

"He took his own life." I blinked. That was certainly news to me. I had to focus to pay attention to Jeremy's next words. "Here in the Graylands, it is hard to leave a traumatic death, especially one that is self-inflicted. We sometimes slip into a state where we experience our deaths over and over again. Coming to terms with facing such a death repeatedly is not an easy thing to do. Try not to be too angry with him."

"I'm not…" And I realized I really wasn't. What was wrong with me? I should be furious with the ghost boy.

"I am. I'd love to ring his sorry neck," said Saleem.

"Not if you can't hold onto him you can't." That got our ghost audience sniggering. Saleem looked pained as if he was recalling his pledge to find the stone. The stone I still had tucked away in my jacket pocket.

"How did you know he betrayed us? How did you know we needed your help?" I asked Jeremy.

"We are everywhere," was all he said.

"We didn't see any of you," I said and then I smiled as the line of ghosts faded away then returned to full power along with dozens more who filled the room leaving almost no space to move.

I blinked, shocked at the number of dead people I was looking at. There was definitely way more to the land of the freshly departed than I ever thought possible. I tried to get my head around the sheer number of dead that populated this plane, but my head just hurt reminding me of how little time I had left. "I see. Okay, so do you know why he betrayed us? Who was the boy working for?"

"He was working for Greer." That would explain a lot, but

what if Jeremy was also working for Greer? I shut the thought out and focused on Skates. "So the boy was acting under Greer's instruction? How? Why?"

"How? We aren't sure. We think it has something to do with the fact that Greer is alive. Maybe that gives her a similar power over the ghosts that the demons have, given that the demons are also alive here in the Graylands."

I nodded. That was possible. Or it could also have something to do with my suspicion of her possible possession by Widd'en. If so, then she could have some demon taint to her that could be working in her favor in terms of controlling the ghosts. But at this point it was all guesswork.

Jeremy continued. "Why? We don't know, but there is a way for us to find out more."

"Well, don't hold out on me."

"We can find the boy and question him directly."

I nodded, liking the idea and hoping at the same time that it wasn't another ruse to ambush us. "Do you have a way of tracking him?"

Jeremy nodded. "Just need to send the word out that we're looking for him and wait. It shouldn't take too long to get the message back. You can't really hide here. Even if you go invisible other ghosts can see your spectral signature."

"So someone, somewhere knows where he is right now?"

Jeremy and a few ghosts behind him nodded.

"Well, then what are we waiting for?"

"For you to take care of yourself before you become one of us." The ghosts sniggered again. Even Saleem chuckled.

Everyone's a comedian.

"Fine." I felt the throb in my flesh and bones and couldn't argue with him.

"And what about Yanuk?" I asked Jeremy. The demon over-lord had disappeared and I wondered when he'd decide to pop out from the blue and surprise me with another punch to the gut.

"Don't worry about him." Jeremy seemed to understand my concern immediately. "A few of the ghosts here are also bound to Yanuk and can track him. We'll keep an eye on him and let you know if he shows any sign of coming anywhere near you."

"Thanks," I said, more than just grateful.

He nodded. "I'll leave you for a while to treat your wounds and eat. We'll be back soon to take you to the boy." With that he left, and one by one the ghosts disappeared like little lights flickering out.

As soon as he left, I headed for the kitchen while Saleem secured the inner door between the storefront and the apartment. I tended to my wounds, re-bandaging them and cleaning myself up as best as I could.

Saleem hovered but it seemed like he knew not to offer his help. Instead, he prepared some tuna and crackers and I ate in silence. I checked my black eye and its busted blood vessel. I looked like a boxer fresh from a match. The loser.

My thoughts stayed with Nerina's possible role in this whole thing. She'd sent us to Skates. Had she known he would betray us to Greer? Was she also on Greer's side? Had that been what she had communicated with my sister when she had attempted her calling?

Skates had seemed so honest, so real. It was hard to accept he'd betrayed us but he had. And yet I forgave him. Because it wasn't his fault. Being controlled by someone else places the blame with the someone else doing the controlling.

Greer.

What was she up to? Why had she sent the boy instead of just meeting us? Was she enjoying playing her games or was she also part of a larger manipulation?

I sat on the bed and stuck a syringe in the wounds, repeating the procedure I'd performed not so long ago. How long ago anyway? I'd begun to lose track of time and that was not a good sign.

A few minutes of raging white fire passed and I lay down for a while. Not that I could sleep. My mind buzzed with questions and possibilities. After a while, when the burning receded and my energies seemed replenished, I rose and replaced my armband, shrugged on my jacket and headed to the kitchen.

I sat beside Saleem, facing the door. I wanted to see whoever entered the kitchen next. After the demon attack, I refused to let my guard down. Lines of fatigue traced Saleem's eyes.

"How long will they be?" I asked Saleem. "Did you get some rest?"

"They should be here any minute now. And no, I'm fine. I'll rest when we are done with this mission."

I knew how he felt. I didn't want to close my eyes in case something happened while I was asleep and I missed my chance to save Greer. At least we now had a way to track Yanuk and we knew where Greer was holed up.

Jeremy entered the kitchen soundlessly, hood up, face still wreathed in shadows. "We can go if you are well enough."

I stood and grabbed my bag and satchel from the table. Saleem fiddled with his bag and came up behind me. "Let's get going."

The cougar nodded and headed out of the building, leading us into the opposite direction to the abandoned sector. Very soon, I began to recognize the area. Jeremy led us to my old school Crawdon High. The path to the front entrance lay bare, unlittered, unoccupied.

I followed him inside the darkened building. He walked with a confidence that said he knew the building or at least knew where he was going. Up one floor, down the hall and right into Mrs. Gallium's English class. Skates sat in the far corner, staring out of the window. He didn't react as we entered though he surely heard our footsteps. He kept his gaze focused on the gray skies.

I walked to his desk and pulled a chair in front of him. I spun it around and sat, waiting quietly for him.

He took his time, though I didn't feel he was being manipulative. He just looked hesitant and guilty. He sighed deeply and glanced up but didn't meet my eyes, his shoulders hunched over. Then he said, "I'm sorry. Hope you know that."

"I think I do." I leaned toward him. "Tell me why."

He looked frantic for a moment, as if he were about to flee. In one smooth move, and before he could blink, I pulled the blue stone out of my pocket. It was small enough that it fit within my cupped palm so he didn't see it until it was too late. I leaned over to him and touched the stone to his bare forearm. He'd shoved his sweater up his arms so it bunched at the elbows, baring a pair of skinny hands that were slowly taking on color and solidity. I gripped his wrist and stared at him.

"I'm not going to do anything to you. I want to talk and I think we both know you'll run as soon as you get the chance."

He stared at the stone for a moment, green eyes gradually gaining color in an olive-complexioned face. "Fair enough." He rocked in his seat, clearly uncomfortable but he didn't fight me, didn't tug at my hand to gain his freedom. "What do you want to know?"

"Everything," was all I said. I kept my gaze on Skates, keenly aware of Saleem beside me. Saleem who now would know I'd had the ghost stone all along.

"I think you must know by now that I have been lying from the beginning. Well, maybe not lying, but I didn't tell you the whole truth." He wrung his hands and that was where I should have been angry but I just couldn't. There was too much shit going on to be pointing fingers. I waited to hear more. "I've been working for Greer all along."

"You call her Greer?" I asked, frowning.

"Yes, it seems knowing her name has no power over her because she is still alive. Yanuk thought otherwise and ended up paying for that with his blood." Skates grinned at the memory of what happened to Yanuk. I wasn't in the least interested at the moment.

"So, she's your master? She has control over you?"

"It's not so simple." He frowned as he tried to find the words. "We have our own master and our master has his own master and we are linked to our master's master that way. And normally, masters don't control their slave's slaves, but Greer saw the opportunity to have more ghosts and demons working for her than Yanuk did so she . . . she lobbied. Like she was going out for class president or something. I think that's the best way to describe it. She talked to a few ghosts and then managed to get a few demons on her side. She never promised freedom but she was nice—unlike the demon masters. She's like a demon master but not. It's kind of hard to explain."

"So how did she end up putting you onto us?" I still wasn't keen on using our names even though the boy had explained it held no power.

"A few days ago, I can't recall how long—all the days are a few days ago to me." I nodded at the apology but he still hadn't really looked at my face. "She got a weird feeling, felt like someone was talking in her head. And then it happened again and she said it was like she could hear a woman speaking to her, asking her if she was okay, telling her she will soon be safe and not to be afraid."

"Nerina." I said.

He nodded. "When Nerina spoke to her, Greer got a little crazy. She was so angry. Said her family must be looking for her, and she knew her Goody Two-Shoes, perfect little Alpha sister would come, and that we needed to start being more alert to the newcomers. She set more ghosts to keep an eye out and watch for new arrivals and just anything odd in general. She suspected that her sister would arrive in the Graylands looking for her, and then you and your friend came. Greer wasn't sure who you two were.

At first she thought you were her sister, but then Yanuk just told her you worked for the Supreme High Council, and she got a bit worried." He paused. "Sometimes it's hard to tell what she's thinking. She has these moments when she goes totally insane and says things that don't make any sense at all."

"Did she hurt you?" I gritted my teeth, swearing Greer would pay if she ever laid a hand on the boy.

He shook his head, but I saw the lie in the quick blink of his eye. I shook his arm.

"Okay, once. She slapped me once. That's all."

"Are you defending her?" I snapped.

"She isn't right in the head. How do you expect me to blame her for everything she's doing?"

My eyes narrowed but I had no argument to that. I'd just made the same excuse for Skates. "What did she want you to do when you saw us?"

"She wanted me to lead you to Yanuk. She thought she could get rid of you easily that way. That Yanuk would kill you for trespassing and her job would be done. I guess she didn't count on you being as smart and strong as you are." He grinned.

"What have you told her? From what I know, master and slave can sense each other but you can't communicate unless you are face to face right?" He nodded. "So have you seen her? And what have you told her about us?"

"How did you call them to the house?" Saleem cut in, his voice cold and hard. Not as forgiving as I was.

"When I went to case the warehouse out, I flitted next door and gave a message to the old woman ghost there. She took the message to Greer, who would have given it to Yanuk."

"You are a fool." Saleem surged forward, putting his face next to the boy's, gripping his chin and lifting his face upward. "Do you have any idea what they did to her? Look at her. They beat her black and blue and made her wounds bleed all over again."

Skates scanned Saleem's face and though his face tightened,

defensive and angry and guilty, he didn't retaliate. Then he looked at my face, probably realizing only then the extent of my beating. My left jaw was swollen and the right side of my face including my eye had doubled in size. Somewhere in the tight, pulpy skin was my bloodshot eye. Then his lower lip quivered.

"I'm so sorry. I didn't realize she would send Yanuk after you. I thought she wanted them to bring you to her. She wouldn't have done that to you."

"No she wouldn't have because if she so much as looked at me, I—" I stopped myself. For someone who wasn't supposed to know Greer, I was getting a bit too emotional. I breathed and calmed myself. My panther nudged for release, but I ignored her. Not now.

"As long as she didn't hurt you," I ended the semi-rant lamely.

"What's her next plan?" Saleem asked.

"She wants to get to talk to you. She's dying to know who you are."

"Have you seen her then?"

He nodded. "Yes, after the demons took you back to Yanuk, I went straight to her thinking she'd have you. But you weren't there and she was happy to have sent you and your friend to your deaths at Yanuk hands. But it wasn't much later that Yanuk arrived to say you'd killed all the demons and that you had escaped."

"Bet she loved that." I laughed softly, strangely happy to have thwarted Greer's plans in some way.

"Yeah, she was screeching mad." Skates made circles at his temple with his forefinger and crossed his eyes at the same time.

I found it strange to think of Greer behaving badly. She'd always been so serene and elegant, so composed. But then I remember her blazing eyes before she jumped through the Wraith's portal. I remembered the hate in her eyes when she looked at Mom.

Maybe Greer wasn't exactly who I thought she was anymore.

CHAPTER 33

$\mathcal{I}$ LOOKED AT SKATES AND he met my eyes head on. "Thank you. For telling me the truth." I leaned forward and patted his arm, moving the stone away from the solid ghost boy and slipping it into my pocket. His body grew shimmery, then a little transparent and gradually became ghostly again. I felt a little rush of sadness as he became colorless and see-through once more.

I gave him the chance to leave but he didn't disappear. Then he nodded sharply. "I'll take you. It's the least I can do." He looked at me and said, "I'm really sorry. I didn't mean for any of this to happen."

Jeremy materialized behind Skates. I hadn't realized he'd been in the room all along. It didn't matter anyway.

"We already have the address. You know that. And we know the way. You don't have to come," I said. It was the truth. There was no real reason for him to come with us except for him to put himself in harm's way in case things got messy.

Skates stood and said, "I know. I still want to come. Can we just go?"

I nodded and got to my feet, avoiding Saleem's eyes. I didn't want to get into anything with him right now. We followed Skates out of the building. The route home was familiar enough.

I entered the building, a tiny bit disoriented having to go left instead of right to the stairs. We ascended the stairs slowly, and as we neared my landing, I withdrew my bow, slipping in a demon vial. I edged toward the wall and peered through the wooden banister at the guard outside my door. I gave myself a mental shake—should I really be thinking about the apartment as mine?

I crouched down as I neared the last step, aimed, and released the trigger. The demon grunted as the vial impacted his flesh, and within seconds, he was a pile of ash and ember, which slowly disappeared into nothing.

So Tara's poison sped up the disintegration process. I liked that.

We hurried to the door, and though I placed an ear to the wood, no sound filtered through. I turned the handle expecting to find it locked, but it shifted. Greer must be pretty confident that her guard would do a solid job of defending the entrance to the apartment. Pity she'd have to be disappointed.

Skates hovered beside me as if he intended to come in, but I waved him off, glaring at him. He moved away but didn't look too disappointed.

I opened the door, letting it swing wide with a little push. Greer sat at my dining room table, on the left of the doorway instead of the right, of course. She didn't look up until Saleem and I moved into the room.

When she did, all color drained from her face. "What are you doing here?" she whispered, her face twisted with what looked like shock, followed closely by worry.

"I came to get you." I didn't trust myself to say much more. I watched her face as she got to her feet and walked slowly to me.

When she threw her arms around my neck and sobbed, I flinched. I stilled the urge to grab her arms from me and throw them away. What was she playing at?

"You have no idea what a stupid thing you've done. You're in danger here." Then she frowned, staring at me long and hard. Too long.

"Were you the ones who arrived here a few days ago?" Her tone had cooled so fast I began to suspect she lacked a solid hold on her sanity. Her mood changes seemed a bit too fast to be healthy.

I nodded and glanced at Saleem. "I did have company when I arrived."

"Dear Ailuros," Greer whispered. "I sent them to watch and to deliver the intruders to Yanuk. I had no idea it was you. I'm so sorry, Kai." She was close enough to get the full brunt of my black eye and pummeled face and grimaced as she examined the damage.

When her eyes filled with tears at the sight of my injuries, I moved away, suddenly uncomfortable being so close to my sister. Must be the blazing spark of distrust in me.

"You know, Yanuk wouldn't have done that to you if you hadn't come." My skin rippled with ice as she spoke, her words freezing me over as much as her tone. Of course it was my fault. I snapped my gaze back at her so fast my jaw tingled with pain, but I ignored it. Greer glared at me, her eyes cold, her expression colder. There she went with her mood change again. One second caring and worried, the next icy cold and vicious. What was going on with her?

"What the hell do you mean, Greer? I came to take you home," I bit out, anger flaring within my veins. Ungrateful bitch.

She snorted. "I knew that. I knew someone was coming, but I didn't think it would be you. Perfect little Kailin, always wants to run out and save the world."

"You don't know what you're talking about. I promised Mom I'd find you and bring you home."

"Mom?" Greer laughed coldly. "What does she care? She betrayed us. Why would I give a damn about her?"

"Because if you'd stuck around long enough, you would have heard her side of the story. She actually had a very good reason for leaving."

"I don't particularly care to know why she left." Greer raised her hand before I could speak. And rightly so. How would she handle knowing Mom left because of me?

But it didn't stop me from being angry with her. As she turned to walk away, I snapped at her, "And by the way, that was a pretty dumb thing to do, jumping through the portal. You are bloody lucky to be alive."

"Don't you tell me what you think is dumb or not. You have no right. Do you even know who I am? You think you can just waltz right in here and tell me what to do?" Greer vibrated with fury as she spoke. Flecks of spit flew from her lips and I stepped away.

"Greer, you need to calm down." I spoke knowing my face showed exactly how I felt, disapproving, shocked.

She glared at me, her face pinched, skin tight, as if she were about to claw out my eyes, but something happened in her eyes. She blinked then refocused on my face. When she spoke her voice was shaky, rattled. "I'm sorry, Kai. I . . . I think . . ."

"I think you've spent way too long in this place. It's time to go home."

She nodded and looked around the apartment. "I can't leave, Kai."

"What do you mean? Of course you can leave—you just come with me."

"No, that's not what I meant. I can't go with you." She seemed uncertain and a little sad but with her emotional extremes she'd just displayed, I didn't trust her. The truth was I had stopped trusting her when I found out she was keeping company with Brand and Uncle Niko, happily going along with Niko's plan to experiment on Walkers. But I refused to go home without her.

"I didn't come all this way to leave without you." I stepped toward her.

Greer flung her hands out, swiping me away, fiery anger burning and dying in the blink of an eye. "Fine. I'll come."

Behind me, Saleem released a long breath. Guess he'd felt the tension between us too. My eyes narrowed as I watched Greer's face. Would she go and change her mind again? I beckoned Saleem. The sooner we got moving, the better. Greer would have less time to decide to change her mind.

"Let's go then," I said, heading for the door.

There wasn't anything she needed to bring with her. She'd arrived with nothing. She followed us out, not even bothering to ask about the missing demon.

As we descended the stairs, the birdcage shuddered and began to move up. I watched the metal elevator as it rose, completely unsurprised to see Yanuk grinning at me.

Greer saw him too and hesitated, but I gripped her arm and moved her along, again surprised at her compliance. The elevator stopped at my floor and Yanuk turned to us. He grinned, wide mouth, dagger-like teeth gleaming. Then he flicked a finger off his forehead, saluting me with a strange expression on his face. His expression changed when his gaze settled on Greer. And though he knew she was leaving, he did nothing.

True to his word, Yanuk seemed happy to be rid of Greer. And though I wanted to just run up the stairs and plant my fist into his face and break his jaw, getting out of the Graylands was now my priority.

I clenched my fists and kept moving down the stairs, watching Greer as she looked up at Yanuk through the metal rails of the birdcage. She had a strange expression on her face, slightly triumphant.

Once outside the apartment, we paused as if expecting to see a horde of demons waiting for us, but the sidewalk remained empty and silent.

"Where to from here?" asked Saleem.

"Dark water," I said.

"Right." He nodded. "This is your territory. You know somewhere closer than Lockwood Park?"

I nodded. "The docks." It was closest.

Greer snorted and folded her arms. "You do realize we'll have to walk all the way there? No cars in the Graylands in case you didn't realize it." Her sarcasm grated on me, but I breathed and tried not to grit my teeth. My jaw hurt too much.

"If we have to walk then so be it. We need to get there." I walked off in the direction of the docks and Greer huffed but she followed. "Besides, we can go Walker speed."

She snorted and I looked at her sharply. "What's wrong with Walker speed?"

She glared at me. "Nothing."

I looked back at Saleem, who followed behind Greer as if he needed to keep watch. And a part of me wondered if we did need to watch her. Either way, I didn't plan on dropping my guard.

A twinge in my side had me grasping my ribs with a hiss. When my hand came away slick with blood, I swore. I'd forgotten about my injury and began to dread the long walk to the docks. The wound was bound to bleed me dry by the time we got there.

"Let's go," I said to Greer and glanced over my shoulder at Saleem. "Meet us there?"

"I'll stay with you." When I frowned, he grinned. "I can move fast too. And I'd prefer you weren't alone." He kept his gaze on my face, but I could tell he really wanted to glance at Greer. Seemed Saleem had taken a dislike to my sister. And here I thought Greer had the drop on all males of all the species with her white-blonde hair, knockout figure and endless legs.

"Suit yourself." I nodded and glanced at my sister. "Ready?"

She just grunted and we set off at high speed, flitting through the streets.

CHAPTER 34

THE STREETS BLURRED AROUND ME and my feet barely touched the sidewalk as we sped through the city toward the water. But something made me want to stop. A ripple of awareness ran through me, making me alert, wary.

Something was wrong.

After a moment's hesitation, I drew to a stop and so did Greer and Saleem.

"What's wrong?" Greer asked, annoyance pinching her features.

I frowned looking around the shadowed street. "I'm not sure. I think we're being followed."

"And you can tell that at warp speed?" asked Saleem with a raised eyebrow.

"I can sense someone else around." I let my eyes and ears transform, channeling my panther and borrowing her sight and hearing. Another scan of the street revealed nothing, but my ears perked, twitching at the faint beat of a heart. An odd, unusual rhythm, but a heartbeat nevertheless.

"I don't think you need to worry about it. This place is filled with ghosts and demons. It's probably one of the more curious ones watching us." Greer shook her head and her lip curled a little. "I really don't think you need to get all suspicious about it." Her eyes shone and she lifted her chin a little.

I scowled. I didn't care what she thought. I'd trust my instincts first. Greer? Probably never. Besides, there was something about her defiance that bugged me. Would she defend the demons of the Graylands? Surely she didn't owe them any of her loyalty?

The single heartbeat was still there, accompanied but the distinct soughing of breath. They were closer now. I nodded to Greer. "Let's go." I didn't miss the look of relief on her face.

We slipped into Walker speed again, but I remained alert. It worried me that someone was following us. Why would they be following us? My side twinged and I slowed. What worried me the most was we couldn't allow anyone to follow us to the docks. Did Greer want someone to follow us there? Is that why she wanted me to ignore our tail? What was she up to?

I stopped so abruptly that Saleem almost slammed into me. Greer hadn't noticed until she was a few hundred yards down the street. I spun around, motioning for Greer to join us.

The demon took it as a cue to come out of hiding. He ran at us, waving two horrific-looking swords. I didn't have time to run to him. Saleem shifted around me to protect Greer while I stepped toward the oncoming demon to meet him head-on. I managed to draw my demon sword from the satchel in time to swipe a wide blow. The clang of the swords sounded dull and hollow to my ears. I was getting used to the strangeness of sound in the Graylands.

The demon danced around me as we exchanged blow for blow. I slammed a sword into his forearm, which elicited a howl of pain from the lamia. He'd moved around me so much that I'd counteracted and moved with him until Greer was almost at my side.

I dodged another blow, happy that so far he hadn't touched

me. He swiped again and I parried, sending the blow off its course and toward Greer. Time slowed and I watched as the sword grazed Greer's forearm, drawing a line of red from her wrist to her elbow.

She shrieked and grabbed her arm, glaring at the demon, her face surprised, shocked. She hadn't expected the demon to hurt her. Her face blazed with anger and she stepped toward the lamia. My jaw dropped as I watched the armed demon stumble away from Greer, his expression fear-filled.

No time to figure Greer out, I rushed at the lamia, swiping wide and hard at his neck. The sword glided through the air, taking his head off clean. It fell to the ground and rolled a few feet until it came to a stop at the edge of the curb.

Greer uttered a shocked squeak and I glanced at her. She still looked horrified, but now as she stared at the head, she also looked upset. I frowned and she looked up to meet my eyes. She held my gaze for a second, then looked away, swallowed hard, and composed her features. I knew it. Greer had known this demon. It had most likely been a setup. The demon meant to follow us to the portal. Who knows what they had meant to do once they knew the location of the dark water. All I knew was the Greer was not to be trusted.

When I looked at the remains of the lamia again, he'd already begun to disintegrate. I wiped my sword clean on a rag from my satchel, dabbed the sharp edge with more demon poison and sheathed the sword.

A quick look at Greer's wound confirmed it was surface only —the cut wasn't deep at all.

"Let's go. We have to move fast. Who knows how many more of them are out there." I tried not to think about it as I slipped into panther speed, keeping a firm grip on Greer's arm. I didn't plan on letting her give me the slip.

She held her body tight even in super speed, as if anger still flowed through her. There was much more to Greer's involvement here than met the eye, and what Skates had revealed had only touched the surface. I suspected Greer would be the only person to tell us the truth and that would near impossible.

Once we got home, we would have to find a way to the truth. For now, we just needed to get home.

CHAPTER 35

WE WERE NEARING THE DOCKS when my side twinged again. This time the pain lanced through my body and straight into my brain. Fiery agony gripped me and I came out of Walker speed so fast I tripped and fell. I curled into a ball and ended up rolling a few feet. Not a comfortable thing when a bag and a satchel full of weapons is strapped to one's back.

I panted, sucking in air as much to ease the pain as for the need to breathe. I lay on the sidewalk assessing my body, admitting that the Wraith poison would have begun to take its toll by now. I twisted my left arm and almost screamed at the agony of the movement. I knew that feeling. The poison had spread, thick and malignant within my flesh and veins.

I needed Logan's fire treatment.

Now.

But common sense said I'd get none. Not from Logan himself, and not from his magical fire syringes either. I'd used the last ones for my last treatment. I was all out of luck until we got home. I'd just have to suck it up for now.

Greer and Saleem finally realized I was no longer speeding along with them and returned for me.

"What's wrong?" Greer knelt beside me. I wanted to laugh, unsure whether her question meant she really cared or she was just making a show of it. Not that I gave a damn either way.

"She was injured very badly when Yanuk beat her. Lost a lot of blood. And she had injuries from back home. The Wraith Lord's sword was poisoned. A piece broke off into her flesh and stayed there too long. Now the poison's in her blood and her body, and we haven't been able to find a cure." Probably the longest speech Saleem had made since I'd met him.

Greer stared at Saleem then turned to bend over me. "Where does it hurt? What can I do to help?"

"Unless you're a Fire Mage, there's about nothing you can do. Logan's fire treatment is the only thing that helps," I said softly through teeth gritted with pain.

"Do you want to take the armband off?" Saleem asked, glancing at my arm. It throbbed in answer.

I shook my head. "It will just hurt more." I waved them off. "I think the super speed is taxing me. I'll just have to walk the rest of the way there. It's not far—just another block."

"Right." Saleem leaned closer. "Hold on." Before I could protest, he scooped me up into his arms and strode off down the street. I struggled, but he just glared at me. "Stop being so stubborn. You don't have the energy to waste, so shut up and be still."

I scowled at Saleem but remained silent. He did have a point —if he could carry me why should I decline an opportunity to conserve my strength? Then again, when did he begin to think he had the right to boss me around?

A few minutes later we arrived at the docks. "Let me down. I can walk from here," I said, determined to walk to the pier by myself.

The docks sat empty and silent, gray sky hanging low over metallic, rippling water. I scanned the area around us, satisfied when I saw no movement, heard no hearts beating, heard no breathing. We were totally alone.

As soon as Saleem let me down, I dug into my bag for the portal key. I was about to head to the water's edge when Greer held onto my arm. My bad arm. I hissed with pain.

"Sorry," she apologized automatically, as if she'd already forgotten what Saleem had revealed about the condition of that arm. Or as if she didn't really care. "Is that the key? Can I see it?"

Reluctant to let go of it, I held it out so she could get a better look. She traced a finger over the metal disk, but when she held onto it as if to take, I didn't let go. Greer glanced up at, anger flashing in her steely eyes.

"Let go," she said, giving it a tug.

"No. I'm not parting with this key for anyone," I said firmly.

She pouted, although her petulance didn't cover her simmering anger. Why was she so angry? Was the portal key part of some plan? Was that why we were being followed? Why Greer had agreed to come back with us so easily? She must not be too happy now that her plans were thwarted.

She held onto the disk for a moment, as if considering whether to take it from me by force. In the end, she relented although her body remained stiff with anger.

"Right, let's go." I made my way down the pier until I reached the dark water of the docks. Around us, silence danced, no wind blew and the water remained still as obsidian. "Saleem, you can go now."

"I'll leave only after the two of you are safely through the portal." He gave me a pointed look. I remembered what Greer had done the last time she took a jump through a portal. Maybe we were better off being careful.

"Fine by me."

I held the disk over the water, keeping it horizontal. There was a familiar pull and the key moved out of my hand and hovered over the water. I waited, holding my breath. A flash of light hit the hole in the center of the key, widening into a bright, blinding column.

Beside me, Greer gasped softly. I held onto her arm. "Ready to go home?"

She hesitated for a moment then smiled brightly. "Yes. Let's go home."

"Okay. Don't let go. The portal key is made only for me. Without me, you can't use it." I spoke firmly and looked her straight in the eye. She held my gaze only a moment then looked away.

Then she lifted her chin, a tiny act of defiance that didn't sit well with me. "Ready?" I asked. Only when she nodded did I say, "Let's go."

I took a few steps backward, still holding onto Greer's arm. She moved back with me, then ran forward as I ran, keeping pace and jumping off the wooden pier as I did.

We hit the light and I felt a pull toward the key, a force that grabbed hold of us and tugged until we flew through the air and went straight into the light, straight into the center of the key.

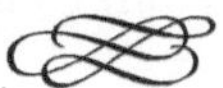

CHAPTER 36

WE ARRIVED AT THE WATER'S edge at the pier, and within moments, the air beside us shimmered and Saleem popped into existence.

The portal key made a whooshing sound and landed at my feet, but when I bent to retrieve it, darkness fed into the edges of my vision and my throat closed. Everything was slowly going black and I ended up falling hard to my knees. I groaned, pain radiating through my body. All I wanted to do was keel over and sleep.

Saleem bent to me, pushing my sweaty hair out of my eyes. "You have a fever. Just stay there and I'll get a car." He didn't wait for an answer, just rose and dialed a number, briskly requesting a car. When he cut the call and dialed again, I knew by the tone of his voice he was calling Logan.

Just the thought of him made me desperate to have him with me. The world tilted, and I turned and settled on the wooden pier where we'd landed, Greer beside me. She'd been silent since we arrived. She hadn't checked on me, either. Not that I expected or wanted it. Just something to take note of.

I shifted and pain spiked through my ribs. A rush of moisture confirmed the wound still bled. How much blood could a person lose before they died? I shook the thought from my head and breathed through the spasm of pain.

The sound of the night was welcome. The waves lapped the docks and the night was as silent as the Graylands so that even the tap of Greer's boot on the wood of the pier was welcome after the odd muffled sounds of the Graylands.

I must have fallen asleep.

Cocooned in warmth, I pushed away hands that seemed to want to move me. I was too comfortable to be moved. Then I opened my eyes and found myself nose-to-nose with Logan. A sigh escaped my lips and I wrapped my arms around his neck. His hand cradled the back of my head and I breathed in the scent of him.

"Be careful with her. She's got a deep wound in her side. Been bleeding for a while. She's probably drained dry by now." Saleem's voice drifted to me and I pulled away from the safety of Logan's arms. A car drew up and two men alighted. They hurried to me, faces intent, scanning me with the intensity of a doctor or a paramedic. Sure enough, they knelt beside me and threw open their bags.

I obeyed their commands to lie down, be still, breathe in. They changed my soaked bandages but could do little else. Logan knelt beside me, withdrawing two ampoules of healing fire.

"Here, I thought you might need this. It's just enough to get you home." I nodded but he still looked worried. "Can you handle it? It'll be more painful than ever simply because you're so weak."

"Do it. I need the energy and I need to go home." I bit out, struggling for breath.

Logan nodded and leaned over to open my armband. The medics gasped as Logan removed the band, revealing the colorful wound. I wanted to laugh. At least I was giving them something to talk about. When last would they have seen a poisoned forearm like mine?

Logan administered the fire, injecting it into a vein on my damaged hand. White-hot agony flared as the needle entered and the fire dispersed into my bloodstream. Logan held me while I shuddered in agony, as droplets of perspiration rose to soak my skin, as fevered heat burned through me. This was worse than any of the other treatments he'd given me.

Way worse.

I wanted nothing more than to slip into blissful unconsciousness, but it seemed I wouldn't get even that relief. I just breathed through the waves of pain until at last it was over and I was exhausted.

Logan drew me into his arms and strode to one of the cars. I looked over his shoulder and saw Saleem grabbing my bags. Greer bent to retrieve my armband, but Saleem grabbed it and held onto it. Greer scowled but didn't challenge him.

They joined us at the car as Logan fastened my seat belt and shut me inside. "I'll drive," I heard him say. Saleem nodded and jumped into the passenger seat. And Logan went around, giving Greer a curious glance. She stalked around the car and jumped in beside me. I didn't pay her much attention. The fire had tired me out so much I could barely keep my eyes open.

I leaned my forehead against the cool glass and thought of my mom. I hoped she'd be proud that I'd brought Greer home safe and sound.

I MUST HAVE FALLEN asleep or fallen unconscious because the sound of distant voices made me open my eyes. I lay in my bed in my own room.

Testing my strength, I sat up and everything seemed okay. When I tried to get to my feet, I figured I needed more rest. I lay back against the pillows and sighed.

Grams was fussing over Greer, who remained strangely silent. Usually, she would shove Grams off and demand her own space.

I eventually gained the strength to swing my legs over and sit on the edge of the bed, waiting for my head to stop spinning, but before I could get up, my cell phone rang.

"Hey, brat. Heard you're back," Iain said, trying to sound casual, but the thread of worry in his voice was clear enough.

"Hey," I answered, unable to hide the puff of exertion from trying to move around.

"What are you doing? Are you okay?" His voice rose.

"I'm fine. Can you stop being so nosy? If you must know, I'm trying to get out of bed to go to the bathroom."

Iain laughed. "Need any help with that? Maybe a bedpan?"

"Shut up."

"I'm sorry. Are you okay? Is Greer okay?" Iain's tone got serious. "I've got Dad here, he's on speaker."

"Hey, Dad."

"Hello, Kai. Are you sure you're okay? You don't sound well."

"I'm fine. Just really tired." I rubbed my temples, feeling the fatigue pull at me.

"We'll leave you to get some rest then."

"Thanks, Dad."

"And, Kai?"

"Yeah?"

"I'm going to have Sentinel do some research on that poison for you. I know your Logan has been using his fire magic to keep the poison at bay, but I do think you need a little more than that to get better." He sounded firm and his tone told me any argument would be a waste of my breath. But he was speaking carefully as if he were afraid of making me angry.

"Thanks, Dad. I guess I need all the help I can get right now."

They hung up and I found I had a little more energy after having sat up for a while. I got to my feet and I'd almost reached my room door when there was knock at the outer apartment door.

I pulled open the room door in time to see Logan and Saleem enter. I must have been sleeping for hours or maybe even days as they were now both changed and shaved and looking much fresher than I did.

"Hey, how you feeling?" asked Logan after greeting Grams and nodding at Greer. Seems even Logan lacked a soft spot for my sister.

"I'm fine, I think." I spoke while taking stock of how I really felt. I felt like shit. No two ways about it, but I wasn't planning on admitting it.

"You don't look fine. Another round of much stronger treatments would do you some major good." He beckoned me into the room and I didn't miss Greer's face as I moved to let him inside.

She looked angry again. I needed to fill Grams in as soon as I got a chance. For now, I left the door wide open and left Logan to wait while I used the bathroom.

Limping back to the bed, I got comfortable while Logan perched on the side of the mattress and waited for me. I could feel Greer's eyes on me, but I refused to let her get to me. I'd done my bit. I'd brought her home safe and sound.

Now she was out of my hands.

WHEN I WOKE UP, Logan was gone and so was Greer. Grams was fiddling in the kitchen as I entered, ravenous and looking for food.

"Hello, dear." Grams looked up from icing what looked like a red velvet cake. I leaned over and dug a finger into the cream cheese icing, savoring the sweet and sour taste. It just made my stomach growl louder. She swatted my hand away turned to fill the kettle.

Soon we sat down with generous slices of cake and mugs of steaming tea. It didn't take long for Grams to ask, "So how did it go?"

"Successful, but strange all the same."

"How so? Was it the place? The Graylands?"

"No. It was Greer actually. Everything the demons and the ghosts that helped us had to say about her." I met my grandmother's gaze, sure the worry was clear in my eyes. "I'm worried about her. Her behavior was so erratic, so unpredictable."

"Why don't you start at the beginning, dear." Gram's sipped her tea and encouraged me with a slow nod.

I launched into the story, giving her every bit, from Skates to killing Lester to Yanuk's beating. Grams' face tightened when she listened to the description of my beating and my injuries. But when I came to tell her about Greer and my conversation with her, she frowned.

"What's wrong?"

Grams shook her head, a little hesitant as she frowned as if confused. "Greer, she didn't mention anything other than that you found her and saved her and brought her here."

"So she didn't tell you she lobbied to replace the demon overlord of the Graylands, then?"

Grams paled. "No. She certainly didn't." Grams placed her mug on the table and stared at it. "What is wrong with that girl?"

"Could it be because she is Pariah?"

"What? Do you think that being Pariah messes with your head?"

"No, I mean that something must have gone wrong in a Walker's makeup to be Pariah in the first place. So maybe somewhere in the problem is the potential to go crazy." I paused, opened my mouth to speak then closed it again.

"Kai, I know what you are trying to say. Niko was also a little unbalanced from early on." She sighed then rose and walked to the window. "Maybe it could have something to do with being an Alpha. We haven't seen this kind of thing happen with Pariahs."

"How do we really know? Don't most Pariahs leave their clans and hide out? There are so many rules that stop them from being part of their clans, so don't most of them leave?" I asked, thinking of Lily and everything she'd been through, everything she'd experienced emotionally because her family, her people denied her.

"Perhaps you're right. Maybe we don't have enough information to speculate that this is an Alpha-related problem." Grams rubbed her arms as if a chill ran through her, then she returned to her seat, a determined look on her face. "Right. So I will speak to your father about looking out for Greer. Keeping a close eye on her, make sure she is okay."

I nodded, relieved but also a little unsettled. I didn't believe that Greer could be helped. But was that just sisterly bitchiness? Or did I still hold her betrayal against her? I remembered her words, her tone, the deep dislike in her voice as she and Niko spoke to each other about what to do with me when he'd captured me.

"Where is she now?" I asked.

"She said she needed some air." Grams looked at me, an expression of worry tightening her features. "I didn't think it would do her any harm. Her cell phone rang and she answered it. She mentioned meeting a friend for coffee. I thought it would be good for her after everything she'd been through." Grams was on her feet, looking a little frantic. "I'd better get Iain on the lookout for her. If what you're saying is true, I should never have let her go off by herself."

"Grams, how did she get her phone?" I placed a hand on my grandmother's arm and waited for an answer.

"Oh, Iain came by yesterday with some of her things that she'd left at Niko's lab all those weeks ago. Now you need to get some rest and stop worrying about Greer. Ailuros knows you've done enough for that child." Grams leaned forward and patted my hand. "Oh, and your friend Tara is going to pop by later too. The note's by the phone."

I nodded. "Thanks, Grams. Did you hear anything from the Supreme High Council about me? About the prophecy?"

Grams face darkened. "I'm sorry, Kai, but they're not prepared to interfere with fate. They're naturally afraid that anything they do may affect the final outcome."

"I would like to know more, Grams. Can you at least let me see what the prophecy says? I don't need any translations or interpretations. Just give me the words." I felt like I needed to beg. Who did I need to go to to get an answer?

She stared at me sadly for a moment then nodded. "Fine, let me see what I can do. And if anyone ever asks, you didn't get it from me."

I grinned. "Thanks, Grams. You're the best."

"I know," she said, giving me a wink as she took her dishes to the kitchen and grabbed her purse. She returned for a quick hug before heading out the door.

Silence settled in the room as the door closed, and I felt the emptiness of the apartment press down on me. And yet I knew what empty really felt like. The Graylands was a different kind of dead. A totality I wouldn't be able to handle on a daily basis. An emptiness that cut to the core.

And though I sat in the empty room it felt filled with emotion and expectation and life.

CHAPTER 37

A KNOCK SOUNDED ON THE door just as I left my room, freshly showered and feeling more alive than I'd felt in a long while. A sniff told me Tara had arrived and I grinned, flinging the door open.

Tara didn't say a word, just wrapped me in a tight hug, squeezing me a little too hard. I didn't protest though. "You are a sight for sore eyes."

I grinned. "So are you."

It didn't take long before we were on the couch and I was relating the story again. I gave a shorter version, leaving out my suspicions regarding Greer.

"That demon sword you gave me? Bloody amazing thing."

She grinned proudly. "I take it the weapon did its job satisfactorily."

"Are you kidding? Demon heads were rolling left, right, and center."

She laughed and raised her hands. "Hey, I just make the weapons. I don't need the gory details, thank you." Then she sobered a little. "Now tell me what's happening with this poison.

I thought you said Logan was working on treating you with his fire?"

"Yeah, we all thought it was working, but it seems all it's doing is keeping the poison at bay. And unless he's had a breakthrough and perfected the treatment in the last few hours, I don't think I'm going to see a cure anytime soon."

Tara stared at me, the look on her face saying her mind was whirling with an idea. "I'll ask mother to see what she can find out. She knows a lot of people, magicians, Fae, alchemists who might know a thing or two about this poison and what could heal you." She nodded to herself as if she hadn't intended to even ask for my consent.

I wanted to protest and tell her not to bother her mother, but who would I be kidding? I needed a cure like I needed to breathe. I'd be stupid to decline her offer.

"Okay. And let me know if there is any kind of payment required." Tara's faced scrunched up, a hurt look swirling in her eyes. I laughed and gave her a quick squeeze. "I meant for whoever your mother finds to help me. If they need payment, I want to make sure they get it."

"Fine. I'll tell her." Tara looked relieved. "And how are you really feeling other than the deadly poison ravaging every inch of your body?"

I raised an eyebrow and snorted. "Tired, but regaining my strength. I'm just glad I have Greer home. Now I can concentrate on getting Mom and Anjelo back."

"When will you go?"

"As soon as I regain my strength. I don't know how long I'll be there and I need to be strong enough to fight if I have to."

"Will you take Lily with you?"

"Most likely." I nodded, wondering where Lily was. I made a mental note to send her a message as soon as Tara left.

"I'm glad you two have each other. She seems to need a little focus right now."

I nodded. "She misses Anjelo."

"So do you," Tara said softly.

"Yeah, so do I," I whispered. "I'm so terrified they won't be okay. What if I get there and they've been killed? What if they're dead because I was too sick to go after them? Because I decided that my sister needed saving first?"

"You did what you had to do. Your mom and Anjelo would understand."

"Not if they are both dead." I made a face and blinked back the sheen of moisture that coated my eyes. Even the thought was hard to bear.

"Even then." Tara grabbed my hands. "It's not about that. It's about you doing the right thing. And your mother would expect you to save your sister first. Especially when you knew she was in danger. Is she okay?"

"You mean, did I save her from going crazy?" I laughed. "No. She's not okay. In fact, she's kind of crazy. Kind of psycho."

"I'm sorry." Tara's face fell.

"It's okay. It's not as if we are close. Not that I would have expected her to be grateful." I shrugged.

"She didn't thank you for saving her?" Tara raised her eyebrows.

I snorted. "Who, Greer? Thank me? Are you kidding? Greer would die first before she thanked me for anything. She's not exactly the grateful kind."

"Well you don't need her thanks or even her gratitude. Just knowing you did the right thing should be enough. Your mom will be proud of you. And we are all proud of you. You went through a lot to get her to safety." Her cell rang just as she took a breath to continue her very uplifting monologue. "Mom. I was just about to call you. Okay. Can you wait for me? I'll meet you there in five minutes. Yes, it's important. I'm with Kai, but I'll be right there." She hung up and smiled. "Mom says hi, and I have to go see her before she heads off again. She's going to Court for another meeting, so maybe she can check with her contacts while she's there."

Tara rose and hurried to the door, throwing a little wave over her shoulder as she went. I locked the door behind her and sent a quick text message to Lily who responded almost immediately saying she was coming right over.

Though I was tired I texted back and said okay. The only way to make Lily happy was to show her I was fine. I wouldn't be able to get rid of her if I didn't.

~

LILY SAT silent and shocked as I related the story for the third time. This was really getting old.

"Wow," she breathed. "Man, I wish I could have come with you."

I shook my head. "Not there. The portal key may have gotten you in but it would have been impossible for you to survive there. I'm still not entirely sure how Greer survived for that long."

"Well, she is your sister. Maybe she had some abilities like you, inherited from your mother," Lily said.

Lily certainly had a point but I was leaning in a very different direction with a very different theory. One involving Wraith Lord possession which I wasn't about to discuss with Lily.

Before she left, Lily put a call through to Storm and passed her phone to me. Storm's voice was soft with concern. He asked a few questions and told me to take it easy, promising to come and check on me soon. At that moment, I decided that should Grams not unearth some information for me regarding the Ni'amh prophecy, I was going to demand that Storm get me some info or else. I hoped that as an Immortal, he still had some major strings to pull. Otherwise I was all out of options.

Lily went home not long after, leaving me with a mind filled with worry and suspicion. Heading to bed, I intended to get some rest. Instead, I shuddered and tried to shove a multitude of thoughts out of my mind. The idea of Greer channeling the Wraith Lord didn't sit too well with me.

What would she do if she were capable of such power?

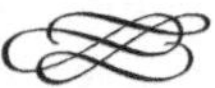

CHAPTER 38

THE MATTRESS SANK BESIDE ME as someone sat on the bed. I sat up with a shock, looking straight into Logan's eyes.

"Sorry, I didn't want to disturb you." His eyes were all innocent and mischievous, no apology in sight.

"Yeah, you just wanted to get yourself killed." I offered dryly as I scooted up against the headboard.

He chuckled then turned to the nightstand to hand me a coffee cup. "Cappuccino. It's a sorry-I-frightened-you cup of coffee."

I snorted and drank deeply. I wasn't about to complain when he'd just brought me coffee. I watched him as I drank, thinking how lucky I was. We were so comfortable together. But it was the trust thing that did it for me. I'd never been able to trust anyone so deeply before. And I was glad I'd taken that chance with Logan.

My thirst sated, I turned and smiled at him. "Thanks. I needed that."

"I'm sure you can find a better way to thank me." He winked.

I grinned and got to my knees. I crawled toward him and

placed my lips on his neck. He groaned softly as I nipped his skin and trailed kissed up his neck to his earlobe. I'd missed him and I intended to have a little fun with him. I bit his lip and was about to return to his neck when he growled and grabbed the back of my head, guiding his lips to mine, crushing his mouth onto mine.

He traced my lips with his tongue—driving me insane. I opened my mouth to him, pulling his closer. He deepened the kiss and we both wanted more. Needed more.

The room was silent except for the sound of our heated breathing. I opened my eyes and gazed at Logan's face. His skin was flushed, eyes hooded with passion, dark with emotion. I thumbed open the top button on his shirt and he blinked, but didn't stop me as I went for the second.

It didn't take long for me to drag his shirt off his body. I'd wanted this for a long time. I hadn't realized how much I'd missed him in the last week.

Logan pulled me to him, his heated skin grazing mine. I sucked in a breath as pain flared in my wound.

"I'm so sorry, Kai," he said as he moved away, but I gripped his arm, held him to me.

"No. I'm fine." I ran my hands over the muscles of his chest and enjoyed the rough breath he took. He pulled my hands away, tugging me toward him and I sighed as our bodies met. I wanted more and so did Logan. He grabbed the hem of my tee shirt and dragged it over my head. I lifted my arms to help him, trying to hold back the wince as the movement of my arms pulled my skin against my wound.

Our bare bodies met and heat sizzled at the contact of fevered skin. My breasts were crushed against his chest and I reveled in the feeling, just wanting, needing more of him.

CHAPTER 39

AFTER LOGAN LEFT, I WENT through my bag and rucksack, laid out all the ammo to take stock and began to clean my weapons one by one. Soon I'd be able to head off to the practice range to make sure the tightness around my wound wasn't going to slow me down if I needed to work.

As I polished the sword, I stiffened. I set the sword down and rushed to my bag, rifling through it for the portal key. I didn't recall seeing it as I went through the bag for the ammo.

And it wasn't here.

Wracking my brain, I tried to remember what had happened to the key after I dropped it. I remembered Saleem picking it up and putting it into the satchel before he dropped the bag on the floor beside me in the car.

After that, I didn't remember a thing.

All I knew now was that the key was gone.

I wasn't too devastated. It was the key to the Graylands portal, and I wasn't exactly going to waltz back there anytime soon. But who would take the key? Greer? Why would she want to go back to the Graylands? Would she even be able to use it?

Saleem maybe? Logan? Could Omega want the key for something? But the key was coded to me. Nobody else would be able to use it, so I couldn't understand why anyone would take it. The thought that it could have been Logan made me shudder.

I shook the suspicion from my head and began to search again. I was lifting the cushions on the sofas when the door opened and Grams entered.

She gave me a funny look as she entered the kitchen and set down her bag of groceries. "What are you looking for?"

I sighed and stuffed the cushions back and plopped onto the sofa. "My portal key to the Graylands. It's gone."

"Omega?"

"I thought about that, but it doesn't make sense. They wouldn't be able to use it anyway because it's keyed to my blood. And besides, they have djinn on their payroll. What would they need my key for?"

Grams nodded. "True. So that leaves Greer, Tara, and Lily."

"And you," I offered with a wink. She rolled her eyes and put a saucepan onto the stove. "Honestly, the only person it may possibly work for is Greer."

"Because you share the same blood." Grams nodded as a shadow passed over her face. "That girl worries me."

"You and me both," I said dryly. "And she's still gone."

"Do you have the other one? The one for Wrythiin?" Grams asked, frowning.

I nodded. "Yes. It's in my nightstand."

"So then, maybe the destination of that portal key is significant."

"Yeah, someone wants to go to the Graylands." I narrowed my eyes, staring at Grams but not seeing her. "Does Greer want to go back?"

"Why would she?" Grams asked, still frowning. I could see she didn't want to believe it.

"She had power there. People obeyed her. She was in charge. Maybe she wants that power back." I paused. "And everything was all so weird about her leaving. She agreed too easily. Especially when she was all demon-overlord wannabe. And she'd wanted that demon to follow us. She'd wanted the location of the dark water to be known. And come to think of it, she'd wanted the portal key too, but I hadn't allowed her to have it. And how she got to the Graylands in the first place ..." I fell into silence.

"What do you mean?" I stared at Grams, wondering if I should keep that suspicion to myself, then deciding for better or for worse I'd best tell her. She listened and nodded and seemed to agree. "You may be right, but it still doesn't fit with why she would want your key unless she knows a way to bypass the blood coding." Grams fell silent for a moment, then she sighed. "I'd better get this info to Sentinel. Greer's been gone too long and that is not a good sign. We need to find her and bring her in ASAP. Whatever she's involved in sounds bigger than just one small Pariah's rebellion."

I shuddered at the thought. "Let's just hope that that is just major speculation." I waved a finger in the air as my chest tightened with fear.

I didn't even want to contemplate the possibility.

CHAPTER 40

*L*ATE THE NEXT DAY, TARA texted asking me to come over to speak to her mother. I was about to head out of the apartment when someone knocked on the door.

Lily grinned at me. "How you feeling?"

I walked straight out of the apartment, ignoring her raised eyebrows. "I'm off to Tara's. Can I meet you later?"

"Nope. I'll come with you," Lily announced. "Seeing as I'm your sidekick and all, I'd better do some side-kicking, shouldn't I?"

I shook my head as we bounced down the stairs. "Gracie's found someone who can remove the poison. I'm not sure how long this will take." Part of me did not want Lily involved.

"That's fine with me. I'm coming with you." She lifted her hair out of her face and marched out onto the sidewalk, keeping pace with me as I headed for Tara's shop.

The bell above the door clanged as we entered and Tara looked up from a ledger she'd been writing in. She stood immediately smiling at Lily. "Hey, come on through." I followed her, the familiarity of the place settling over me eerily. Tara noticed. "What's wrong?"

"Nothing," I answered her, pasting a smile on my face. "Just tired."

She looked at me, suspicion bright in her eyes but said nothing as she led us through to the kitchen. We found her mother sitting at the table. She wasn't alone.

A man sat with her, hooded and cloaked in a purple robe so dark it was almost black. They both glanced up and the man stood to greet me. Gracie pulled me into a quick hug. "I'm glad you are feeling better, Kailin." I smiled and thanked her. "This is Darian."

Darian bowed and then stood upright to look directly at me. His face, though shadowed by the hood, held a curiosity and empathy that surprised me. He had an air of hardness, like he'd lived a long and terrible life. I couldn't tell his age although the lines in his face and the slight stoop to his shoulders would define him as old. But he could be centuries old for all I knew.

"Kailin, Darian is an Ancient. He can heal you," said Gracie.

"Thank you for doing this," I said to Darian, meeting his gaze. He inclined his head and stood.

"I will need a place where you can be comfortable. A bed preferably," he said to Gracie.

She nodded and got to her feet. "You can use Tara's room. It's down the hall to the left. Do you need anything else?"

"I have what I need, Your Majesty. You may join us." Then he turned to me. "If there is anyone you wish to call, anyone you would like to keep you company while I perform the removal."

I thought for a moment, then shook my head. "Just Tara and Lily are fine."

I'd thought of calling Logan but he'd spent weeks trying to perfect his fire so he could cure me, I wasn't so sure how he would feel to watch someone else take the poison away. Of course, I was yet to see proof that Darian could pull it off.

We entered Tara's room, the same one I'd slept in while in the Graylands. I sat on the bed and Tara brought a chair for Darian. I watched him. Despite his age, his movements were elegant and soft, nothing to say he was old and decrepit.

I removed my leather jacket and set it beside me since Darian would probably need access to the wound. My forearm was dark with purple bruises. Although the last fire treatment had worked, it seemed the poison was as strong as ever. It had spread again, strong and thick within my veins in only the space of a few hours.

My gut clenched. Could Darian really remove the poison from my body? Suddenly, I wasn't so sure. I wasn't so sure anybody could. And what if that was true and I was destined to die of the poison?

I pushed the thought away and watched as Darian brought a crystal bowl out of the leather bag on his shoulder. Beside it he placed a small jeweled knife.

"Lay your hand on the bed, child. I will need to make a cut in the skin. Blood must be drawn from your veins to make this work." I did as he asked, watching his veiled face as he bent over my hand to make the incision.

A spike of pain traveled up my arm and I hissed. Lily came around to the other side of the bed and sat beside me. "You okay?"

I nodded. "I'm fine. It just hurts way more when anything gets near the original wound."

Darian cleared his throat. "I think perhaps this might be a little harder than I originally thought. It sounds very much like there may still be some of the obsidian left within your arm. If that is the case, I will need to remove it before I can do anything to help you."

I nodded even though my stomach twisted so tightly I wanted to throw up. I knew from his description and the somber look on his face that it wasn't going to be an easy procedure.

I almost wanted to call Logan over. Or maybe Grams. But I wasn't a baby. I could handle this. I lay back and tried not to think of pain. Normal pain I could handle. Walkers had a fairly high pain threshold, but the pain from the poison was insidious, debilitating. It ate at me, not just my energy, but my strength and motivation too.

Darian brought the knife to my forearm. "Can you tell me where you think the original piece of obsidian was embedded?"

I pointed and suppressed a shudder, looking away as he lowered the viciously sharp blade to my skin.

"Shouldn't you take something for the pain?" Tara stood rigidly at the foot of the bed and interrupted the knife's descent.

Darian shook his head and met my eyes. "We would have to procure a powerful tranquilizer. Something we do not have time to obtain."

"Wait. Kai, can't you call Logan and see what he can get for you?" Tara looked at the knife and then back at me, her face pinched with worry. I hesitated. "You can't have this done while you're awake, Kai. It's insane. It's going to hurt too much and you're already too weak from the poison."

I glared at her, hating that she was probably right. "I'm sorry, Darian. Do you have time to wait? If Logan can get me the drug, I doubt it would take him long to get here."

"Very well. Make your calls. I will wait." He didn't sound too annoyed, so I relaxed a bit. I watched him walk slowly out of the room.

As soon as he left, I called Logan, listening to the phone ring once, twice.

"Hey." I could hear the smile in his voice.

"Hi." I spoke fast. "I need a favor and I'm not sure it's something you can pull off super-quick." My tone was a little too serious and I knew he'd sense something was up.

"What's wrong?"

"Gracie found someone who may be able to cure me. He knows about obsidian poison. The only problem is he has to reopen the wound to make sure all the obsidian is gone."

"Kai, how the hell would he be able to tell? You'd need to be in the hospital, under a surgeon's knife to be sure." Logan sounded angry and frustrated.

"I think he knows what he's doing. He's an Ancient." I tried to convince him, and from the silence on the other end of the phone when he heard the word "Ancient," I think I had him convinced. "And I trust Gracie, so I trust him. Please, Logan. I need a drug that will put me to sleep. Something stronger than the normal kind."

"Fine, I'll get it. But I'm going to stay for the procedure." His tone brooked no argument.

"Thank you. How long?"

"Give me half an hour. I need to pop into the lab for this."

"Thanks, Logan."

"Don't thank me. I just hope you know what you're doing," he said with a disapproving grunt.

Me too, Logan. Me too.

THE DOORBELL CLANGED in less than twenty minutes and I sighed, relieved that I didn't need to wait any longer. Logan's expression was angry and worried when he entered the room, ushered in by Tara, who came around to sit on the foot of the bed.

Logan handed me the little bottle and a syringe, then moved to stand against the wall behind Tara. On cue, Darian entered the room. He inclined his head in Logan's direction, a neutral, respectful greeting from the Ancient. Darian didn't need to be nice, but he was careful and meticulous. It made me more curious as to who and what he was.

"Kailin, once you receive this drug you will be asleep. I am hoping that you will awaken and be free of this poison." He patted my wrist and waved Logan forward. "You may administer the drug."

Logan moved toward me, quickly and efficiently preparing the syringe. I felt the pinprick of the needle as it entered my vein. Logan was good. I barely felt it break my skin. Barely heard Lily's intake of breath as she watched next to me. Except for the one question, she'd been oddly silent the entire time.

Beside me, Darian withdrew his bowl and dagger again and placed it close to my hip. Gracie entered the room with a sheet of plastic and a stack of towels. She placed the plastic beside me and spread a few layers of towels over it. I blinked as I watched her activity. An iciness gripped my throat, a dry, tight feeling that made me repeatedly swallow to bring some moisture back into my mouth. It didn't help.

I heard her formally introduce Darian to Logan, but it all seemed so far away, so garbled.

I blinked again, wanted to tell Logan something was wrong. I could feel my heart speeding up, my panther snarling as the drug filtered into my bloodstream. I took a breath but couldn't speak. I just stared at Logan until the image of him became two. Then everything in my vision blurred until I could handle it no more and shut my eyes, shut everything out.

CHAPTER 41

*L*OGAN STOOD AT THE FOOT of the bed, watching as the old man readied his knife. He was a bit startled when Darian raised his eyes and asked, "Kailin never got to tell me exactly where the obsidian had embedded within her arm. I do hope you are able to tell me. It will make this easier for both the girl and for me." Darian's voice was soft and calm and confident. He managed to put Logan at ease.

Logan bent forward and pointed just halfway along the scar that Kai's wound had left. She'd healed incredibly well, leaving only a fine line, as thin as a hair.

"Here," Logan said, praying the man knew what he was doing. Kailin was asleep, breathing the long, deep breaths of the unconscious. Her friends Tara and Lily still sat beside her, worried looks on their faces. Lily looked up, giving Logan a soft, encouraging smile and he realized he must look a mess.

He watched Darian bend over Kai's hand and winced as the old man pressed the blade to her skin. He made a deep incision and blood welled from the cut, dripping down the side of her arm onto the waiting towels. Logan gritted his teeth, the urge to hit Darian so strong that fire began to rise within his blood.

Darian set the bloody blade on the towel, then turned Kailin's hand allowing the seeping blood to drip into the waiting crystal bowl. As the blood touched the stone, the dark red liquid began to shimmer with streaks of silver. Little forks of lightning spread within the blood and Logan frowned. The bowl must have some magical properties, something that reacted to the poison running through Kai's veins.

Then the old man held his hands over the wound for a moment, hovering there as if his palms released some kind of invisible energy. Logan concluded that Darian was some kind of Mage—exactly what kind he was still to discover.

When Kai's arm began to glow with silver lightning striking beneath her skin, Logan stepped closer to the bed to get a better look. Darian didn't react.

The cut shimmered as the open wound also emitted the silver sparks. One particular area, almost exactly where Logan had pointed, glowed stronger, like an x-ray pickup detecting metal.

Darian nodded and gripped the dagger again. This time holding it perpendicular to Kai's hand. He looked like he was about to stab her arm but he made no sudden movements.

In fact, Darian moved very slowly, with a sure, steady hand that was a comfort to Logan. The point of the dagger entered the open wound and though Logan flinched and though he expected Kai to flinch, she didn't move a muscle. The tranquilizer he'd brought was doing its job.

Darian's dagger sank further into Kai's arm and Logan wondered how deep the old man intended to go. He feared Darian may damage vital nerves and muscles in his quest to remove the obsidian he thought was still within Kai's arm. Logan hadn't expected this level of surgery.

He opened his mouth to question how wise it was to perform such a procedure in this kind of environment when Darian let out a hiss of breath. Logan bent closer, careful to keep out of the old man's way. He watched as Darian slowly lifted the point of the deadly sharp knife, bringing with it a tiny sliver of black, so thin it was barely wider than a strand of hair.

The dark tip of the black crystal rose slowly, lifted by the point of Darian's dagger. He brought it only high enough to be visible, then looked behind him at Gracie, who'd remained at the entrance to watch. "Tweezers please. Or some kind of equipment to serve a similar function."

"I'll only be a moment," Gracie said, already halfway out the door. Less than a minute later, she returned with a small pair of tweezers, the metal glinting in the light of the bedroom. Darian took the instrument without a word, returning his attention to his patient almost immediately.

Logan peered closely at Darian, even Gracie and Tara bent forward to watch as the old man place the teeth of the tweezers on the fine tip of the hairline-sliver of obsidian. Darian closed the tweezers onto the obsidian and began to pull the sliver out of Kailin's flesh a tiny fraction of an inch at a time.

The process was so slow, so nerve-wracking that even Logan had perspiration dotting his creased forehead. Nobody breathed as Darian continued to pull at the sliver. Then he stopped and put the tweezers down and everyone looked at him, concerned, worried he'd done something wrong.

"I need to rest my hands. I fear my age is not conducive to such fine work." Darian smiled wryly.

"Would you like me to take over?" Tara offered and Logan almost nodded, knowing the kind of work the metal-singer did, but Darian shook his head.

"I wish I could take you up on your offer, and I am certain you have a much steadier hand than mine, but unfortunately, there is a ripple of magic here that I am working with. The power is just fine enough to allow me to lift the obsidian piece but I have to concentrate very hard, the fine magic and the tiny piece of crystal is a difficult and dangerous combination."

Tara nodded, her face clouded with worry. Darian smiled encouragingly at her. "Do not fear. I am almost there."

Then he turned his attention back to the sliver of obsidian sticking out of Kai's arm. Logan swallowed hard, slowly appreciating why his fire had never worked in totality. The piece of obsidian still stuck in her flesh had worked against every effort he'd ever made, leaking its poison into Kai's flesh constantly ensuring she never got better.

Darian picked up the tweezer and bent over Kai's hand again. He gripped the obsidian carefully and began to pull. Nobody breathed as he inched the sliver out of the wound. Not until Darian finally held the inch long, hair-thin piece of poisonous obsidian up for all to see.

Lily's breath hissed from her lips as if the mere sight of the obsidian infuriated her. Logan knew how she felt. That tiny piece of crystal had caused Kai so much of pain and everyone else so much worry. Logan felt as if a weight had been removed from his chest, something that had been suffocating him all these weeks.

He glanced at Tara and noticed the sheen to her eyes. She looked about to burst into tears and Logan knew just how she felt.

Darian's voice broke into his thoughts. "This tiny piece of crystal has much power." He held it up to the light, staring at it. Logan wondered if his ancient looking eyes could see it at all as the old man scrunched his face up to examine the piece.

"How is it possible it was so debilitating? It ravaged her body. We were barely keeping it at bay." Logan rubbed his face, the memory of Kailin's suffering haunting him.

"It is the power of the obsidian. The dead magic of the Wraith stone. It is filled with the power to kill, to poison. And unfortunately, it is very powerful, very insidious."

Dead magic. Odd choice of words Logan thought, but he didn't question Darian further. The old man wiped off his blade then fished inside his leather bag and retrieved a smaller pouch, tied off with a leather thong. He untied the bag and laid it flat—it turned out to be a large square piece of leather with dozens of needles pinned to it. Along one edge a variety of threads were coiled and tied off.

Darian picked a needle, threaded it then moved to the open mouth of the wound. Logan flinched as he watched the needle enter Kailin's skin, as he watched the thread pull at her flesh while Darian proceeded to sew the incision shut with a small row of neat, precise stitches. He tied the thread off and cut the ends with his blade. Kai was still unconscious, for which Logan was grateful.

"Now that is done, we can begin the purge." Logan glanced at Darian. He'd thought it was over but clearly the old man had more to do. "Once I begin, please do not move. Remain as silent as possible or please leave the room."

Though Darian spoke quietly, his tone clearly indicated there'd be hell to pay if he was disturbed. Logan, Lily and Tara remained where they were. So did Gracie. Darian stood at the side of the bed, pushing the stool away. He held his hands over Kailin's body and muttered a few words in a language Logan did not recognize.

As Darian chanted, the air around Kailin began to shift and move, twisting and roiling onto itself. The air took a hint of cloudiness that made it seem like Kai lay encased in a large, oval glass bubble.

Darian chanted and little strokes of silver lightning shot between Kai's body and the inside of the bubble. The silver lightning slowly darkened until minutes had passed and the forks of bright sparks turned a sinister black. Everywhere the black strikes touched on the inner surface of the bubble it took on a dark tinge, until the entire bubble began to darken as if it filled with a shadowy smoke.

Logan's heart beat too fast and he had to force himself to calm down. His gut told him Darian wouldn't hurt Kai, but what he saw looked pretty darned life-threatening. He fisted his hands to prevent himself from lashing out at the old man.

At last, the entire bubble turned a solid black and the rhythm of Darian's chant changed, became faster, darker. His voice took on an eerie echo sending chills up and down Logan's spine. Darian waved his hands around the top of the bubble, making large circles with his palms.

His hand moved faster and faster until at last he threw them up in the air. With that movement, the bubble popped and transformed into a black smoke that writhed around Kai's body like a snake. Darian moved his hands over the smoke, urging it, guiding it until it sinuously coiled, twisting and moving toward Darian's crystal bowl.

The blackness sought out the bowl, swirling within its center until it disappeared, as if the white crystal was swallowing the smoke. And perhaps that was exactly what was happening. Logan's eyebrows rose as he watched the pure white crystal darken slowly and become off-white, then silvery gray until it grew so dark it rivaled obsidian.

Logan blinked as the smoke dissipated and the bowl sat empty. Darian sighed and Logan realized only then that he'd stopped chanting altogether.

Darian faltered then stepped back. Before Logan could move to help him, Gracie pulled the stool to him. She put a hand on his shoulder as he sat heavily. "Are you well, my lord?" she asked softly.

"Yes, Your Majesty. I am well. This process is very draining. I only need a few moments to collect my energy."

"Do you need anything? Can I provide you with food or drink?"

Darian shook his head. "Thank you for offering but I am quite fine." His gaze returned to Kailin, bringing Logan's attention back to her as well. Her skin looked a much healthier color than it had in the last few weeks. Something Logan found to be a great relief. He took it as a sign that she was well on her way to a full recovery.

Logan looked at Darian who silently packed away his implements and bags. "Is she going to be okay?"

The old man looked up at Logan, his eyes clear and his expression open. "Yes. She will be fine. Usually this kind of poison would have needed only the extraction of the dead magic, but the piece of obsidian had to be removed before I proceeded."

Logan nodded, accepting what he took to be an apology from Darian for whatever damage he may have done to Kailin's arm. Darian got to his feet, hiking his bag up higher on his shoulder. He pulled the hood of his cloak back over his head and gave Logan a bow before offering Tara the same greeting.

Then he turned to Gracie. "Your Majesty, it would make me very happy if you would convey my best wishes to Kailin."

"I will tell her myself." Gracie held her hands out and grasped Darian's hands, squeezing them.

Logan stepped forward and cleared his throat. "I don't wish to be rude but . . . reimbursement for Darian's services . . ." Logan trailed off unsure how to ask, wondering if it were an insult to ask or an insult not to.

Darian grinned. "Young man, I am grateful you wish to reimburse me, but I have done Kailin a service of my own free will. And please tell her I am at her service if ever she needs me again." Then he turned back to Gracie. "Your Majesty, please feel free to tell her how to contact me should she ever need me."

He bowed again and exited the room. Gracie followed him out and the room fell into silence. Logan wasn't sure what to say, and it seemed neither did Tara. When Kailin moaned and tried to turn, Logan went to her side, using the stool vacated by Darian.

"What exactly was he?" Logan asked, still curious about the old man.

"He is an Ancient," Tara said softly.

Logan's eyebrows shot up. Kai had said he was an Ancient,

but they were almost unheard of in this day and age. They were immortals with a Druid-like system of magic and worship. Some said the druids were instructed by the Ancients but Logan wasn't sure of the details. "Interesting."

"Mother used her contacts back home to find him. He was very happy to help."

"We're all happy he helped." Logan pressed his temples then folded his fingers and leaned forward on his elbows, his eyes on Kai's face. Lily still sat beside her as if afraid to leave her friend alone. "I'll sit with her if you have anything you need to do," Logan said to Tara.

She nodded and shifted off the bed. "Thanks. How long will it be before she awakens?"

"It might be a couple hours. They weren't specific. I guess it's different for each Walker and with Kai being an Alpha, the dosage was fairly high."

Tara nodded, her forehead creased with worry. She left the room and Logan felt a similar twinge of fear in his gut. He hoped the dosage had been correct and that Kai would regain consciousness soon enough.

CHAPTER 42

MY THROAT WAS PARCHED. I tried to swallow, but it just made the scratchy feeling worse. I wanted to cough but no sound left my throat. I blinked and was relieved to find that my eyelids opened. My eyes felt gritty though, sand-papery, and blinking hurt.

A sound beside me made me go still. A sough of breath I recognized as belonging to Logan. He was still here? I turned my head to face him and he looked up at almost the same moment to meet my gaze.

He grinned. "Welcome back."

"How long have I been out?" I croaked the words out.

"In all, about an hour and a half. I'd expected you to be out for a whole lot longer. Darian left about half an hour ago." He leaned closer and smiled. "How do you feel?"

"Weird," I said. "My throat feels raw, and my arms and legs feel like rubber."

"Rubber is good considering the condition of your arm." Logan's face darkened and his expression worried me. I glanced at my forearm to see the thin line of skin stitched together with a handful of elegant stitches. It was a pretty neatly finished job, so I was happy the incision would heal nicely. "It looks good."

"Mmh, if you were the one watching while Darian did his little surgery, you might think otherwise."

"Okay then, spill." I stared at him, daring him not to speak. But he seemed relieved to tell me what happened. I let him talk without asking too many questions and when he rounded up saying Darian had offered his services to me whenever I wanted them, all I could manage was a soft "wow."

After a few moments I said, "That actually sounds pretty cool. I'm sorry I missed seeing it."

Logan shook his head and snorted. "You never fail to surprise me."

"I like keeping you on your toes." I grinned.

Logan stared at my face. "I like it when you keep me on my toes." He leaned forward and kissed me on my temple. And though his voice had turned husky and his eyes smoldered he did no more than that. I couldn't deny I was disappointed, but it was neither the time nor the place for a make-out session.

Footsteps in the hall announced Tara and Lily's arrival. "You're awake," Tara said as she looked from me to Logan. "So quickly?"

Lily remained oddly silent.

Logan nodded. "Must be something to do with those Alpha Walker Hunter genes she has."

I snorted not feeling distinctly Alpha Walker Hunter at the moment. I had to admit I did feel much better than I had expected, though. My worry that the drug would have adverse effects was unfounded, although it was disconcerting to know I'd been pumped up with an animal tranquilizer. Despite my panther's constant company, despite my transformations into full animal form, I'd never really considered her to be a true animal.

A hybrid creature sounded better than a pure animal. But what was it that I became when I changed if not a pure animal? I blinked the thoughts out of my head and pulled myself up to rest against the headboard.

"Hey, you should take it easy," Logan admonished.

"I'm feeling much better actually." And I truly was.

"How about some food?" Tara asked.

I nodded, suddenly ravenous. Logan stood. "I'll get it. Burgers from O'Hagan's all round?" He looked from me to Tara to Lily and grinned when we all nodded eagerly. "I'll be back soon. You, don't go anywhere." He shook a finger at me and then left.

I leaned against the wooden headboard at my back and sighed. And for the first time, I noticed something that wasn't there any longer. The persistent ache, the ever-present throb in my arm, the dull pain within the muscles of my body. Now that it was gone, it was so clear to see how bad a burden the poison had been.

I lifted my arm and pressed the flesh around the wound. Nothing. No pain, no ache, no tenderness. Just a normal, healthy arm again. I was more than thrilled.

"Feeling better?" Tara asked as she sat beside me.

"Absolutely." I nodded. "I'm back to normal now. I really hadn't realized how much of a toll that wound and the poison had taken on me."

"You do look a lot better," Tara said, nodding at me. Then she patted my wrist. "Maybe get a little more rest until Logan brings the food."

I nodded then reached for her hand. "Tara, thank you. For staying with me. And Lily..." I turned to my side-kick who had a moist sheen to her eyes. "Thank you."

"You're my friend. There isn't anything I wouldn't do for you." My breath hitched at her words. It meant more to me than I could say knowing the depth of my friendships.

CHAPTER 43

*L*OGAN ARRIVED A FEW MINUTES later bearing food, and from the look on his face, bearing bad news.

"What's wrong?" I asked, and Lily turned her gaze from the paper-wrapped burgers to Logan's face.

"I'm going to have to eat and run. We have a problem."

I raised an eyebrow and waited. Logan looked like he wanted to avoid telling me but something told me I needed to know. "What is it?"

After a long pause he said, "It's Brand."

"What about the jerk?" My skin still rippled with disgust at the thought of the slick murdering bastard.

"He's escaped." Logan didn't pull any punches. The words dropped on me like fiery hot stones.

"What?" I leaned forward, food forgotten. "What about all your fancy security?" I couldn't help the accusation in my voice.

"We're not sure what happened. The supervisor is convinced there's a mole in the police department."

"What if there is a mole in Omega?" The words left my mouth before I realized the ramifications. But I was stretching my worry a little. Grams' mole wouldn't do this. Brand must have a contact who helped spring him. How else would he have gotten out?

Logan spoke, reminding me I'd asked him a question. "We're not sure where the leak is. Both Omega and the CPD are investigating."

I was silent for a moment. "This isn't good."

"Damn straight it isn't. You're not safe."

I glared at him. "You are so not going to throw police protection at me."

"How else do you expect me to keep you safe?"

"I can take care of myself. And besides, what makes you think he'll come looking for me? Doesn't he have a drug ring to head up? Won't he go straight underground?"

"We don't think so. The assumption is that he would come for you first. You are unfinished business."

I snorted and swung my legs to the floor. "Let him come. He'll get more than he bargained for."

"You aren't in any condition to defend yourself." He raised an eyebrow and scanned me head to toe.

"I'm fine. The Wraith poison is gone. It's no longer draining my strength. The tranquilizer is gone too—my metabolism has probably processed it fully by now. In fact, I feel totally fine. Better than ever actually." I got to my feet to prove my point, and for a moment, I feared I'd be proven wrong and keel over in a dead faint, but I didn't. I really was fine. Strong and healthy once again. I grinned. "Let's eat."

Logan looked at me strangely but didn't protest. He just followed Tara into the kitchen, his shoulders stiff, the cords in his neck taut.

He knew when he'd lost an argument.

CHAPTER 44

*L*OGAN WAS ON TENTERHOOKS AS the three of us left Tara's. He insisted on walking me straight home.

"I can walk myself home, you know." I tried to assure him. "Plus, I have Lily."

Lily nodded.

"I know you can, but I don't trust Brand." He scanned my face, his eyes shadowed with worry. "How are you feeling?"

"Fabulous actually. I'm a little surprised at how good I feel. I guess I realize now how much the poison had affected me these past few weeks." I frowned, thinking about my trip to the Graylands. "Even while I was in the Graylands, the poison managed to take a huge toll on me, but I didn't let it control me. It's the same with Brand. Yes, he's free, but I'm not going to allow him to control my every move. Then he wins."

"Still, I'm putting a car outside your apartment and I want you to call me when you need to go out. Just until we know where he is and what he's planning." Logan touched my arm. "Okay?"

"Fine. Do what you have to. But it doesn't mean I have to like it." I snapped, not caring if he was hurt by my attitude. All he wanted to do was to protect me. But I'd never liked being coddled.

And now as we walked the few blocks to my apartment, the hairs on the back of my neck began to stand on end. Lily and I both glanced at each other. She'd smelled it too. We settled into a comfortable silence while Logan checked his messages. I let my panther hearing loose, allowed my sense of smell to expand.

We were being followed. The footfall of the stalker was soft, controlled, as if they knew just how to prevent someone from hearing them. His breathing was even, calm. His heartbeat remained steady, unaffected. Whoever he was, he was certainly well in control of his senses. He knew what he was doing and confidence emanated from him in much the same way as the stink of him.

Leopard Walker stink.

Logan didn't know how right he was, but I wasn't planning on telling him. Brand was mine to deal with. Brand and I definitely had unfinished business. Unfinished business that did not have anything to do with Logan.

This time I meant to finish it.

We neared my apartment and I paused outside to tell Logan not to worry to come inside. Instead, he cut me off. "I'm coming up, Kai."

I snorted. "It's not as if you can smell if anyone is inside my apartment, you know."

"It doesn't matter. I'm still the one with the gun."

"I have a weapon too." I tapped my lower thigh, pointing at my boots where I always strapped my daggers. These days I never left home without them.

Logan just grunted and hurried up the stairwell to my floor. At the door, he glanced over his shoulder. "Panther power please."

I rolled my eyes but let my senses loose. Safety first. "It's empty."

"Good," he said as he used his key and entered the apartment. I followed him inside and after a quick scan of the still empty apartment he turned to me. "I have to go but I'll be back later."

"You go do your thing. I told you I was fine." I folded my arms and glared at him but I couldn't really be angry. Lily shut the door behind him and we went to the window that opened onto the street outside the front of the building. Sure enough, a shadow lurked in the entrance of the opposite building. I peered through the netting but he didn't move. Clearly, he planned to stay and watch my movements. Was he waiting for me to leave the apartment or was he planning on breaking in after dark?

I wasn't going to give him the satisfaction. I grabbed my satchel and threw in my scimitar and my bow. A part of me said I was wasting my time with the weapons, even while I tried to imagine finding a place from which to shoot him from a distance.

I glanced up at Lily. "You come as far as the street then you go home. Brand is too powerful for you." I spoke a little too harshly, but I was worried about Lily. With their history, Brand was the last person she needed to meet face-to-face right now.

I went to the window again. The shadow still lurked across the street. I moved away from the curtain and beckoned Lily to follow me out of the apartment. Locking up, we headed down the stairs to the back entrance. Would he have had someone watch the alley?

I had to try.

Shoving the door open a tiny bit, I glanced outside, letting my Walker senses out to check the alley. Sure enough, a Walker lurked at the alley entrance. He was looking out into the street, his hands in his pockets, the hood of his jacket hiding his face. I slipped out the door and motioned for Lily to follow. I closed it as quietly as possible behind us. A dumpster, an old car, and a bunch of trash cans were my only hurdles.

I watched the guy, then ducked behind the dumpster, calling for Lily to do the same with a quick flick of my head. I watched

Brand's guy, knowing I couldn't tackle him where someone could possibly see us. I needed to get him to come to me. Peering around the dumpster, I looked around for something to throw.

Nothing.

Then I glanced at the metal door I'd just exited. I raised my booted foot and kicked it hard. Hard enough for the metal to vibrate and ring loudly. I drew my bow from my back and checked it for ammo. This time I'd loaded Walker ammo, a poison strong enough to kill a Walker—tamping down a twinge of guilt. And I was prepared to use it even though this was one of Brand's thugs and not the bastard himself.

I listened, waiting to hear the footfalls of Brand's guy. And it didn't take him too long to come investigate. His shoes hit the concrete of the alley as he drew closer—louder and louder until he was around the corner of the dumpster. I tucked myself against the wall with Lily scrunched behind me and waited, finger on the trigger, until he turned the corner and looked at the door.

His attention had first been drawn to the door and not me, sitting not five feet from it. I raised the bow and aimed it at him. The movement drew his attention to me and his eyes rounded in surprise, then horror.

I pulled the trigger, and an instant later, he lurched backward, stepping slowly toward the far wall. His back hit the wall and he looked down at the front of his chest. He gaped at his chest where hundreds of tiny poison-tipped darts were embedded. Little drops of blood began to leak into the fabric of his hoodie, converging together into a large stain.

Lily made a soft, squeaking sound behind me.

He held a hand to his chest, gasped, then slid slowly down the wall until he sat, legs akimbo, against the moldy brick. I blinked and watched as the life fled from his eyes and his head lolled forward, his arm slipping into his lap.

I swallowed. What had I just done? I'd just killed a Walker.

One of my own. And even though I knew he'd have killed me on the spot given half a chance, it didn't make me feel one iota better. I gave him one last glance and tore my eyes off his corpse.

The alley was still empty and I got to my feet and tucked my bow back into my bag. I peered around the dumpster in case Brand had decided to come looking for his goon. I crooked a finger at Lily and she followed. We crept to the corner of the wall and looked right, up the street. Clear. I didn't bother going any further to check if Brand was still watching. I knew he'd still be there.

I pointed a finger across the street, meeting Lily's defiant stare. She let out an exasperated breath and walked off, her shoulders tight. She was mad at me, but I could take it. Brand was not the kind of Walker she needed to mess with.

Spinning on my heel, I headed down the block away from my apartment. I made a right and crossed the street, hurrying into the first alley on my right. I went straight through and met the street on the other side. A good place to keep an eye on Brand. Heading to the entrance of the alley, I peered around the edge, looking right again and made out Brand's shadow. He still stood where I'd seen him from my apartment window. He seemed happy to wait too. No pacing, no fidgeting. Just calm stillness, like a leopard waiting for his prey.

I snorted and settled against the wall to watch him. Shadows lengthened and darkness fell. A chill set in but I didn't pay too much attention. At around eight, he headed across the street and into my building. I gave him five minutes and it took almost exactly that before he came racing out the entrance and around the block, heading for the alley.

Moments later, he hurried back up the street, crossed the intersection, and headed down the block, away from my apartment and away from me. He seemed unaffected by the death of his thug.

Typical.

I left a fair distance between us. I wasn't afraid to lose him. All I needed to do was track him by smell.

As he led me deeper into the abandoned part of town, past the red-light district where the absence of the under-aged prostitute was clearly obvious, toward the abandoned warehouses, I knew where he was taking me. Back to where he'd last had me dangling from chains, where he would have had me for dinner, literally, had it not been for Logan and his excellent timing.

He walked ahead, neither fast nor slow, seemingly sure of himself, not looking at all like the vicious criminal he was. Brand had always been suave, so I wasn't surprised.

I stopped at the last corner and watched him enter the building. He turned to look up and down the street before entering the building and pulling the wooden door closed, leaving it slightly ajar as he disappeared inside the warehouse.

Shrouded in darkness I didn't need to worry about being seen. Even if he'd used his leopard night-vision, he wouldn't have seen me peering around the corner.

Night fell heavily around me and the lack of streetlights in this part of town didn't help any. I felt the weight of my cell-phone in my pocket, urging me to give Logan a call. I bit my lip. Should I call Logan or maybe Lily? I struck Lily off my mental list. She was mad at me but I preferred she stay mad and alive.

I tapped Logan's number and waited for his answer.

"Logan, I need backup." I just cut to the chase.

"Kai, what's wrong?"

"I'm outside Brand's warehouse in the abandoned quarter."

"What the hell, Kai. I thought I told you to stay put." He growled, his annoyance clear in his voice. I could almost see him wipe his face in frustration.

"He was outside the apartment. When he left, I followed him. I didn't want to lose him. What was I supposed to do?"

"Fine. It doesn't matter now." Logan snapped. "Stay where you are. I'm on my way."

He cut the call without waiting for my answer. Not like I was going to agree with him. He'd better get his ass here fast or I was going in. A little niggle of doubt worried me. The last time I didn't wait for him, I almost got myself killed. It was all a bit too déjà vu for me.

This time, I intended to wait. I leaned against the wall and kept an eye on the warehouse.

CHAPTER 45

THEY CAME UP BEHIND ME so fast I heard them only at the last second—too late to do anything but struggle as they grabbed my arms and manhandled me across the street. I tried to elbow the guy on my right, but all he did was twist my arm up my back so high I was sure it would slip out of its socket.

I tried to look around, but the thug behind me grabbed my hair and bent my head back, so I was blind to where I was going and had to concentrate as the two other attackers dragged me toward the warehouse.

Just my luck. Even when I had decided to be careful, trouble came looking for me. Logan was going to be so pissed. I guess I'd only care if I actually survived.

They shoved me through the entrance between the hulking pieces of abandoned metal and gigantic coils of metal wire. My heart thudded as memories of my last experience here filtered through my mind. I so did not want a repeat.

The three pushed me into an open space just a few meters away from where Brand and his men had made a meal of that poor human girl the last time I was here. This time he was seated at a rickety metal table, one ankle resting on his knee. His eyes met mine and he stared at me, the expression in his partially transformed golden leopard eyes unreadable.

I couldn't even tell if he was angry.

The relaxed set of his body said he was fairly happy. No anger tensed his shoulders or tightened his jaw. I was confused.

"What do you want with me?"

Brand laughed and his men snickered behind me until he gave them a murderous glare and they all shut up in unison. They let me go and took a step back. When he returned his gaze to my face he said, "Do you really not know what I want with you?"

I shook my head. I knew he wanted vengeance, but I wasn't going to give him the satisfaction of answering his question. I may be his prisoner, but I didn't answer to him.

"You, my little panther Alpha, have been the true bane of my recent existence." He got to his feet and moved toward me. I thought for a moment that I had a chance to run, but one of the men behind me grabbed my hair again, gripping it close to the scalp, so close that if I decided to make a run for it this minute, I'd need to leave my scalp behind.

Brand walked up to me and stared down into my upturned face. He bent until his nose was a fraction of an inch from my neck and then he took a deep breath. "I'm glad you could make it. I was surprised at how easy it was to get you to follow me." His eyes glittered.

"Not as easy as you think. Did you check on your little friend in the alley?" And as Brand lifted his head, his nostrils flaring, I realized how stupid I'd been. I'd been so sure I could track him by smell if he got too far away from me. Why had it not occurred to me then that he could track me just as well? A normal Walker had pretty solid tracking skills. An Alpha was much better, stronger, and faster, but it didn't mean Brand was incapable. In fact, he'd just proved that. Even if he hadn't known where I'd hidden in the alley across the street, he certainly had known when I'd followed him.

"Yes. That was a bad move, my dear. I'll have to make you pay for that too." The smile he gave me was so clear, so friendly, it was easy to see how the Walker had run a club and had kept his drug-dealing a secret for so long.

I kept my mouth shut, beginning to worry where Logan was. I had a bad feeling that this time he wouldn't make it here at the last minute to save my ass. I watched Brand, and let my senses free for a moment. I needed to know what I was up against. His men were no match for me if I had my hands free to fight. Three of them and Brand.

And something else teased my senses. An odor that was familiar. Too familiar.

It smelled like Greer.

My heart thumped in my chest. Had Brand abducted Greer? But from what Tara had remembered of them when Brand had ordered Niko's metal claws, Greer seemed to be happy enough with Brand. What if she'd returned to them? Was Brand the person who'd rung Greer? Was he Greer's real coffee date?

I flicked the thought away, having too many other things to worry about right now. Brand hadn't moved. He seemed to be waiting for something. "What do you want?" I folded my arms across my chest. With my fingers out of sight, I let my claws lengthen. They were, in fact, my only weapon. I wanted to turn around and check which one of his men now had my bag of weapons. Not that it mattered anyway. I wouldn't be able to get to them. Even the knife in my boot couldn't help me now.

But my claws just might.

"I want you to pay. There are a few things on the list. You've destroyed a good few things of mine. And you put me in jail."

"Not that you spent too much time there," I countered sweetly.

Brand was pacing. "True, but I'm a busy man. I can't afford to spend too much time away from my business, my dear. I'm sure you can understand how it is. Things just don't do well when left unattended. And imagine my shock when I returned to find no sign of any of my drugs. Clean streets are not good for business."

"I'm sorry. I've been away. Had no idea the streets were clean." I didn't sound sorry and he knew it. He stopped walking back and forth and stared at my face again.

"You know, it's a real pity you aren't working with us. We could use someone like you on our side." His eyes raked me from head to toe.

I wanted to shudder, but stilled the urge. "That's never going to happen, so quit dreaming."

"I thought so. Never mind. So tell me what happened to my partner Niko?"

"He's dead." My voice remained expressionless.

"So, it is true. So how am I going to get my drugs back on the street?" He was talking to himself now. He sounded focused, determined.

"What's wrong with just running your club and not ruining peoples' lives?"

"Are you crazy? You have no idea the kind of money there was in the Synthe. I need that formula."

"I don't need an idea. I just know the toll it took on peoples' lives."

"You know sometimes you sound a bit too much like Niko. Despite his need to experiment, he often felt guilty for what he ended up doing to his 'patients.' The problem with him was he often went a bit nuts while experimenting on them. And then of course there are the Wraiths. I'm assuming they will be a lucrative source if I can get back in with them."

I raised my eyebrows but he didn't take the bait.

"That Wraith Widd'en? He was very keen on seeing the Synthe on the streets. Said it made the Walkers more susceptible to possession. Said Walker possession had been unheard of, but the Synthe depleted their defenses and allowed the Wraith to possess them. The only problem he and Niko had was once the drug wore off, the Walkers body expelled the Wraith immediately."

This was very interesting. Brand was filling in the many blanks we'd had about Niko and his activities. We could have interrogated Greer, but Grams seemed worried that any kind of questioning could set her off, and we had no idea how crazy the Graylands had made her.

A sound at the entrance drew Brand's attention and at the same time, the dude holding my hair loosened his grip. I tugged my head loose and took the opportunity to spin my arms in a wide arc and rip my claws into Brand's abdomen. He screeched and held his hands to his belly. I sped around a gigantic coil and came at his men from behind in a blur of speed.

A quick swipe with one hand opened up the first Walker's jugular. I avoided the spray and ducked behind him to close in on the second thug. He spun around, his lynx eyes glaring, his hairy-tipped ears sprouting in the blink of an eye. He bent low and growled at me. But I didn't wait for his next move.

I sank low and swiped at his thigh, obliterating the muscle. He howled in agony and grabbed his leg as blood sprouted thick and fast. I landed a punch to his jaw, putting the full force of my strength behind it. My fist connected with a thud, and I felt the crunch of bone beneath my knuckles. He fell heavily to the floor, his eyes rolling back in his head.

The third guy had left to attend to Brand and both were now gone.

Darkness lay thick and ominous within the warehouse and my heart thudded in my chest. I breathed and released my panther senses in full force. The dark became lighter, clearer, shapes more defined. I could smell everything around me. From the sweat on my own body to the blood from the two thugs I'd decimated. Oil and gasoline and metal mingled to remind me how big this warehouse really was. I could even hear the soft murmur of the pigeons that sat within the rafters high above our heads.

And I could smell Brand.

Probably just as well as he could smell me, but I didn't care. I moved to step over the Walker whose jugular I'd ripped open when I had an idea. I bent to rub my hands in his blood, wetting my palms, then wiping the still warm liquid all over my neck, arms, and face. I swiped the rest of the blood off on my clothes, then rummaged in my bag for the demon sword. It seemed more appropriate for fighting a creep like Brand, the curve of the blade, the jagged tip, all saying don't fuck with me.

I breathed in and out, lowering my heartbeat, calming my breathing until I was so quiet I would sound much like a rat or a similar small animal. That should confuse the hell out of Brand. I eased myself past stacks of metal, huge broken chunks of what looked like engines, but nothing like I'd ever seen before.

I concentrated on Brand's scent and followed it through to the other end of the warehouse. He leaned against a pile of scrap metal, inspecting his stomach while the last of his men stood guard, waiting for me. The nervous cougar's eyes darted back and forth, but he saw little in the darkness. His night vision power seemed limited. Was he Pariah too? That would make a lot of sense. All these Walkers banding together, all different levels of Pariah. Probably what had drawn Greer to them. I couldn't blame her if she'd been looking for fellowship, but I could blame her for betraying her family.

I looked around for something to throw and found a small tin can, opened and empty. I tossed it off to the side and waited until the Walker disappeared into the row of metal stacks.

"Be careful, she's probably around here somewhere," Brand called.

I frowned. What the hell was wrong with him? Why didn't he

just transform and use his leopard sight to look for me? Unless I had hit something vital.

Sniffing the air softly, I followed the scent of fear and Brand's blood that emanated from his goon. He wasn't hard to find. None of Brand's men seemed trained or strong. They were just as hard and just as much a fighter as the next man on the street. Brand had recruited green Walkers to follow him in his quest to regain the streets as Walker drug lord. Selfish asshole.

I ran up behind the cougar Walker and tapped him on the shoulder. As he glanced left, I ran around the other side of him and waited for him to look back at me. When his gaze swung back, it was filled with fear, and for a tiny moment I wanted to spare the guy. He had no idea who he was up against. But then he charged at me, yelling like a madman and leaving me no choice but to swipe hard at him with the demon sword.

I let the blade slide through the front of his neck, just enough to sever his life's last threads. I wasn't keen on seeing a headless Walker corpse anytime soon. The thug fell to his knees holding his throat as if it were possible to keep it closed, or to keep himself alive. Blood spilled over his fingers and he sucked in air through his severed throat. He choked, coughing blood everywhere until he grabbed his neck harder before slipping slowly to the floor, dead.

Three down, one to go.

I gave the cougar one last glance. I still hadn't gotten used to killing my own. Wasn't sure if I ever would.

Then I went in search of Brand.

And found him still leaning against the stacked metal. What was wrong with him? Had prison made him soft?

And then I smelled Greer again.

Brand laughed, a loud, braying sound that would have startled me if I weren't on high alert. "Come here."

"Not a chance, asshole." My eyes narrowed as I glared at him, my sword ready at my side.

"Not you." He grinned at me, then looked over his shoulder. My gut clenched as Greer walked toward him, her face impassive. When she got to Brand, he grabbed her arm and faced me.

"Whatever you were planning to do to me, you'll have to do while I have your dear sister close to me."

"Greer, are you okay?" I frowned and glanced at her face.

Her eyes were glacial as she looked at me and folded her arms. "What do you think?"

Ailuros tell me why I had to keep saving Greer's ass even though she behaved like an ungrateful bitch every single time?

"Fine, just stay out of the way." I gave her one last dismissive glance.

"Sure, I'll try my best," she snapped.

"Enough with the sibling chats." Brand shook Greer's arm and she glared up at him, but something about the familiarity of her expression bugged me.

I just confirmed that Greer had come back to Brand willingly.

But why was he holding her hostage? Was he just pretending or was he using her?

I didn't plan on wasting any time thinking about it. "Let her go," I said, knowing it was a waste of time, but it was still worth a try. "This is between you and me. Why do you want to hide behind a girl?"

His ego took the bait and he shoved Greer aside. She stumbled and bumped into a pile of metal. "What the hell?" she yelled, rubbing her hip. He gave her a sneering look, his lip curling to reveal a yellowed canine. Poor Greer. The object of her loyalty seemed a little unappreciative.

Brand walked forward. What may have been intended as a strut turned into little more than a limp. If he'd expected to instill fear in me, he'd failed badly. The look on his face said he knew it.

I kept Greer in my peripheral vision. I didn't trust her not to try and defend this creep. Certainly I knew I could no longer trust my sister.

I held the sword at my side and waited as Brand moved in a wide circle around me. Perhaps he thought it gave him an advantage over me to be the one moving while I stood still and watched.

It didn't.

All his movements did were allow me to predict where he would be next in case I could strike.

As he moved, his claws released and he allowed himself a partial transformation. His eyes and ears and forehead and chin transitioned slowly to his Leopard Walker form. But he didn't look right. Not like a normal Walker transition.

His jaw and the bones in his chin looked lopsided. "What's wrong with your face? The last time I had the privilege of seeing this side of you, it wasn't this bad."

"Concerned are we?" he asked, still circling.

"Not concerned. Just curious."

"Well if you must know, it seems that Niko forgot to tell us one little detail about using Synthe. It has a side effect in Walkers like us." His face twisted but I couldn't figure out his expression. I assumed it was disgust given the topic of discussion.

"You were using the drug that you were peddling?" I was blown away. I'd have expected dealers at least to stay clean, but maybe my expectations were a little unrealistic since Pariahs had to deal with a plethora of emotional imbalances, and judging from Lily's past reliance on the drug, I shouldn't be surprised that Brand had used.

He snorted. "Of course I used. Everyone did. It made us feel better, didn't it, Greer honey?" Brand asked the question but kept his eyes on me.

I stiffened, unsurprised by his new revelation. Maybe Greer's side effect was her going crazy. But then I'd actually never seen Greer in a partial transformation. She could be just as disfigured as Brand now was.

Tightening my grip on my sword, I stopped moving in

tandem with Brand. I was tired of him circling me. I wanted to get this business over and done with.

Brand continues to circle me, then frowned when he saw I hadn't moved and he'd come too close to me for his safety. He backed off.

I made him nervous and I liked it.

Something came flying through the air and hit him on his temple. He growled and looked behind me. "Ah, you have a little friend, I see."

I knew what he meant. Lily was here.

Damn it.

CHAPTER 46

I DIDN'T NEED TO LOOK to know Lily hadn't listened. And I couldn't waste time reprimanding her. Later would have to do, if we made it out alive.

"Take care of Greer," I said and rushed at Brand using the distraction of Lily's arrival, swiping my sword in a wide arc. The curved blade caught him on his upper arm. The jagged slash in his bomber jacket began to redden and he growled, his misshapen face clenching, making him look more hideous.

He sprang at me, his claw-tipped fingers extended, aiming for my face. He lacked speed and I sidestepped him easily enough.

I raised my sword again and ran at him, but something stopped the smooth arc of the blade. A hand pulled on my wrist.

"Stop. You'll hurt him," Greer pleaded.

"That's the fucking point. He wants to kill me in case you didn't realize it."

I struggled with Greer, pulling her fingers off the handle of my sword. "Lily, get her off me." I snapped and felt Greer being pulled away. Brand took the opportunity to run at us, his claws flared for the most damage. He jumped as he closed in, bringing his claws downward.

A glance behind me confirmed Greer had somehow managed to knock Lily out. Damn. I knew the girl wasn't up to this.

Greer struggled against me, tugging hard. I saw the danger and relaxed my hand a little, hoping the momentum would propel her backward, but she stopped hard and leaned forward again to try and grab the sword again.

She moved right into Brand's strike path.

His eyes widened and his arm stiffened but it was too late to stop the blow. His claws struck Greer full and came away bloody. She slumped back against me and Brand stumbled to the side, watching me with hooded eyes.

I slipped to the ground, cradling Greer in my arms, and when I looked down at her, my heart sank. Her throat was slashed open. Four neat incisions spewing blood all over her neck and the front of her clothing.

She'd never survive the wound.

I lay her carefully on the ground and rose, spearing Brand with a glare that should have killed him instantly. "What have you done?" I growled at him, the sound ending in a high-pitched keen. He had killed my sister and he was going to pay.

"It was an accident. I didn't mean to kill her. She wasn't supposed to die." The note of despair in his voice almost made me feel sorry for him. But it wasn't enough to save him.

I ran for him, landing a blow to his jaw, putting my whole strength behind it. I heard his jaw crack and enjoyed the sound. He stumbled back then regained his balance. He came at me, swung his fist, then feigned and caught me in the ribs, doing damage with both claws and knuckles. I gasped and stumbled backward, bending at the searing pain. But I found I could handle the agony, channel it with my anger.

I surged forward and caught Brand with another fist to the side of his head. He staggered backward and hit a stack of compressed metal. The stack shook, threatening to topple over. I paid little attention as I waited for Brand to come at me again.

This time I struck as soon as he was within range, sweeping the sword at him, but he threw himself aside, avoiding the jagged teeth by a fraction of an inch. Damn. How did he suddenly get so fast? He was very erratic in his movements. Was this what the Synthe did to the Pariah? Not only physical deformation but erratic strength and accuracy?

Greer moaned, the sound really more of a gurgle than a moan. Brand looked at her at that moment, and though I wanted to look too, I saw this as my only opportunity to catch him off guard. I threw the sword at him, but my hand shook and my aim was off. The sword whirred as it spun at him passing within a hair's breadth of his cheek.

It struck the stack of metal behind him with an ominous thunk. Brand's gaze snapped to the blade still swinging from side to side, its point stuck in the metal. I raced at him, grabbing him around the neck.

He reached his claw-tipped hands backward for me and I tilted my head away. He growled as his fingers met air. I held tight to his neck despite his struggle. He moved his jaw to the side as if he wanted to try to bite at my hand, but I grabbed his jaw with my hand, gripping firmly to his chin.

With a deep growl, I pulled hard, seeing only Greer's face and her bloodied neck, seeing again the poor human girl as Brand and his men attacked her, seeing Lily's face filled with self-hatred for falling into the clutches of the Synthe.

When I heard the crack and then the rip, I shook the memories from my mind and gritted my teeth as I pulled his jaw from his face and flung it away from me. Brand slumped against me and I shoved him off, letting him stumble headfirst into the stack of metal sheets. The impact loosened the pile, setting them sliding off the stack in every direction, bringing the fifteen-foot stack of metal down to five feet, and half burying Brand.

My stomach tightened and I retched. But thankfully I didn't give in to the urge to vomit. I just stared at the sight of Brand's face, his jaw ripped away, his upper teeth yellowed and exposed, his throat convulsing as he drew painful breaths. The damage to his jaw was not life-threatening. Not for a Walker anyway.

I had to finish the job.

I hurried to retrieve my sword, which had landed a few feet from Brand. With a single blow aimed at his neck, I ended his pathetic life.

For a moment I stood there, sword hanging beside me, surprised that the sight of his decapitated head no longer made me queasy. I was getting too used to the violence.

Then I remembered Greer and rushed to her side. She was fading, her wounds irreparable. He'd slit her throat, opened her jugular. And she'd last only as long as it took for an Alpha to bleed out.

She couldn't speak and I wasn't sure if that made me feel better. What could she say? Not apologies, not regrets. All I could do was support her head in my hand as she gazed at me, droplets of red marring her white hair.

She shifted a little and something hit the ground with a small thud. I felt around the floor and my fingers touched metal. I grabbed hold of it bringing it close to inspect it.

The Graylands portal key.

So it had been Greer who'd stolen it from me. And now I'd never know the reason for her betrayal.

Her face had lost all color and she reached for my hand. I gave it to her and she clenched it hard. When she entwined her fingers with mine, my eyes filled with tears. I blinked them away and bent close to her face unsure what I should say to her.

I opened my mouth, grasping for something to say to make her feel better. But it was too late.

She was already gone.

CHAPTER 47

I sat there with my sister bleeding out on my lap in the ominous silence of the abandoned warehouse, surrounded by bloodied, dead bodies. I sat there until lights flashed outside and until I heard Logan's voice asking me questions I couldn't decipher.

I heard Lily's moans as she sat up.

Hands grasped my shoulder, more hands moved Greer from my lap. I sat back and let them do what they wanted. A part of me was aware that Logan was there, talking to me, holding me, that even Jess stood close, giving off her calming energy.

I tried to focus on my next step, tried to ready myself for my mission to save Mom and Anjelo.

All I could think of was what my mom would say when I told her I had lost Greer.

Saved her and lost her within the space of a week.

I stood on shivering knees amongst the white noise of the cleanup crew, blinking back tears I couldn't understand. I'd felt only bitterness for Greer these past few days, so what place did grief have in my feelings?

I backed away from the scene, my sword clutched within

gritty fingers. I must have reached for it automatically when I stood up. Officers were flashing past, speaking into walkie-talkies, pointing off into different directions. Everyone had something to do.

Except me.

All I had to do was to stand here, helpless and hopeless.

I wanted to scream, to throw something. But with a sword in one hand and a portal key in another, neither were suitable throwing objects for any occasion.

The portal key.

I blinked.

I didn't dare look at it. Didn't dare waste a single second more hanging around the warehouse. I scanned the area for Logan, but couldn't see him. Good. Slipping behind stacks of metal, I hurried to the entrance, spotting my discarded bag of weapons right where Brand's thugs had left them.

Omega's teams were concentrating on the bloody mess I'd created and paid me little attention apart from a few respectful and sympathetic nods as I passed. I retrieved the bag and headed for the door, walking fast around the corner, pausing only when I was three blocks away to lean against the brick wall of another abandoned building. I put a shaky hand to my throbbing fore-head. I stared at my dark, stained fingers, nails caked with Ailuros-knew-whose blood. I'd ended so many lives this night. My shaky hands were a testament to many a soul now passing through the Graylands. And it didn't bother me that they were also headed straight there.

Hiking the pack higher up onto my shoulders, I set off at Walker speed toward the docks.

CHAPTER 48

There was only one place I knew to go to find Greer in the Graylands, and that was my apartment. And my instinct had been right. I moved slowly up the stairs, allowing my panther senses to take control, lengthening and furring up my ears to catch every sound within the room above.

Greer wasn't alone.

Someone else moved around inside the apartment and their size made me nervous. I let my panther senses filter into the apartment, heard the odd beat of the other person's heart, the sough of breath.

I stiffened, ready to pounce the moment I sensed Greer was in danger.

"Come on, Greer. You do realize how perfect this is. With you human and alive, our plan would have worked, but with you as a ghost, it will work even better." Yanuk chuckled, his gravelly voice grating on my nerves, causing my fury to well up uncontrollably.

I burst into the room moving swiftly and straight for the red oaf so fast all he could do was stare at me with his big red eyes. I had him flat against the wall, the curve of my blade snug against his throat before he could take the next breath.

"Leave him, Kai," said Greer from behind me, her voice calm, almost serene. I didn't loosen my grip although I did glance around to get a look at her. She stood to my left, still dressed in her jeans and jacket from the warehouse, the multitude of grays hiding the blood-stained remnants of her recent death.

Her throat showed no sign of her mortal wound. In fact, she seemed almost alive, if a little insubstantial. Not that I hadn't expected that.

"Why should I let the bastard go? He'd kill me if he had a chance. Almost did in fact." I glared at him, still regretting not killing him before.

"He didn't know who you were then."

"Greer, that makes no sense. He's a demon, for Ailuros' sake. The demon overlord of the Graylands. Why would he care who I was?" For a moment, I stared at her. Then I flicked the red, winged demon a dirty look. To be honest I didn't give a damn what his motives were. My purpose here was to talk to Greer before she crossed over. "Look, Greer. I really don't care about Yanuk. I came to speak to you."

Greer walked toward me, but she looked over at Yanuk. "You see? This is precisely the reason I can no longer help you."

I frowned, confused, already releasing the demon who rubbed his throat gingerly but remained where he was. Seemed he had some sense after all.

"Greer?" I called her name but it was as if I wasn't there. She stood in front of me, a gray specter, wavering in the air, and turned her head to speak to Yanuk.

"The plans we had would have worked perfectly had I been alive—preying on Walker souls, demons living on Walker strength. And maybe you're right. Our plans would work just as perfectly now that I am dead. But you see, things are different now. I see things so differently now . . . things can never be the same."

"What do you mean, Greer? Why does it have to change?" He came away from the wall and would have taken a step toward her, but I turned my head and gave him a glare that said 'make one fucking move and you are dead'. He took a step back and resumed position against the wall.

Greer was still looking at him as she spoke. "Because what we want to do isn't right. I can see now how terribly wrong it is. And I wonder how I could've possibly considered doing such a thing. I think something happens when you die. Like a blindfold being removed. All anger and envy and negativity is removed, and you can see clearly for the first time. I can see now, all the things I've done in the past, all the times I made decisions thinking others were against me, when in truth it was me who was my own enemy." Then she turned to me, her face filled with sadness. "So many times I hated you. Hated how hard you worked, and yet you were always true to yourself. You were a true Alpha and I was always jealous of you. Probably why I aligned myself with all the wrong people, Niko, Brand, Yanuk—for all the wrong reasons. So many times I pushed you away and yet you still came to help me, to save me. I didn't deserve you. I don't deserve you." Tears glistened in Greer's eyes and I felt a tightening in my chest.

A part of me felt guilty to think I'd often done what I'd done out of duty to my parents and not out of love for my sister.

"This isn't necessary, Greer. I only came to make sure you were going to be okay. That you weren't going to end up being Yanuk's pawn for all eternity." I gave the demon another dirty glance.

"No. I was never his pawn." Greer smiled, and her face seemed to glow a little. "Oh, and can you give Mom a message for me?" Those words made me want to burst into tears, but I swallowed them and nodded. "Tell her that I'm sorry I didn't stay and give her a chance to explain. I know she wanted to, but I was so angry."

"If you want, I can tell you what she would have said," I offered.

Greer nodded. "I'd like that." I gave her a quick version of the events that led Mom and Dad to part ways and repeated Mom's apologies to me in Wrythiin, hoping they would give Greer the solace they gave me. From her expression, it seemed to have done her some good.

"You know, a lot of what you were going through may not have been entirely your own fault," I said, recalling my conversation with Grams regarding the possible Pariah gene affecting the development of the Walker's brain.

"How so?" Greer frowned, although the glow on her face hadn't faded.

"Grams and I were talking and we think the Pariah gene may also affect a person's mind as well as their body. The way it affected Niko." I didn't want to say more in case I offended her, but it seemed Greer was immune to offense. She nodded slowly as if the possibility made a lot of sense to her.

"That would explain a lot." She looked up at me, an almost pleading expression on her face. "Kai, you must get them to research that. If it's true, then that research could help so many Pariah Walkers work through what they are feeling right now. It's terrible what we have to go through. All those horrible emotions. Feeling broken, not feeling whole, not belonging. Not being able to change is the worst of all. If you could do something to help, anything at all . . ." Her voice faded away and the glow in her face brightened.

She looked down at her hands and stared at them for a moment. My stomach clenched and I knew her time had come. The light was calling her and she had to go.

Greer looked up at me, her expression still waiting for my answer. I nodded. "Yes. I will. I promise."

"Thank you, Kai." She smiled and gave me a small wave.

She began to glow so brightly I had to shade my eyes against the pain of the glare.

I blinked and she was gone.

"No!" Yanuk yelled and came rushing at the bare spot that had held Greer only seconds ago.

I wiped the blood off the curved blade of my demon-sword and returned it to its sheath at my back, then shut the door of my Graylands apartment.

Time to go home.

~ TO BE CONTINUED ~
The SkinWalker Series continues with Last Chance.

ACKNOWLEDGMENTS

To my ever supportive Inklings gals – you rock!
To the Indie Inked ladies – not a day goes by that I don't look to you amazing girls for support and encouragement.
To my proofreaders Cassie, Karen, Cath and Dharsh – I know ... I enjoy keeping you cross-eyed ;)
To my editor and friend Amy Eye – Girl, you and I, we've seen some major ups and downs, but nothing ever keeps us down, does it? Live strong, woman!
To my super amazing PA Cath Cowley – I just can't imagine how I survived each day before you came along. You're a dynamo!
To my little family – always there in the background, ensuring I remain sane, hydrated, fed, and alive. I am quite glad you haven't traded me in as yet.
And to my readers. Keep on turning them pages...

FREE STARTER LIBRARY - JOIN MY NEWSLETTER

Get the following titles FREE when you subscribe to my newsletter.

Tee's Newsletter

http://smarturl.it/TeesMailingList

ABOUT THE AUTHOR

I have been a writer from the time I was old enough to recognize that reading was a doorway into my imagination. Poetry was my first foray into the art of the written word. Books were my best friends, my escape, my haven. I am essentially a recluse but this part of my personality is impossible to practice given I have two teenage daughters, who are actually my friends, my tea-makers, my confidantes… I am blessed with a husband who has left me for golf. It's a fair trade as I have left him for writing. We are both passionate supporters of each other's loves – it works wonderfully…

My heart is currently broken in two. One half resides in South Africa where my old roots still remain, and my heart still longs for the endless beaches and the smell of moist soil after a summer downpour. My love for Ma Afrika will never fade. The other half of me has been transplanted to the Land of the Long White Cloud. The land of the Taniwha, beautiful Maraes, and volcanoes. The land of green, pure beauty that truly inspires. And because I am so torn between these two lands – I shall forever remain cross-eyed.

Stalk Tee here:
www.tgayer.com
tee@tgayer.com

facebook.com/TGAyerAuthor

twitter.com/TGAyerAuthor

bookbub.com/profile/t-g-ayer